DARK NIGHTS OF THE SOUL

Andrew Langley

LPS CREATIVE MEDIA 2016

Cover image used under licence from Shutterstock.com

Typeset in Minion Pro

British Library Cataloguing in Publication Data. A catalogue record for this book is available from the British Library.

ISBN 978-0-9554137-5-9

Published by LPS Creative Media
www.lpscreativemedia.com

AUTHOR'S NOTE
This novel is a work of fiction. Names, characters, places and incidents are either the product of the author's imagination or are used fictionally. Any resemblance to actual events, locales or persons, living or dead, is entirely coincidental.

To discover more about the Nathen Turner novels, and read news, views and extracts, visit: www.andrewlangley.co.uk

DEDICATION

For my wife and son, my creative team.

CHAPTER 1: THE ALCHEMIST

Kenny Florian gazed up at the tall figure in the loud Hawaiian shirt like he'd drifted into the shop from another planet. With wide eyes, Kenny read again the note in his hand and then flicked it deftly onto the glass counter beneath him. Drifting down over the largest of the good-luck charms cocooned beneath the counter, the offending paper sat silent, totally unaware of the reaction it had caused.

'Consultant? A psychic consultant?' Kenny blurted, seeing visions of a bowler-hatted figure in a three-piece suit holding a crystal ball like a fine wine. 'You've got to be kidding, right?'

Kenny moved two paces from behind the counter and put his hand on the man's shoulder. Given the height difference between the pair, this proved more challenging than he'd first realised. He ended up tottering a little, raised precariously on his open-toed sandals.

'So what – like you're going to put on a suit and go all corporate on me?' Kenny mimed, placing a tie on the man's open-necked shirt, relieved to lift his open palm off the shoulder into a more comfortable position. 'I'm sorry, Nate. I don't get it … I mean what exactly is a psychic sodding consultant? Some nine-to-five business man with a spiritual leaning?'

Kenny was a flower-power dropout who owned and ran The Alchemist, a small purple-fronted spiritual shop in the heart of the bustling seaside town of Whitby. For him, anything remotely resembling mainstream society was as attractive as a greased-up pig in a Savile Row suit. He believed in the power of nature, and had little time for those who worshipped at the foot of the money tree, where the pursuit of 'success' usually came with its own particular dress code, and the constant craving for more and more things. As he saw it, the best things in life were not things. The prospect of one of his oldest friends moving anywhere near that world was not something he relished.

Scattered around the shop's colourful interior, lines of haphazard driftwood shelves cascaded with row upon row of tarot cards, talismans and beautiful crystals propped in neat wicker baskets. Little handwritten cards signposted each section, with slogans such as 'for health', and 'ideal for meditation'. Behind him, above the glass counter, framed press clippings showed the two men in happier times, posing for the cameras outside a range of spooky-looking buildings.

The tall man looked up sheepishly from his snakeskin cowboy boots with the burnt toes and smiled. 'I'm still the same person, Kenny. I'm changing what I do, that's all.' He reached a long arm over to retrieve the note off the counter and reread what he'd written in untidy black pen:

NATHEN TURNER – PROFESSIONAL PSYCHIC CONSULTANT

Develop your natural psychic ability with one of the UK's most talented spiritual workers. Whatever your level of reading experience in tarot, crystal ball, palm reading or astrology, Nathen Turner can take your skills to the next level. Beginners welcome.

Then there was a scrawled email address and a mobile phone number.

'Maybe you're right, Kenny. Consultant does sound a bit pretentious – I didn't see it that way. I thought it would make me come over as a more professional type. How about coach? Yes … psychic coach.' Nathen Turner looked over hopefully at his pony-tailed friend in the tie-dye T-shirt and tight white jeans.

'Honestly, Nate,' Kenny said, shrugging his shoulders, refusing to call him Nathen as it wasn't cool in hippy speak, 'I don't see what's wrong with psychic medium, like before. I mean you've used that for years. Worked out pretty well so far, don't you think?'

Turner was forced to admit that it had. For over a decade he'd worked as a psychic medium and been well rewarded for it. The spiritual sessions had been a sham – a combination of observation, background research and good acting had meant that Turner could freak out the most sceptical of people. When he'd thrown in a few conjuring tricks for good measure, his clients had become lifelong believers in his 'special gifts' (albeit they were completely fake).

Turner himself had never believed in any spiritual realm. He'd seen the psychic medium job as simply an actor playing a role, and had justified his deception on the grounds that he was helping people. In reality, he'd been preying on the grief of others and making a good living from it. But, just over a year ago, the real ghost of a dead girl had come calling at his door. A genuine spirit, hell bent on revealing her brutal murder to the world, had appeared to him for help. All his scepticism had disappeared – it had turned out that the fake psychic medium wasn't as much of a fraud as he'd thought he was. With no alternative, Turner had helped the ghoul and nearly died in the process. A messy police case had followed, and, worried at being labelled as a nutcase, he had managed to keep all reference to the supernatural out of it. His girlfriend and housemates had all been involved so there was no way to pretend it never happened – they'd all lived through it, and none of them had been the same since. Ashamed of his past deceptions, Turner hadn't been able to face going back to his sham psychic act, and as a direct result his income had dried up. He'd figured that maybe he could stay in the psychic realm by helping others to explore their gifts, instead of being the centre of attention himself. So the 'Nathen Turner – psychic consultant/coach' idea was born.

Kenny had no idea about Turner's ghostly visitor of the past, and Turner planned to keep it that way. 'Look, Kenny, can you get something designed properly and printed up for me as an advert? I want to give this a go. I may not be the best teacher in the world, but at least I can try.'

Relieved that his friend intended to keep his wacky dress sense, but a little bemused by the change in business direction, Kenny simply muttered, 'Of course.' After agreeing terms, and that the new advert would be placed in a prominent position in the shop, Turner, with his Hawaiian shirt, jeans and cowboy boots, headed out into the cool afternoon air.

The heavy tang of the sea enveloped Turner as he clip-clopped his way across the cobblestone street, travelling the short distance to his terraced house overlooking the marina. Seagulls, sentry-like on top of the empty lobster creels and Gothic lampposts, stared down at the assortment of tourists bustling along the crowded paths, ready to pounce on the next available dropped chip or battered treat. Occasionally, a bolder bird would swoop crying from the sky, dive-bombing open trays of crabsticks left unguarded beside the fishmonger stalls. Colourful boats, showing the scars of a lifetime battle with the sea, motored their oily way in and out of the swing bridge that connected the two sides of the town. Pedestrians and motorists crowded together, watching them go by, ready to sprint forward when their way over the River Esk clicked slowly back into place. Such was the ebb and flow of Whitby, and Turner adored it.

Pushing open the solid-wood door that led from the front of his house directly into the kitchen, he was pleased with his morning's work. Finally, comfortable with a possible way to make a living that played to his strengths and had the potential to help others without scamming them, he felt calm and at peace with himself.

'What on earth are you reading?' a green-eyed Japanese lady called up from the kitchen table, making him jump from his reverie and waking the sleeping dog in the corner. Three seconds later he was on the floor, being licked and pawed by the hairy hound, pushing his face vainly away from the putrid breath. Half Siberian Husky, half Rottweiler, Turner had rescued the dog some years before and it had been his boon companion ever since. The unfortunate downside was that it tended to show its gratitude by rugby tackling him whenever he came home, then covering him in its particular version of affectionate, and smelly, doggy kisses.

'Kyle, come here,' the woman called to the dog, who immediately sprang to its feet and padded softly to her side. Gently, she stroked the thick fur at the base of the neck, and watched its bushy tail swish excitedly back and forth. 'Serves you right for waking him up.' She giggled at the drool dripping off Turner's chin. 'So, tell me, what are all these about?' A dainty hand raised a tatty leather volume high in the air, wrinkled pages flapping open against the broken spine.

Not sure if he was in trouble or not, Turner scanned the pile of dusty volumes littering the kitchen table, trying to figure out which one she was holding. He'd spent the early morning reading from his bizarre book collection, munching through piles of toast and downing copious cups of green tea. 'It's called the *Malleus Maleficarum* …'

'Don't try and confuse me with pseudo Latin – English please.'

'It's usually translated as the *Hammer of the Witches.*' Turner quickly pressed on before she had time to comment.

'Basically a how-to guide on witch hunting … very interesting.'

'Only you could say something like that and truly mean it! You are one unusual man, Nathen Turner.' Laughing, she stood up slowly, pulled down the skirt on her tight-fitting black dress, and hugged him gently before kissing him playfully on the cheek.

Known affectionately as Jade, due to the unusual green colour of her eyes, she and Turner had been inseparable in the past few months. Turner had never truly been in love before, but somehow this felt different. Sure, he'd been 'in lust' many times, but nothing compared with how he felt about his dainty, book-waving companion. Looking at her made him feel good, and he felt an insatiable drive to make her happy. They were practically living together, Jade abandoning her London flat at every opportunity to spend time with him. Turner knew this was deeper than friendship; for the first time he was beginning to imagine himself being with the same woman for the rest of his life. Whether she would have him, and his somewhat unusual way of making a living, was an entirely different question.

'The airline's been on. I've been called in to cover long haul again,' Jade said, more seriously this time. The Texas drawl in her accent was faint, but unmistakable. Jade had been schooled in the States and remnants of her childhood still lay on her tongue, and most certainly in her uninhibited personality.

Turner looked downtrodden. His other housemates were away travelling across Australia and he faced an empty house, caged in with his loveable, but boisterous, hound. Jade worked as an airline stewardess, and long haul meant she'd be globetrotting for at least a week, maybe two. The best he offered was a mumbled 'OK' in response.

Jade waved a hand carelessly over the dusty pile of books littering the table, spotting his sombre expression. 'I'll be back before you know it – you've got your weird books for company. What more could you want?'

'Maybe, but the books can't do this ...' Turner pulled her gently into his arms, feeling the warmth of her breath on his neck before he kissed her softly on the lips. She smelt of roses and lavender as her body sunk willingly into his embrace. They stood holding each other tenderly, like lovers sheltering together for comfort against the storm of life. After long moments, Jade slowly pulled away.

'Look, I've got to pack. Give me half an hour, and then we'll go out, OK? Take a walk on the beach with old fur bag.' Jade smiled down at the dog, who was pacing around the kitchen after hearing the word 'walk'. 'Then, maybe later, we can continue our conversation upstairs ...' Jade pointed up to the bedroom and then kissed him again playfully, before heading for the stairs. Turner looked lustfully at the swinging of her hips in the tight dress as she stalked off sexily, silently thanking again whatever god had brought this beauty into his life.

Alone, he starting flicking through another of the crusty volumes on the table, stopping occasionally to examine a woodblock print of some gory witch interrogation from the seventeenth century. Page after page of graphically detailed scenes flooded his gaze as he quickly turned through the crumpled pages. As part of his work, Turner prided himself on collecting old texts relating to the bizarre, occult and supernatural. Much of the knowledge was long forgotten, and the child inside him relished the idea of rediscovering ancient secrets written in darker, more superstitious, times. Lately, though, the images had been giving him nightmares, waking him up in cold sweats, as the horrific scenes of demons and torture came to life in his dreams. Quickly, he closed the book and turned his mind to more romantic thoughts of the evening ahead.

CHAPTER 2: ALONE IN THE WILD

Four hundred miles north, Mike Fletcher was living through his own particular nightmare. A nightmare from which there was no escape; one he was forced to live with every single day. Twelve months ago, Fletcher had lived the high life – an apartment in central London, a flash sports car, and a beautiful girlfriend had made up his world. As a freelance photographer, he'd been a camera for hire, anyplace, anytime, selling his images to the highest bidder through his agent in Fleet Street. Everything had seemed perfect, but then, on the eve of his thirtieth birthday, he'd become blind. In three days the vision had gone completely in his left eye. No reason, no warning, just blackness. As a blind photographer, with mounting bills to pay, his girlfriend had decided she was better off out of it and left him, throwing him her flats keys as she headed tearfully out the door. His agency had cooed soothing words of sympathy, offering to re-market as much of his photographic back catalogue as they could, but at best he'd have been earning just enough to cover his mobile phone bill after they had deducted their fifty per cent cut. Within two months he'd lost everything, except the car, and was staying with his sister in a small terraced house in Dorking.

Fletcher's doctor had referred him to an eye clinic, where a crowd of chattering students had dropped various painful potions onto his pupil, before staring intently through a high-powered microscope at his retina. Fletcher could smell the stale beer and pizza on their breath from the night before as they leaned ever closer, trying to figure out the cause. After much mumbling and head scratching, he'd been sent for a brain scan. The huge white MRI machine looked like something out of a science-fiction movie, and everything seemed to move quickly as they clamped his head to the sliding table that fed the machine, and stuck a pair of plastic headphones over his ears. It got worse as the headphones filled with the strains of Barry Manilow singing 'Mandy', and the table slid into the menacing white mouth of the resonance chamber, his nose almost touching the top of the tube. Claustrophobia overwhelmed him, and he started to panic. An emotionless voice cut through the music saying, 'Please stay still, Mr Fletcher. We'll be starting the scan in a second,' before the music drifted agonisingly on. Fletcher couldn't give a damn about Mandy and wished the big-nosed Yank would shut the hell up. The white cocoon smothered him in waves of mechanical noise, like a car crunching through gears, and inched slowly up and down, pounding loudly above the nauseating singing. Fletcher felt like he was trapped inside a steel barrel that someone was randomly attacking with a sledgehammer.

A week later, he was sitting in front of a pale neurologist, who fidgeted constantly with his medical report. Fletcher knew it must be bad news, and the guy was desperately trying to figure out a way to break it to him gently. Then six words tore his life apart. The consultant took a deep breath, looked him in the eye, and almost whispered, 'Mr Fletcher, you've got multiple sclerosis.' Almost in a daze, Fletcher listened as he was told his immune system had begun to eat away the insulation surrounding his nerves. Effectively, his body was short-circuiting itself, cutting off nerve impulses randomly and for no apparent reason. There was no cure, and attacks could happen at any time for the rest of his life. He was likely to experience paralysis, spasms, loss of bowel control and chronic fatigue, to varying degrees. The consultant explained, almost apologetically, that there was nothing the medical profession could do except try to slow down the progression of the disease, and alleviate the symptoms as and when they happened. Fletcher's vision could return, but, if it did, it would never be the same as before. His nervous system was playing Russian roulette with him on a daily basis, and nobody could tell him when the bullet would come.

Every day for the next three months, Fletcher woke each morning, gradually moving limbs, toes and fingers to see if they were still working. Then he checked his eyesight – the pupil in his left eye was completely open and didn't respond to light. Picking anything up with monocular vision was proving a real challenge – he was always a little to the left or the right, as he had no sense of perspective. Gradually, the blackness turned to a grey haze, and then he could make out shapes. After more intrusive medical assessments by the DVLA, he was deemed fit to drive, but would need re-assessing every three years for the rest of his life. Cautiously, he began to regain his independence, driving one-mile round trips, then two, and then ten. On and on it went, until, finally, he felt his confidence returning, comfortably motoring for hours, and aimlessly heading anywhere to get away and try to clear his head. Photography was all he'd ever known, having left school with no qualifications and a passion to get his work published. With no prospects, no money, and no hope, it was his sister who'd finally managed to get him back out in the world.

'Look, why don't you get away for a while. Get your head sorted out. You'll make some money on the car – use it and get away,' Rose Fletcher pleaded with him. She'd watched him spiral into depression, sleeping later every day and then slouching around her house. 'I'll help you sell it. Find a place where you can think for a while and sort out what you want to do.'

A search for a quiet retreat in the reference section of the Dorking Library had yielded little, except for the odd spiritual hideaway or expensive holiday abroad. Finally, Fletcher found what he was looking for. A remote village on the north-west coast of the Scottish Highlands had an old croft to rent. There was no electricity, but water was piped from a local stream, and he could cook and keep warm with a wood-fired stove. To him, the sheer isolation and back-to-basics living sounded like heaven. Since moving to his sister's house, Fletcher had lived his life through a TV set, with little or no social contact. He might as well feel alone in a beautiful wilderness setting, he thought, and so agreed to rent it for three months, starting in October, then come back to his sister's house for Christmas. Buying an old Land Rover from the sale of his fancy sports car, he still had three thousand pounds left over – more than enough to support his brief wilderness existence.

With every mile of the ten-hour drive to Scotland, Fletcher could feel his cares and his old life slipping behind him. The Highland roads were narrow and invigorating, with sheer drops on each side, causing him to concentrate hard as he trundled through the breathtaking scenery. Finally, the road ran out – it simply stopped at a small pull-in area at the edge of a dense pine forest. According to his on-board satnav he still had five miles to go to the croft. Turning the car around, he headed to the nearest village about ten miles back.

'Can I help you, son?' the smiling face of the post-mistress asked him in a thick Scottish brogue.

'I'm trying to get to Lanner's Point Croft, but, well … the road's run out.'

The post-mistress laughed, the curls of her grey hair bobbing up and down with her mirth. 'There is no road to that place, sonny. Didn't they tell you? You have to walk or boat – only way in or out is either the forest trail or a boat from Benlogan across the bay. There'll be no boats at this hour, so if you want to get there tonight you best get your walking boots on.'

Fletcher agreed to park the Land Rover at the edge of the pine forest and walk to the croft that night, carrying his bare essentials in a pack on his back. He left the rest of his luggage with the post-mistress; she'd promised him that one of the fishermen from Benlogan would bring it over in the morning.

Picking his way downhill to the croft, through the overgrown forest trail on the springy carpet of pine needles,

Fletcher had never felt so alone, and he liked it. Surrounding him, the warm tints of autumn were already appearing, painting the hills in a sea of warm brown and amber. Coppery bracken poked through the greenery that covered the lower slopes, before giving way to swathes of purple heather and the gloom of the towering grey crags. The tranquil scene filled him with such a sense of wellbeing that he began whistling an upbeat tune happily to himself. Here, in the middle of nowhere, without a map, following a haphazard forest trail in the growing gloom, he finally felt happy and at peace. The path was opening into a clearing and Fletcher got his first glimpse of the stained whitewashed walls of the croft about half a mile ahead.

Looking below at the tranquil scene, Fletcher felt like he was somehow part of an ancient picture postcard – part of a primordial landscape, where he could visualise woolly mammoths and sabre-tooth tigers roaming the woodlands that flanked the tiny speck of the white croft sitting centrally in a glade of cleared middle ground. The sea glimmered in the warm evening glow, carving a horseshoe-shaped bay that separated the isolated peninsula from the nearest evidence of humanity. Glimmering lights of a town were flicking into life across the water, and Fletcher guessed this must be the village of Benlogan, from where hopefully some obliging fisherman would be bringing the rest of his luggage in the morning. A large brown eagle soared overhead, gliding in the air currents bouncing from the grey crags that rose inland like huge, jagged fingers of rock, jutting into the sky. Directly in front of the croft, a smaller building, with a rusted metal roof, stood isolated and alone, and Fletcher could make out a rocky path that led from it to the edge of the sea. Way in the distance, he could hear the sound of rushing water coming from the far treeline. It sounded like a huge waterfall that he guessed had been carving its way relentlessly through the landscape for thousands of years. Other than the buildings, the entire area looked untouched by human hand and he breathed in the fresh pine-scented air like a man reborn.

Almost jogging along the sloping path, feeling excited at seeing his new home up close, he made the rest of the trip in less than ten minutes. The white croft walls had not seen a lick of paint for many generations, and bare masonry showed in patches around the wooden shuttered windows. Broken slates from the croft roof lay haphazardly scattered on the mossy ground around the building; historic remnants from its last repair. A quaint chimney poked its way upwards at the end of the house, currently serving as the perching place for a black and grey crow. The bird spotted him moving down below, and squawked off noisily into the trees. A little further down the slope, in front of the croft towards the shore, the metal-roofed building he'd seen from the trail looked like a small run-down byre, possibly used for storage and animal shelter by the previous tenants.

The croft's heavy wooden front door had no lock, just a simple long bolt on the inside. Pushing his way in against the creaking hinges, he stepped excitedly into the main living area. Upturned fish boxes, covered in hessian sacks, surrounded a wood-burning stove at the end of the room. These makeshift chairs framed a huge fireplace with blackened pots hung on the walls, and piles of roughly hewn timber at each side. A thick workbench had been pushed against the outer sea-facing wall next to a rectangular porcelain sink. Filleting and carving knifes, all adorned with deer antler handles, lay neatly placed in size order on the well-worn surface. Hidden underneath were two oil lamps, a container of oil and a huge box of matches. Fletcher made his way over and lit one of the lamps so that he could explore further in the growing gloom of the building. It dawned on him why the room was so dark. In his excitement, he'd forgotten to open the outside shutters on the windows. With a quick trip outside, he restored what exterior light there was, and the place seemed to take on a much cheerier aspect.

The only other room was a bedroom, again with overturned fish crates to provide a base for a thick straw mattress. A side door to a small toilet lay in one corner, but other than that the room was empty. Fletcher threw his sleeping bag on the bed and made his way back to light the stove. Someone had thoughtfully left the fire already prepared with wood shavings and crumpled paper, and in no time it was a roaring blaze of heat and crackling pine, filling the room with a scent that reminded him of the campfires of his childhood scouting trips. For years, he'd been surrounded by the noise and dirt of London, and a hectic work schedule that varied each day. From celebrity luncheons to hard-luck cases, he'd photographed them all, never taking the time to step back from his life and live it. Work was, or rather had been, the thing that defined him. Finally, he had a chance to take stock and find a new meaning, a new direction.

There was something about the simplicity of the place that soothed him and he felt comfortable in his own company, free of the distractions of the modern world. It was totally uncomplicated, sparsely furnished and designed to provide just enough comfort to survive. The flickering flames in the stove filled the cold and cheerlessness interior with life, and he imagined to himself the type of characters that had carved out an existence there in years gone by. How many had lived off the land, brought up families and thrived in this remote and beautiful setting? he wondered. Pulling out the basic supplies in his rucksack, he busied himself making a simple meal of bacon, eggs and mushrooms, using one of the large frying pans hanging above the fireplace.

Outside, night was covering the hills like a dark blanket gently dropping from the sky. Throwing his dirty pots in the sink, Fletcher stepped out into the starlit landscape, taking in the vast veil of silence that surrounded the cottage. Down at the water's edge, the twinkling lights of Benlogan greeted him from across the bay, much brighter than he'd seen on his woodland walk. The gentle lapping of the waves on the shore sounded like soft music, sent to wash his worries away. Fletcher reached down and cupped some of the water in his hand and, on an impulse, tasted it. It was salty, the taste of the sea. The peninsula faced into the vast ocean's gulf stream and he felt the fresh clean breeze on his face. Wandering further down the shoreline, using the pale moonlight to guide him, he dodged in and out of rock pools like a child at the seashore. The air felt heavier, a distant rumble of thunder booming from over the top of the craggy mountains. Fletcher had been warned not to trust the weather – 'If you don't like the weather in the Highlands, then wait a few minutes. It is always changing,' advised one of the people he'd got chatting to at a petrol station further south when he'd told them where he was going. 'Make sure you've got clothing for summer, monsoon rain and arctic conditions and you won't go far wrong.' He'd taken the advice and bought some extra clothing at one of the villages along the route.

By the time he was closing in on the cottage, the rain was bouncing off the ground, hammering his face and body. The temperature had dropped rapidly, so, rushing indoors, he snuggled up to the stove and warmed his wet limbs as best he could. In the firelight he could make out the glint of two green eyes staring back at him from the corner of the room. Thinking his faded vision was playing tricks on him, he rubbed his eyes and looked again. The two gleaming eyes were still there, surrounded by a dark furry shadow. Slowly, he inched forward to take a closer look at the figure sitting nonchalantly in the gloom. First, he spotted a blunt tail ringed with black markings, gently flicking from side to side as he moved nearer. Then more brown fur, and black markings that ended on top of the head in the shape of a capital M. It was a huge cat, like a large brown tabby, but the beast was the largest cat he'd ever seen, more the size of a small dog than a domestic feline.

As Fletcher got closer, the cat stamped down its two front paws, arched its back and hissed loudly at him. 'It's OK. I'm not going to hurt you,' he said softly, grabbing some of the bacon scraps left from his meal and throwing them towards the noise. The cat didn't move, just stood its ground, hissing at him. Rather than take on the angry creature on his first night, he sidled his way round to the other side of the fire and pulled up a fish crate. If he was going to live here for three months, he'd have to get used to the local wildlife, and they'd have to get used to him. Somehow, the angry bundle of bristling fur had sneaked its way inside to shelter from the storm, and Fletcher gave a little shiver, thinking about what other unwelcome visitors he may find. Coping with a stray cat was one thing, but what else lurked in the wilderness? he wondered. Images of the Loch Ness Monster flitted into his head, making him chuckle at how easily the dark and isolation had turned on the fear button in his mind after only a few hours.

Cracks of fizzing lightning shattered through his thoughts as the room briefly flared with light and trembled under the angry clamour of the thunder. Through the roar, he could hear stones falling, and what sounded like chunks of metal crashing to the ground. Warily, he peeked through the small window at the front of the croft to watch as the byre wall on the side nearest the house crumbled and fell. The metal roof of the byre had grounded the lightning and paid heavily for the privilege. At least attempting to repair the shattered building in the morning would give him something to do, he thought, praying silently that the worst had passed. Nature was providing him with work, something to make him feel useful again, and he silently congratulated himself on his decision to get away from it all.

CHAPTER 3: REPAIRS AT DAWN

Fletcher woke with the light of the dawn, stretching wearily in his sleeping bag on top of the straw mattress. The bed had proved surprisingly comfortable, and, whether it was the clean air, or the aftermath of the long drive, he'd slept soundly and well. Padding barefoot into the living room, he was relieved to find no signs of his furry visitor from the night before. The stove had gone out, so he busied himself cleaning and relighting it, before sticking on a huge pan of water for his morning brew and wash.

The steaming liquid hardly filled the porcelain sink as he splashed his face and bathed himself as best he could. If the weather got warmer, he thought he could use the sea as his giant bathtub, and then have a swim further down the coastline to explore a little more. The unspoilt and unpopulated environment invigorated him after years spent racing through crowded streets in the city, and he was determined to make the most of it. Slurping loudly as he drank his tea, he looked around the small room again, seeing what he'd missed the night before. Squinting occasionally, to manage the haziness that still surrounded his left eye, he wandered around like an eager estate agent surveying the property.

Two small windows, one facing the front of the house towards the byre, and one to the back, looking up to the hills and trees that surrounded it, provided the only source of natural daylight. Huge windowsills sat underneath each opening due to the thickness of the solid stone walls. Neither window had curtains, which didn't surprise him, as, he guessed, the threat of a peeping tom out here was non-existent. Faded green wooden shutters were hinged to the outside of each window, and these had remained secured where he'd left them in their open position, despite the battering from the storm last night. Inside, the walls had been painted white at one point, but now they were a dirty cream with stains of soot and smoke around the brick fireplace. The absence of any pictures, or wall decoration of any kind, gave the room the atmosphere of a stark, simple dwelling. He noticed a small drawer under the workbench next to the sink. It was set back from the edge and he hadn't seen it when he'd grabbed the oil lamps the previous night. The contents were uninspiring – simple cutlery with antler handles and a couple of smaller cutting knives. All the flooring was made of huge slate tiles, which, he'd found to his cost, were extremely cold if you walked on them in bare feet. With no rugs or mats in sight, he decided it would be socks or shoes for him from now on. In the farthest corner sat a straw broom, wedged right in the angle against the wall, hiding a rusty steel dustpan and bucket behind it. The bedroom was sparser, with one window facing the front of the house, similar to the one in the main living room. A metal spike had been driven into the wall above the bed, which he assumed was there to hang an oil lamp from at night, or put clothing on ready for the next day.

Exploring outside, the damage to the byre was worse than he'd thought. Half the corrugated metal roof lay in tatters across the lawn, and part of the supporting wall facing the house had fallen in and around the building. Heading into the byre to investigate further, he pushed hard against the door, the rusted hinges groaning against his efforts. The door was a two-part split affair with cracking green paint, and he needed to lean his entire body weight against both panels to get them to move.

Two of the inner walls of the byre were hung with rusty tools – several axes, a medium-sized wood saw, and an assortment of spades and garden tools. The best find lay horizontally on the back wall – a ten-foot fishing rod, still with line, hooks and a reel. A small rusted biscuit box underneath held different-sized hooks, lead weights, and an assortment of floats and various spinners to use as bait. This was great news, and he looked forward to chancing his luck, casting on the shoreline.

At the far end of the rectangular byre interior, a strange stone bench lay in ruins after the lightning strike. The base was made from a hollowed-out square of rough granite about six feet across. On top of this had lain another slab of what looked like sandstone. It had been split in two by the lightning strike – one half still on top of the granite and the other angled precariously over the side. He tried to move the dangling slab, but it was too heavy, so he went outside to find a branch to lever it safely to the floor. Then he froze. On the top inside panel of the door, a symbol had been neatly drawn in what looked like red paint. It was a pentagram about the size of a large dinner plate, with strange hieroglyphic cursive text inside it. The weird thing was the way the paint dripped from the edges, almost like the symbol was bleeding. Dots of paint and uneven streaks hung from each edge in a bizarre design that created a surreal, and slightly unnerving impression. He pushed out quickly into the light, gasping for air, and cursed himself for being so superstitious. All the New Age shops in London had this symbol on display, and trendy spiritualist types proudly wore it as jewellery, for goodness' sake, so what was he worried about? he thought, heading around to look at the damaged wall from the outside.

His mental scolding was interrupted by the sound of a boat engine coming across the bay. Fletcher watched the small fishing boat expertly push onto the stony beach below the croft, before a giant of a man stepped out and quickly tied it off to an eyelet set into a heavy boulder on the shoreline. With huge squelching strides, the enormous figure made his way up the path to the croft, and spotted Fletcher.

'You Fletcher?' the huge figure barked.

He nodded back at the man meekly in a 'yes' gesture.

'Got your stuff. Come and give me a hand.' And off the giant trudged back to the boat without a backward glance.

Fletcher followed at a half trot, panting slightly as he tried to keep up.

'C'mon, son. Get in the water. Don't be afraid to get your feet wet.' Fletcher had hesitated at the water's edge. He plodged into the foaming waves up to the side of the boat as his companion thrust the first of his bags roughly at him. 'Here, get that on shore and I'll pass out the rest.' Fletcher did as he was told and within ten minutes all his spare clothing, food supplies and basic camera kit were onshore. He was determined to try photography again, so had packed a simple kit with a multitude of spare batteries and a solar-panel charger.

'Got to catch the tide to lay my pots – be back later to make sure you got everything, OK?' It wasn't a question, it was a statement, so Fletcher nodded meekly again in reply and watched the colossus motor off expertly out to sea.

Fletcher hauled his bags up the slope and unpacked. Most of the food he'd brought was tinned or dried; he wasn't expecting to find any refrigeration or long-term storage capability at the croft. He stacked tins of sardines alongside soups, macaroni cheese, and pots of steak and kidney pudding. Next to these came the vegetable assortment – mushy peas, beans and a huge bag of rice. He pushed a large holdall of dried meals from an army surplus store under the bench, followed by small sacks of onions, potatoes, carrots and several giant spiced salamis. Not exactly cordon bleu, but enough to keep him fed and alive. There was enough bacon, eggs and mushrooms to last for another couple of days, and he sealed these neatly in a large plastic container next to the sink. He heaped his clothing in the corner near the fire to air off, and then started laying out the camera gear on the floor.

The equipment was a stripped-down version of his professional kit – one Nikon digital SLR camera body, a short-range zoom and a telephoto lens – plus ten batteries, five memory cards and a solar charger. There was no computer to view an enlarged version of the images, and, frankly, he hadn't wanted to bring one. With no Internet or printer, he hadn't seen the point. Satisfied, he packed it away again in an all-weather camera rucksack and placed it next to the pile of clothes.

Back outside, he continued hunting for something to lever the broken sandstone slab off the bench in the byre. After about ten minutes of searching, he found the remains of a fallen birch tree and headed back inside, deliberately ignoring the strange symbol on the inside of the door. Carefully, he wedged the end of the small trunk between the granite base and the overhanging slab, before heaving it backwards to flip it safely on its back with a crash. Now he could explore further without the threat of the thing falling on him.

Fletcher rushed to get one of the oil lamps from the house, and then set about examining the strange stone workbench. Removing the broken slab had exposed the hollow construction of the granite base. It was an incredible piece of masonry. Somehow a huge boulder had been hollowed out to provide a square framework for the sandstone top. He assumed this must have been done to minimise the weight when moving it, as the slab could have sat happily on the solid rock. Half the sandstone top still lay safely in place, and he thought it must have made an excellent work surface before being split in two by the lightning from last night's storm. On the floor, the other remnant lay on its back, the smooth top surface facing down in the dirt. He brought the oil lamp closer. The entire hidden face of the stone had been expertly carved with Latin text and strange illustrations. In the centre, under a large arc, were three figures. The central one looked like some religious figure holding a cross, flanked by a double-headed eagle on one side and a lion on the other. Only half of the figures were visible and he assumed the rest of the carving must be hidden under the other part of the slab.

Fletcher turned his attention back to the hollow base. Peering inside, he found it was much deeper than the height of the external walls. Overall, he estimated the hole in the centre at about five feet deep, and the external walls at three. Fletcher carefully squeezed himself inside the base. From here he could look under the other part of the slab, and, sure enough, the rest of the carved figures and more writing were there. As he shuffled about in the cramped space, his boot kicked over something metallic concealed by the build-up of earth inside. Cautious of cutting himself in case it was a discarded nail, he bent down carefully and picked it up. It was a round disc caked with dirt, about the diameter of a small tangerine.

With tales of buried treasure in his head, he bounded inside and started to wash it under the tap. Perhaps he'd found a secret haul, hidden for centuries by ancient invaders. Laughing to himself at his childish notion, he scrubbed away until the markings on the metal disc became visible. It was a coin, or possibly a medal of some sort, made of base metal, and the markings on it were definitely religious. One side contained a robed figure, again holding a cross like the one on the slab. The entire surface of the reverse was dominated by a single cross that looked more like an ornate addition sign than anything else.

The sound of the boat motor resounded again off the walls of the croft, and he headed out in time to see the gigantic fisherman striding his way up the rocky path, clutching a blue-brown struggling lobster in one hand.

'Present for you, son.' The giant fisherman thrust the angry shellfish into his hand, causing Fletcher to drop the medal in a panic. 'I'm Peter Davis but most people round here call me Hulk.' Hulk thrust out a huge calloused hand and grinned as Fletcher held the lobster at arm's reach like an unexploded bomb.

Fletcher juggled the slippery sea beast into his left hand and reached out to shake the giant paw. There was no need to ask why he had the nickname – the only difference between Hulk and his comic-book namesake was that he wasn't green. 'Mike … I'm Mike Fletcher. Thanks for hauling my gear … and this …' he said, trying to sound enthusiastic, raising the lobster briefly in the air.

Hulk let go of the vice-like handshake and reached down to pick up the medal Fletcher had dropped. 'What's this? Well, I'll be – I haven't seen anything like this for years. You religious, son?'

'Not particularly. Why? I found it in the byre.' Fletcher pointed back at the broken building and its gaping wall.

'That's St Benedict, that is. There, the guy holding the cross. They used to sell these things back home. Not sure what it's doing here – probably left by some Catholic renting the croft.' Hulk seemed pleased that he'd solved the mystery.

'There's more than that – look.' Fletcher headed to the croft so he could temporarily house the lobster in the sink, then led Hulk into the byre to look at the sandstone slabs. 'See the carvings on the stone – that looks like him again in the middle of the figures, doesn't it?'

'Hard to tell, son. Could be anyone. Looks too worn to make anything of it.' Hulk turned around and gasped. 'You do that?' He pointed a slightly trembling finger at the bleeding pentagram on the door.

Fletcher felt a touch unnerved by the look of fear in the giant's eyes. 'No, it was already there. You seen that before?'

The huge man paused as if choosing his next words carefully. 'Yes, but not here. My old fishing partner back home used to have a son that dabbled in that sort of thing.'

'What sort of thing?' Fletcher asked, a little curious, assuming he meant making pagan jewellery.

'Witchcraft, son, witchcraft.' Hulk involuntarily crossed himself as he said it.

'You're kidding me, right? New boy in the wilderness, trying to scare him? Well, it won't work – I don't believe in all that stuff!' Fletcher took a step forward and gazed challengingly into Hulk's eyes, surprising himself at how quickly he'd bridled at the fisherman's remarks. He thought, wrongly, he was being made fun of by this man of the sea.

Hulk laughed hard and long at the smaller man standing boldly before him as if he was getting ready for a fight. 'I'm not trying to scare you, son. That's a symbol witches use, and it looks like that one's been drawn in blood, doesn't it? Look for yourself – no normal person would create that thing. Pagans lived here long ago and carried out all sorts of weird and wonderful rituals. It's probably some hangover from then, and they've reused the wood on the door. Nothing more than that. But, honestly, I'm not too fond of things like this, myself. Bad omens and all that – not good for fishermen.' Hulk crossed himself again.

Fletcher took a step back, slightly embarrassed that he'd read Hulk's intentions incorrectly. 'Who's the guy you mentioned? The one who knows about this stuff? Will he know what it is, or what it means?' In truth, Fletcher felt a little uneasy at the mention of ancient rituals, visions of burning effigies filling his thoughts. Sleeping in a croft next to some bleeding pagan symbol, in the pitch black, on his own, miles from anywhere, was beginning to fuel his desire for answers into a worrying inferno.

'Very likely, but I haven't talked to him since after his dad died and I moved north. He's back home in Whitby, where I come from. He's a psychic, and a good one by all accounts. Bit of a specialist in the weird and bizarre side of life. Why?' Hulk began walking back out to his boat, pleased to be out in the clean air again after the dry musk of the byre.

'Can you get in touch with him? I'd be interested in talking to him about the symbol,' Fletcher said, a little out of breath as he followed the giant and tried to keep pace with his huge strides. At least, if someone who knew about these kinds of things told him it was nothing to worry about, he would definitely sleep easier.

'Maybe – he's well known in Whitby. Someone there will have his phone number, but your mobile won't work out here. Nearest place to get a signal is in Benlogan.' Hulk stopped and thought for a moment. 'I suppose you could call him with the satellite phone on the boat … but I'd have to charge you. It's a bloody expensive bit of kit.'

'No problem – I'd be happy to pay the call charges. Can you get me his number? At least it will help me fill my days. What's his name?' Fletcher said, still chasing after Hulk as he strode off again, relaxing a little inside at the thought of solving the mystery of the symbol.

'His name's Turner, Nathen Turner. His dad – Dave – and me were partners in a fishing boat. Seems like a million years ago. I'm back out here in a couple of days. I may have something by then. Look, I've got to go. The light's fading and the bay's a bugger to cross in the dark.' Hulk stepped into his boat and started the engine.

With that, he was off, salt spray streaming back as he gunned the motor out to sea. Fletcher could hear the boat engine echoing down the bay as he headed back into the croft. Things were definitely interesting in the wilderness, and it was certainly taking Fletcher's mind off his health worries. Now the main problem was how the hell he was going to cook the lobster.

CHAPTER 4: A VOICE FROM THE PAST

Nathen Turner's ears were burning. According to the old wives' tale, that meant somebody, somewhere, was talking about him. In his case, he'd been sitting too close to the fire. For the last half hour, he'd been toasting his toes close to the roaring flames, after a freezing walk along the beach with his dog had chilled him to the bone. The dog lay curled at a more sensible distance, snoring gently in the warm glow.

Turner was alone in the tall Georgian terraced house, built into the cliffside underneath the foreboding Whitby Abbey, made famous by the Dracula myth. His best friend and housemate, Lee Melone, had headed off to Australia with his girlfriend for a two-week holiday. That was six weeks ago, and last he'd heard they were hitchhiking through the outback, picking up bar work and odd jobs along the way to fund their travels. Lee Melone, and his girlfriend Sandra, were always living for the day and the next 'experience'. Lee was an ex-musician and used to life on the road. Whenever he stayed still too long his biological clock forced him to explore and try new things. Lee had become Turner's road manager when he was working as a fake psychic medium and it had paid dividends for both of them. When Turner had decided not to do the psychic work anymore, Lee turned his hand to doing odd jobs and studio recording work to make ends meet.

Finally, saving up enough money to fund his travels, he was off and out exploring again. Turner's girlfriend, Jade, was somewhere mid-Atlantic and wouldn't be back for at least another week.

Turner had spent his time alone developing a six-step programme to support his new psychic coaching venture. After numerous enquiries from Kenny Florian's shop that hadn't led to a booking, he was finally expecting his first student that evening. He stretched out his baking feet, letting the blood return to the icy digits.

A loud knocking at the downstairs door announced the arrival of his guest. He was pleasantly surprised to find an attractive twenty-something beaming somewhat nervously back at him.

'Mr Turner?' He nodded back 'yes' from the doorway. 'I'm Emma. Am I too early?'

'No, no, please come in. Take a seat.' Turner offered her a place at the kitchen table. The kitchen served as the main entrance of the house, with all living accommodation scattered throughout the floors above. 'Can I offer you a drink?'

'No thanks, I'm fine. I've brought the photograph you asked for,' Emma said, reaching into her small black bag and removing a colour image of a couple beaming happily at the camera. Emma wore a smart dark-purple uniform with a Chinese-style wraparound top and wide trousers. A logo in gold on her left breast said 'Sade's Health and Beauty'.

'So, Emma, what makes you think you have a psychic gift?' Turner asked politely, pulling up a chair opposite and leaning back comfortably. The whole teaching idea was new to Turner, but he had a natural way of putting people at ease and he hoped it would carry him through.

Before answering, she seemed to spend a long time taking him in. At a slim six foot three, with shoulder-length blond hair and a goatee beard, Turner was certainly out of the ordinary. The beard had been Turner's girlfriend's idea – she thought it made him look more professorial for his new venture. Still feeling a little awkward, Emma said, 'Well, as I told you on the phone, I'm a hairdresser and I talk to clients all day long. But sometimes I get a premonition – like something good or bad is going to happen to a client and I don't know how to tell them, or put it into words. Last week a lady came in, and I had this strange feeling of danger about her. Later that day, she was involved in a car accident – maybe if I'd said something she could have avoided it.'

Turner nodded to show that he understood, reached for the photo and flipped it face up. Turner looked over the smiling faces in the image, taking in their bright clothing and the holiday setting, and spotted the similar facial features on the older lady in the photograph to the younger one sitting in front of him. 'Your mother looks very happy,' he said, glancing across the table.

Emma gasped. 'How did you know it was my mother? Do you know her?'

Turner was pleased that his guess was correct from his brief examination of the facial features, but the man in the image was an enigma and he could spot nothing in common with his seated guest. He took a risk. 'I feel this man is not related to you, but cares for you deeply,' he said, ignoring the question about whether he knew Emma's mother. Turner figured this must be right, as he'd asked Emma to bring a picture of people she cared about. She'd have forgotten this by now, so his obvious statement would seem miraculous to her.

It did, and she gasped again. 'It's my mum and step-dad, taken last year on their holiday in Tenerife. You are psychic, aren't you? They said so at The Alchemist.'

Turner felt ashamed of his little parlour trick and guesswork, using the skills that had made him a successful, albeit fake, psychic for so long. He wanted to try to get away from his past scamming ways as far as he could, but he was slipping back into them far too easily, and it made him uncomfortable. He tried a different approach to try to cleanse himself of his past.

'They seem like a lovely couple. I have to ask, sorry, but neither of them are in the spirit world, are they?' Turner assumed that he already knew the answer to his question as she'd told him the picture was taken last year. It would be highly unlikely they'd passed away since then.

Emma giggled. 'No, don't be silly. My step-dad's probably in the pub at the moment and that's the closest he's got to spirit so far.'

Turner smiled back, enjoying her joke. He stood, opened a kitchen cupboard, and pulled out a cutting board with a short vegetable knife; then he sat back down. Placing the photograph centrally on the cutting board, he offered her the knife as he said, 'I'd like you to stab the picture, please. Each person in turn – preferably several times.'

Emma stopped giggling and looked across at him like he'd gone completely insane. Reluctantly, she picked up the short knife and raised it, with a trembling hand, directly above the image. Her eyes looked down at the smiling faces in the sunny setting. She raised the knife higher, ready to strike. Something inside her made her pause, a horrible feeling like she was about to harm her loved ones. She stopped short and gazed pleadingly at him. 'I can't do it. I simply can't do it.'

'But that is just a piece of paper, not your parents. No harm will come to them.' Turner looked directly at her as he spoke, challenging her.

Emma threw the knife down on the table with a clatter. 'No, I won't, and you can't make me.' She was starting to regret booking herself on Turner's course, and he could tell. Maybe he wasn't cut out for this after all, he thought.

Turner tried pressing his point to help her follow what he was trying to show her. 'You see how we attach meaning to things that are more than they are?' Turner said softly, and reached over gently to hold her hand. 'Something in you is telling you there is a connection between that image and the wellbeing of your parents. Something beyond logic; a fantasy, if you like. You think, if you stab that picture, some harm will come to your parents, and it will be your fault. Those feelings are real for you, aren't they?'

Emma hesitatingly nodded 'yes', and said, 'But I'm still not sure I understand.'

Turner smiled reassuringly, relieved that she was calming down. 'Many think that psychic phenomena and the spiritual world are fantasy, but they're not, they're real. Your feelings are real, and most people wouldn't deliberately harm an image of their loved ones. Call it fantasy, instinct, whatever you want – it is in this area of our mind that the psychic skill lies. Our job is to help you develop your gift.'

Intrigued by what Turner was telling her, Emma leant forward, listening intently.

After a sketchy start, Turner felt pretty good about his opening gambit and silently congratulated himself on his progress so far. 'Look, in school, all we usually learn is how to use the left part of our brain – the bit that does all the logic and reasoning – and we get pretty good at it. We learn times tables, our left from our right, and how, if we do things in certain ways, we get a predictable result, right?' Emma nodded in reply, thinking back to her dusty classrooms and badly dressed teachers. 'But we are never taught much about our right brain, our creativity, our intuition, our imagination. There is so much we don't know about it. We all have some psychic ability, some more than others. I'm going to teach you how to develop those skills and nurture them like a newborn child. Then, most importantly, how to use them to help others.'

He fished out a series of ten small postcards from the chest pocket of his loud blue Hawaiian shirt and scattered them, face up, on the table. 'Pick one of these – doesn't matter which one.'

Pushing them around, she could see that they were a collection of various landscapes and cityscapes with a variety of people in them. Turner had pulled the images from news stories off the Internet and printed them onto postcard-sized photographic paper. She settled on one showing a young couple sitting in a forest scene.

Turner spoke softly, talking to her almost in a whisper. 'Start breathing slowly; feel a calmness building up inside you. Look at the image, but don't try and think about it. Let your subconscious take over; use your intuition. Who are these people, what do they do, what is their life like?'

Emma's body began to relax as she held the image in front of her, almost looking through it, rather than directly at it. After studying it for a couple of minutes, she said, with a confidence that surprised her, 'They are a young professional couple. Probably with good jobs in the city, maybe trying for a family. I don't feel they've got much money, like they are starting out in life. Maybe they've moved to a new area or something, but I feel like they're making a new beginning somehow. How was that?' Emma looked up at him like someone asking for a test result and hoping for the best.

Turner flipped over the card and read the typescript on the back out loud. '"David Kitt, accountant, and Martha Kitt, unemployed. David's mother died two weeks before the photo was taken," it says. So you picked up on difficulty with money – the wife is unemployed. The "new beginning" you felt – that could be the death of the husband's mother.'

Emma gasped, startled by her ability to sense things from the photograph.

Turner smiled across at her. 'So, you see, if you let go and trust your own ability, you are able to sense things psychically. That is what I'm going to help you develop – your psychic "sixth sense", if you like.' He passed the card back over to a positively enthusiastic Emma so she could see for herself.

Over an hour, the rest of the postcards were picked up

and read as before. Roughly half returned a positive result, but on others she was completely wrong. Turner explained that her results were well above average for her first attempt, and next time they'd go on to use the same technique to decipher common tarot card meanings. By the third session, she should be able to try her hand at doing a sample tarot reading for someone. Moving to pull out a small velvet bag from another kitchen cupboard, Turner slid it over and said, 'Please take this, Emma. It is my gift to you.'

Emma carefully opened the drawstring bag and gently tipped the contents onto the table. A set of loose tarot cards spread out slowly, followed by a beautiful purple crystal.

Turner picked up the polished crystal, displaying it in his fingers like a fine gemstone. 'I want you to practise with these until we meet next week. This is a Vera Cruz amethyst; they are very rare and sought after by spiritual healers. Amethyst is a powerful crystal for helping with your advancement and meditation – this particular stone is one of the best ever found. Here, please hold it in your hands.'

Emma picked up the gleaming lavender stone and placed it in her palm.

'I want you to close your eyes and breathe in the energy from the stone,' Turner said softly. 'Feel the energy filling your body – starting from your solar plexus, then your heart, into your throat and finally into the "third eye" on your forehead.' Turner watched as she followed his instructions, her body visibly relaxing as she continued to breathe rhythmically. 'That is the energy you are searching for before you try any session to develop your gift. Feel it, and remember it. Please open your eyes again.'

Turner reached down and spread the tarot cards, fan-like, in front of her. 'This is the Rider-Waite tarot deck. It is a good one for beginners to try, although I use a different one myself these days.' He turned over a couple of the cards to show her the colourful illustrations in more detail. 'As we did with the postcards, I want you to look through the deck before our next session and see what they say to you. Whatever you do, you must not read anything from a book or on the Internet about them. You must come to connect with the cards and how they make you feel first, before looking at how others interpret them. Does that make sense?'

Emma picked up one of the cards for a closer look and nodded 'yes' as she continued to glance through them, fascinated by the imagery. With Turner's help, she carefully packed everything away again.

'That was wonderful, Nathen. Thank you. You're a great teacher.' She reached in her bag and handed over the fifty pounds for the lesson like someone paying for a once-in-a-lifetime bargain at a sale. 'I can't wait for next week – is it OK if I tell some of my friends about you? I'm sure they'd like to try this as well.'

Nathen Turner was delighted. 'Yes, of course, please do. I'd be more than happy to see them.' The first try of his new venture could not have gone any better, and he felt good about helping the girl. What's more, he truly believed every word he was saying and knew his six-step teaching programme was going to work well for him.

Turner watched her stroll back into town with a wave, before heading back up to his toasty boudoir above. Kyle, the dog, hadn't moved so much as a hair and was still snoring gently on the rug. He glanced down at his watch, decided it was well past 'booze o'clock', and poured himself a large Crown Royal whisky. His thoughts turned to his beautiful girlfriend, Jade, and he wondered which continent she would be on right now. Turner was lonely and felt it deeply. The loud ringing of the telephone downstairs interrupted his melancholy.

'Hello, Nathen speaking.' He had to answer like this as most of his housemate Lee's boozy mates rang and thought he was Lee.

'Hey, Nathen. It's Hulk. Sorry it has been so long, but you know how life seems to get in the way. I'm still up here in the middle of nowhere trying to catch enough to keep a roof over my head. Most of the time, things pan out, but you know what it's like – real hit and miss. How are you?'

Turner was taken aback. He hadn't seen or spoken to his father's ex-partner for close to seven years. 'Hulk? Is that really you? Good grief, man, I thought you'd bloody died!'

Peter 'Hulk' Davis laughed. Same old Turner he remembered. 'I'm calling you from my satellite phone on the boat; we don't have much in the way of modern communications up here. Listen, you still involved in that psychic, spiritualist stuff?'

'Yeah, sure, but not the same as before. I don't perform anymore, just well … teach people about it. Why are you asking?' The dog had padded down the stairs to see what all the fuss was about and patiently sat at Turner's feet as he spoke, tail wagging.

Hulk pressed on, trying his best to describe what Fletcher had found. 'We've got a guy up here. A guest staying in one of the old crofts. Anyway, he found a couple of things and was trying to figure out what they meant, thought you might know. One is like that souvenir coin thing you get at Whitby Abbey. You know, the one with St Benedict on, except this one looks old and it's bigger than the usual tourist charm type.'

'So tell him it's a souvenir from an abbey,' Turner said bluntly, bemused as to why Hulk would ring him about such a common object.

'OK, point taken, but that's not the main thing. He found one of those witch's symbols. You know, the star thing?' Hulk superstitiously crossed himself again at the other end of the line as he mentioned the symbol.

'You mean a pentagram? Down here, I can't walk ten yards without seeing one. So, what's the big deal?' Turner was growing impatient, his warm tot of whisky and toasty fire calling to him from up the stairs.

'Well, it's painted on the inside of a door. And the weird thing is, it looks like it's bleeding. Really creeped me out. You know how I feel about things like that.' Hulk shivered slightly as he remembered the bleeding paint.

Turner remembered Hulk and his superstitions well. The giant couldn't walk past a magpie without saluting, believing them to be an omen of bad luck. Plus, he never went out to sea on Friday the thirteenth, something that was a constant source of annoyance to his late father. Remembering something from his background reading about witches in his bizarre book collection, he asked, 'Was there any writing inside the pentagram, like hieroglyphics or a weird language?' Turner now had his full attention on the call.

'Yes, how'd you know?' Hulk hoped Turner wouldn't say he'd had a bloody psychic premonition and laugh at him.

'And you said it looks like it's bleeding?' Something flashed into Turner's mind. 'In pagan times, symbols like this were used to protect from evil. If it's on the inside of the door then something evil was inside that building at one time, and the symbol was meant to stop it getting out. If the symbol looks like it's bleeding, then maybe whatever it is has got out.' Turner had spent countless hours in the past week or so researching this very thing. He spoke urgently into the phone, trying to make sure Hulk understood him.

'C'mon, Nathen. You're trying to scare me. You're trying to wind me up because you know I'm superstitious. Are you telling me something dangerous has been let loose up here? That's nothing new – if the cold doesn't get you, then another thing will. It's a rough place up here, you know.' Hulk shook his head, expecting to hear Turner laughing back at him down the line.

Turner's frustration was mounting as he tried to get his point across to his old friend. 'Look, I don't know how to convince you. These sorts of things are real – I've seen stuff you'd never believe. Whoever this guest of yours is needs to be careful. Can he protect himself, do you think? Physically, I mean, if it comes to it?'

Hulk chuckled, still not taking it seriously. 'Don't be silly – he's a city boy up here on a break.' The fisherman was beginning to regret making the call. He should have known better than to try to get a psychic to give him good news.

'You need to tell him to keep his eyes open for anything unusual. Let me know – maybe I can help somehow.' In reality, Turner had no idea what he could do, but felt compelled to offer.

Hulk would much rather keep well away from all this superstitious talk; it was beginning to make him feel uneasy. 'OK, will do. I'll pop over tomorrow and tell him. Can he call you direct?'

Turner happily agreed, and the rest of the call was spent catching up and exchanging pleasantries. He made Hulk promise to tell the guest about his warning as soon as he could, and then they said their farewells. In sombre mood, Turner grabbed his whisky and made his way up the stairs to his bedroom on the top floor. Carefully, he began to comb through his books on witchcraft and the occult, looking for the study on the symbol he'd read about a few days earlier. Deep into the early hours of the morning, he found what he was looking for in an old Elizabethan text from 1684. He read the Latin translation in modern English as:

The Symbol of the Pentagram

The Pentagram is a five-pointed star representing the five elements – Earth, Fire, Water, Air and Quintessence. When enclosed in a complete circle it is used as a talisman by Druids and Witches for rituals and spells and sometimes called a Pentacle. Symbols within the circle indicate the type of spell used, but the language of these symbols is often coded. The symbols can be drawn in chalk or sandstone, but it is believed that the most powerful rituals use animal blood. If the spell or charm fails, it is common for the symbol to appear to bleed …

So he'd remembered correctly – something had caused the charm to fail, whatever that was. He knew 'Quintessence' was the old word the alchemists used for the 'spirit' or 'energy' they believed dwelt in all things. Now, it appeared, something best kept hidden had escaped, and was roaming across the remote wilderness in north-west Scotland.

CHAPTER 5: VISIONS IN THE NIGHT

Back at the croft, Mike Fletcher's struggle with the lobster had proved conclusive and delicious. With a side order of tinned potatoes, he felt like the laird of the manor, sitting in front of the wood stove, polishing off the last of his feast. He hadn't felt this good in ages and the mood of optimism got him thinking about his camera gear.

Carelessly pulling over the rucksack from the corner, he grabbed the camera body and short zoom lens. It felt good in his hands and he expertly manipulated the controls by touch. He raised it to his damaged eye; the image was still hazy, as if the lens had misted over with condensation. By instinct, he checked the lens and viewfinder, but the precisely engineered glass surfaces were fog free. He tried the other eye. It felt awkward, like trying to write with the wrong hand. There was no haze this time, but the image remained blurry after the autofocus had kicked in. Slipping off the rubber eyecup protecting the viewfinder, he gently turned the dioptric adjustment dial until the image came into focus. So far so good – at least the camera was adapted for his vision. Flicking up the on-board flash, he eased the shutter down and took a shot of the empty lobster shell discarded on the plate in front of him. Not exactly an award winner, he thought, but a first step, perhaps, to regaining his confidence.

To check the results, he pressed the replay button on the back of the camera before zooming in to check the quality. For professional work, everything had to be perfect, from the exposure to the focus. Slightly nervous, he manoeuvred the zoom area over each part of the image before minutely examining the detail. It didn't look too bad – the edges of the shell were sharp and the vivid red colours showed through, true to life. He needed a more severe test.

Heading outside, Fletcher needed to find a subject with some fine detail and a range of colour tones. The symbol on the byre door would be perfect, with the thin outline of the red against the cracking green paint of the door. The half broken-down wall and missing roof panels let in some natural daylight, so he could try with and without the flash, and see how he did. By instinct, he moved around, constantly changing shot position. High, then low; wide, then close up. His feeling of unease about the symbol melted away – working his camera, as always, was taking his mind off the subject as he concentrated on getting the shot. After an adrenalin-pumping ten minutes, he was back inside, examining his results. He'd taken a total of twelve shots, of which three were blurry and unusable, four were not bad, and five were probably acceptable. The five were a mixture of close-ups and general images showing the whole design. Again zooming in using the LCD on the camera back, he went over them bit by bit.

Fletcher knew from experience that digital imaging would often show detail not visible to the naked eye, particularly under direct flash lighting. That was certainly the case here. The straight edges of the pentagram were sharp and clean towards the inside, but runs and streaks spotted the outside, as if dripping from the line. The hieroglyphs inside the symbol were much easier to read, and he could make out what looked like the rounded capital letters E and M, but the others bore no relation to any alphabet he'd ever seen. Inspired by his progress so far, he went out and tried again. As with most professional photographers, it had become almost like an addiction for him, always looking for a better image, a better angle. He'd never yet met a pro who was one hundred per cent satisfied with their photographs.

After another dozen attempts, his strike rate had got a little better. This time, half of them were probably acceptable and he felt proud of himself. Carefully, he compared his first set of images with the latest ones and then sat back, confused. He'd covered the same areas as before, but this time the blurring of the lines on the outside had changed. There was no mistake; he checked over and over again. In the second set, the dripping was definitely longer – not by much, but it had certainly changed.

It was now too dark to try again and double-check his results. A little unnerved by the changes in the images, he wandered out down to the shoreline to clear his head, following the route of his moonlit walk the previous evening. He'd noticed a change in his confidence since his MS diagnosis. The slightest thing seemed to worry him and he found himself second-guessing all the decisions he made – like he wasn't good enough and needed a second opinion on everything he did. With nobody around to check over his camera results and see whether he was imagining things, he needed a distraction to push away the fear that was starting to eat away inside him.

A light breeze fluttered across the water, making the air taste crisp and salty. Over the bay, he could make out the glimmer of lights from Benlogan, and he wondered idly what the residents' lives must be like, and what had brought them to such a remote area. Were they, like him, looking for a break from the day-to-day rat race, trying to find some sense of meaning and purpose in their existence? Possibly, he thought, although maybe many had been born in the area and didn't know any different. He decided to ask Hulk next time he saw him and see whether he could convince the giant to take him over for a look around. At some point, he'd need more provisions, so the town would be as good a place as any to get them.

Stars twinkled brightly in the ebony sky like tiny specks of glow in the dark dust clinging to a blanket. Fletcher had never seen so many; the fog and haze of London were not the best fit for aspiring astronomers. At most, you counted yourself lucky to get a half decent view of the moon above the skyscrapers and towering streetlights. Silently, he congratulated himself again on his decision to get away from it all. Though the accommodation was incredibly basic, he felt blessed to have found the place. Already, one day in, he was starting to feel more relaxed as he eased into a slower pace of life.

On the way back up the rocky path to the croft, Fletcher caught the green glimmer of a pair of eyes and a blunt ringed tail up close to the byre, highlighted briefly in the light from the croft window where he'd left one of the oil lamps burning inside. Following the orange glow bathing the path, he trotted back up to the croft door, searching for the cat. He had hoped it would come back. Maybe the smell of his cooking had roused its curiosity and it was on the hunt for an easy meal. Hopefully, it was in a better mood this time. If he could convince it to become a regular visitor, he felt sure the hairy beast would make an interesting companion.

'Come on, I won't hurt you. Let me get inside and I'll get you something,' he called gently, for some reason assuming the cat understood English. Moving as silently as he could, so as not to scare it, he skirted in a wide line away from the byre and up to the front door. There was no sign of it; even his Ninja-like approach tactics had been too loud. Alone again inside, he bolted the door and made himself ready for bed. Realising this security measure was totally unnecessary in this remote wilderness, he'd still been unable to break the habit of locking the door. You could take the man out of the city, but not the city out of the man, he mused silently to himself.

Washing plates and cleaning up didn't take long, and he found himself returning to the images on the camera. They were definitely different and he was at a complete loss for how to explain it. The best he could think of was that, somehow, the flash lighting had picked out more detail in the second series of shots. As the flash was a small, low power unit that popped up from the top of the viewfinder when required, this didn't make sense. With a setup like this, the lighting couldn't move, so all the images would receive the exact same illumination every time. Anyway, it was the best explanation he had, so he turned his attention to searching for the elusive cat through the living-room window.

The moon was at its height and spreading its silvery rays across the byre and the slope down to the seashore. It was a beautiful peaceful scene, the shadowy pine trees majestically framing the view, guarding sentry-like each side of the glade the croft was snuggled inside. The left of his face where he'd gone blind was aching badly – it always did when he tried to use his vision more. Though he'd been using his right eye to photograph, he'd given his damaged one more work to do, and it was letting him know. If he was ever going to get back to work, this was something he'd just have to learn to live with.

As Fletcher's gaze adjusted to the soft illumination bathing the beautiful scene outside, something caught his eye straight in front of the croft through the broken-down wall of the byre. There were two small pinpricks of light inside the byre that flickered in and out, moving up and down inside the building. He saw the tiny lights emerge, attached to a dark substance that seemed to slither over the pile of rubble and weave its way towards the house. It looked like the glimmering lights were two eyes, reflecting in the moonlight, attached to something human sized and moving on two feet, not four. Whatever it was, he realised with horror, it certainly wasn't the cat this time. Moment by moment it drew nearer, increasing in stature and bulk as it approached, as if it was wearing a cloak, flowing and spreading in the breeze. Now and then he lost it in the long shadows stretched across the rocky path. Then it appeared again, larger than ever, still coming directly towards the window, where he stood rooted to the spot. He felt gripped by an uncontrollable fear and wanted to scream, but his voice was paralysed, his tongue glued to the roof of his mouth. Then the terrifying object, drawn to full height, turned to one side and moved around the house and off into the trees at the far side of the glade. From the light of the window, he thought he glimpsed the edges of a dark cape being pulled tightly in around the figure, standing about the same height as he was, as it increased speed and disappeared into the night.

For over an hour, he sat staring out of the window, unable to take his gaze off the byre and the path outside. Sometimes he imagined he saw a shadowy shape shifting in and out of the treeline near the shore, but it was nothing more than the rippling water playing tricks on his eyes. His vision always got worse at night, so how much of what he thought he saw, and how much his imagination had added to it, he couldn't be sure. Realising that if something was out there he'd be an easy target in the croft, he felt compelled to investigate. Shrugging off the fear gnawing at him ever since he'd found the pentagram, he grabbed an oil lamp with a trembling hand and stepped quietly outside.

Nothing looked any different from the doorstep as he examined the short distance to the byre and tilted his head, listening intently for any sound. The mossy ground was still soft from the thunderstorm, so his boots made no noise as he sidestepped slowly down across the front garden. Pushing on the byre door, the creaking hinges sounded like a gunshot going off in the dark, and he carefully prised it open to peer inside. Light from the lamp only revealed the space a couple of feet ahead, so, shaking and a little anxious, he took a step forward. At first everything looked the same. Tools still hung in their regular spots, the fishing rod was still in place … and then he saw it. The other part of the sandstone slab, the one that had remained on the granite bench, was no longer there. It lay overturned on the opposite side, some five feet away as though flung like a discarded toy. Fletcher paused, gripped with a sense of sheer dread he could not understand. What manner of thing could move so heavy an object as if it were nothing? he wondered, lifting the lamp higher to get a better look at the bizarre scene. Marks in the dirt floor spread out haphazardly from a small brown object trapped underneath one edge of the overturned slab. He knelt down carefully for a closer look and gasped in horror when he realised what is was – a withered human finger.

Fletcher sensed something watching him from outside, something peering over the top of the broken-down wall. Spinning around quickly, he caught a glimpse of a slithering shadow. Cautiously, he raised the oil lamp to get a clearer view. Scrabbling over the top brick, clawing and grasping its way slowly forward, was a bony hand that disappeared into a black shadowy figure. Skin brown; dry, cracking like a fallen leaf in autumn, the forefinger absent. Slowly it was scraping its way forward, moving directly towards the terrified photographer. Fletcher jumped to his feet and then ran as fast as he could, screaming into the night.

Running across the clear ground, he crashed headlong into the pine forest, desperately trying to find cover and hide in the woodland, ignoring the pain as the sharp branches cut and tore at his flesh. In his fear, he'd dropped the oil lamp and was running blind, his bruised body smashing from tree to tree. Too afraid to look back, he pressed ahead for what felt like hours. Now he was falling, tumbling helplessly, grasping desperately for anything that would slow his descent. With a sickening snap, his world went black.

CHAPTER 6: ROAMING THE HILLS

For Maggie Douglas, every day started much like any other. Rise at dawn, a light breakfast, then eight miles of difficult walking amidst the steep slopes of the Highland fells. All she'd ever known was working the land; it was in her blood. For more than five generations her family had been serving the remote peninsula, from its more inhabited beginnings as a thriving crofting and fishing community, to its now isolated and barren state, with the odd herd of red deer and her flock of Blackface sheep.

Maggie shared the tiny estate lodge with Callum Benvie, the grandly titled head keeper. In truth, he was the only keeper responsible for the entire six-and-a-half thousand-acre estate. The remoteness, and changeable weather, had driven away the modern tourist looking for convenience and twenty-four-hour room service. Even the stalking parties, organised by the London money set, had abandoned the area for the convenience of taking their Range Rovers to more hospitable dwellings, with electricity and chefs on call for their boozy evening feasts.

Maggie headed out into the largest outbuilding, which served as part garage and part workshop, to find the stocky white pony missing. That meant one thing – Callum was up and out before her and hunting for red deer. Throughout the year, he meticulously managed the stag and hind population, culling the old and weak to maintain the strongest herd possible. Callum used the pony to transport the carcass back to the lodge, shunning the Argocat and quad bike for his more traditional method. The full-grown animals were a heavy burden, often weighing fifteen to eighteen stone, so he always called on the help of their only neighbour, Julian Etienne, to join him in the pursuit. She guessed Julian was used to his early-morning tweed-clad surprise visitor, and looked forward to a delicious venison meal as much as she did. Julian was an enigma. Completely self-sufficient, but always the first one to offer help, without any thought for himself. His carpentry skills were extraordinary, and their fine carved fireplaces and bookcases were proud examples of his expertise. She guessed he was in his sixties, but it was hard to tell; he had one of those faces that didn't seem to age. The three of them had happily co-existed on their little isolated strip of land for as long as she could remember, with little interference from the estate managers and landowners. For her, it was idyllic. Despite the hardship of the environment, she felt at peace and as one with the wonder of wild nature.

The squat, toad-like profile of the green eight-wheel drive Argocat stared back at her as if to say, 'Drive me.' In truth, she did feel a little tired this morning, so maybe a petrol-assisted trip to her flock would not be such a bad idea. Settling on the red Honda quad bike, she strapped an axe and chainsaw on the rear cargo rack, and manoeuvred the bike carefully forward through the wide doorway. After the recent storm, it was likely she'd come across maybe one or two felled trees that would make ideal firewood to add to their winter stock. Driving the quad was much more fun than the caterpillar-like Argocat. She was positively excited as she pushed the starter and it boomed noisily into life.

The four-wheel drive of the monster machine made light work of the narrow muddy track as she roared through the golden glow of the morning rays. She tore forward with a huge grin on her face, red hair whipping messily around her freckled features. The key job this morning was to check the health of the lambs. She'd be sending them off to market shortly, so it was vital that they were doing well, both for themselves and the state of her future bank balance.

After fifteen minutes of bumpy motoring, she found them on the lower slopes of Bean-nighe crag, its towering grey presence dominating the upper reaches of the mountainside. It was named after the Gaelic Bean-nighe spirit, or 'washing woman' in English, the grotesque contours of its granite face appearing to form the outline of a strange sitting lady in the shadows of the morning. According to legend, on moonlit nights a small and squat childlike figure could be seen below the mountain, washing bloodstained shrouds in one of the many remote rock pools throughout the vast corrie. As this mountain spirit ceaselessly beat and wrung the water from her macabre laundry, she could be heard crooning a sorrowful lament all to herself. The traveller who dared to speak to her would hear the names of those about to die, or, if he wished it, his own fate foretold. Julian was an expert storyteller and had many such tales of the area's history, providing Maggie and Callum with plenty of spooky entertainment well into the depths of the night.

Half a dozen sheep ran up to her, baaing in delight at the familiar presence, expecting some form of treat for their trouble. Spooning out a handful of turnip scraps from her deep parka pocket, she cast them amidst the purple heather and watched as the curly horned bundles of wool began to search for them. The coarse straggled coats looked in good condition for the time of year, and the lambs were gaining weight from their lowland foraging. Out of the corner of her eye she saw a mass of brown fur slinking towards her. It was coming out from the treeline on the lower part of the track and making a beeline for the quad bike. To her complete surprise, she recognised it immediately as a large Scottish wildcat. There was no mistaking this beast of ferocious reputation, but it was unusual to see one in daylight. As with most wild animals, the wildcat was a shy and elusive creature, preferring to run away unless cornered. It stopped about twenty yards away, sat down, and fixed her with a hard stare from its green eyes.

Curious, she slowly moved forward to get a closer look. The black and brown tabby markings provided excellent camouflage amongst the pines, but she spotted the round tip of a blunt tail disappearing back into the trees. A large head, with whiskers twitching, popped back out around a tree stump, and she laughed. It was like the cat was playing a game of hide-and-seek with her. Pressing on cautiously to the tree stump, she watched the tail disappear again through the woods, and then, sure enough, the furry head popped back out again. Intrigued, she followed her stealthy companion down through the woodland to the ravine at the bottom.

The ravine was a huge cleft in the rock, formed over millions of years by the ebb and flow of the bubbling waterfall noisily gushing at its head. Swathes of pine lined each side, blanketing the steep slopes in an array of towering green trunks, tottering in the light breeze. High over the top, towards the east, several miles of dense woodland covered the ground before dipping back to the sea and opening into the glade that held Lanner's Point Croft. Hooded crows circled in the sky, their sooty-feathered wings and heads contrasting with the light grey of their bodies. Maggie hated the things. The ghastly bird was an indiscriminate and cruel predator, responsible for maiming members of her flock at the slightest opportunity. Many times she'd found trapped ewes with an eye pecked out or some other ghastly injury inflicted by the sadistic creatures. Seeing them circling in the sky like this meant one thing – death.

From her vantage point, she could see the cat expertly pad down the steep slope and move towards a brown shape lying near the bubbling stream at the bottom of the bank. Once at the shape, it stopped, sat down gently, and then looked back at her again. The brown contour was too thin for a deer, and somehow it seemed to look unnatural. Using a fallen branch as a walking staff, she picked her way down, slipping and sliding on the mix of loose stone and pine needles. Almost running the last few yards with her downwards momentum, she fell with an undignified thump on the mossy ground. Her feline guide stood emotionless, watching the performance, tilting its head curiously as if to see whether she was hurt.

With horror, Maggie realised that the peculiar brown shape was the body of a man. One leg was bent sickeningly back in ripped cargo trousers, with a congealed patch of thick red ooze soaking through the cloth on the thigh. The face was badly bruised, one cheek ballooning out unnaturally below the eye and an untidy mess of black hair. All the areas of exposed skin she could see were scratched and torn, as if the body had been dragged through a thorny hedge. With heart racing, she felt for a pulse in the neck and pressed her face close to the mangled features to see whether she could hear any sounds of breathing. For what seemed like hours, but in reality was a few seconds, she could sense nothing from the cold figure. Then he coughed – painfully, retching up a bloody froth from his lips.

With no means of calling for help, her only option was to get the man back to the lodge somehow, then get hold of Callum and Julian. The nearest hospital was over a hundred miles away – she doubted he'd survive the bumpy trip back up the mountain, let alone a longer journey. Both Callum and Julian had learnt the hard way how to deal with field injuries, and Maggie prayed they'd know what to do with this wounded stranger, if, that is, she could get him back to the estate lodge. With a great heave, she propped the man on his side and stuck her fingers in his bloody mouth to check for any blockages. A short red tuft of moss came out sickeningly in her fingers and she threw it away into the stream. Tilting his head back, she checked again that he was still breathing. Removing the moss seemed to have helped a little, and for the first time she could clearly see his chest moving under the tattered brown shirt. Carefully making her way up the ravine, she followed her trail to the quad bike and began to manoeuvre it slowly down the bank. It was dangerous and heavy work. One slip would mean that both her and the seven-hundred-pound quad would go tumbling down the slippery slope. Stubbornly, Maggie refused to wear head protection when using either of the outdoor vehicles, and she was beginning to regret her pure disregard for safety. For over an hour, she zigzagged her way downhill, reducing the steep angle by travelling in long convoluted spirals. When she couldn't go any further, she cut a path with the chainsaw and axe, and inched her way over the sliding rocks.

To her relief, he was still breathing when she pulled the noisy quad alongside. He'd have to go on the front cargo rack so that she could keep an eye on him as they travelled. Fortunately, he was of medium height with a skinny frame, so, she figured, with a little effort, she could get him up there. Cutting a sturdy piece of pine shorter than the length of his leg, she strapped it tightly to his misshapen limb using two of the bungee cords from the cargo racks. At least that should keep it from getting any worse, Maggie hoped quietly to herself. Next, she stripped four prickly pine branches and cut them so that they extended about a foot each side of the quad. Laying these together over the black cargo frame would provide a temporary stretcher and also shield him a little from the heat of the engine. Bit by bit, she secured each branch, pushing them tightly together on the front of the quad before stepping back and checking her handiwork. Not perfect, but it would have to do.

The prone figure hadn't moved, and the cat had disappeared back into the hills some time ago. With no way of getting the man to help her move him, she knew she'd have to lift him in one go. Anxiously, she knelt down and eased one of her hands through the hollow made by his pelvis, and the other under his shoulders. Thrusting up furiously with her legs, she had him balanced precariously on her chest as she tottered to the bike. As carefully as she could, she rolled him onto the makeshift stretcher, where he lay corpse-like, his swollen face drained of all colour. Thank God the years of manhandling sheep had made her strong enough for the task, she thought gratefully. After more work with the bungee cords, she felt happy enough that he couldn't move from his temporary resting place, and began the slow ascent up the ravine.

Going uphill proved easier, and the extra weight on the front helped to prevent the quad from tipping over backwards. Retracing the path she'd cut on the way down was a simple task as logs and branches lay scattered either side. By the time she'd reached the top, there was no sign of her flock of sheep. Maggie guessed that they'd probably moved on to forage on the other side of the corrie, following the sun as it journeyed westward. The light was fading fast as she approached the lodge, and she felt relieved to see smoke pouring from both chimneys and the stocky white pony grazing in the meadow. Both fires lit meant that the kitchen and living room were seeing some action, so, hopefully, Julian had stayed to share in the venison feast.

The men heard the noise of the quad and came out to greet her. Callum always wore the same clothes – tweed trousers, a plain blue shirt and gaiters covering heavy boots. In colder weather, he'd add a green fleece body warmer and a waterproof wax jacket, but that was the full extent of his exploration into the world of fashion.

Callum's craggy features shouted over to her, 'What the hell have you got there? We've already got a beautiful stag in the larder. Don't tell me you've got another deer!' His voice boomed over the sound of the engine.

She cut the motor and motioned them over urgently to take a look. Julian had a green wool hat pushed down over his ears, and he yanked it off quickly in surprise when he saw the figure. The result made the mottled grey and black tufts of hair either side of his large bald patch stand on end, making him look like a weird impression of Bugs Bunny. In other circumstances, she would have laughed out loud. Not sure why he'd removed his headwear, and feeling the cold on his shining brow, he stuck the hat back on.

'Who on earth is that?' Julian asked in surprise. He never swore and was always proper and polite. It was one of the things she loved about him.

'I've no idea, Julian. I found him over by the ravine down from Bean-nighe.'

'He alive?' Callum said quickly, always direct and to the point in times of crisis. He believed in sorting out what needed doing first, then talking later. Maggie nodded 'yes' at him. 'Good – Julian, give me a hand. Let's get him in and take a look.'

Between them, they lifted the broken body like a weightless rag doll, and placed him carefully onto the wooden floor in the lamplit living room. Using his short gralloch knife, Callum cut away at the sodden cloth matted around the misshapen leg. To his untrained eye he couldn't tell whether the leg was broken; the entire thigh area was a mess of mottled purple bruises. The swollen limb bent awkwardly outward and congealed blood caked around a four-inch gash above the knee.

Callum looked downtrodden as he spoke, like he felt he was condemning a wounded animal to its death. 'We're going to have to straighten out this leg, and stitch up that wound, before we do anything else. Maggie, can you make me a pot of boiling water, and Julian, can you get the first-aid kit from the shed, soon as you can? If we can't sort this leg we're going to have to get him to hospital – if he survives the night.'

The keeper made himself busy, whittling sturdy wooden splints from the woodpile by the fire, while the others set about their tasks silently. For thirty minutes, they worked on the leg, cleaning and stitching the wound first, before Julian pulled hard and straight on the ankle to set it back into a normal position. The man screamed and struggled weakly before passing out again. Callum quickly bound the straightened limb with the splints and tight bandages before they moved on to his other injuries.

Everything else proved, thankfully, superficial. There was much more bruising and scratching, but nothing that needed stitching. Finally, they worked on the swollen face. As Maggie wiped carefully over the balloon-like cheek, the man opened his eyes. They had a strange look in the flickering light of the lamp. One pupil was permanently wide open, while the other opened and closed normally with the passing of the soft illumination.

'Can you hear me, sir? Can you see me? We found you on the hill. You're in the estate lodge – you're safe now. We're trying to help you. Don't try and move – your leg is in a pretty bad way, could be broken, but I don't think so. I'm Maggie. What's your name?' She leant over him, staring into the strange blue eyes, looking for a response.

The man tried to lift his head, then slumped down again as if exhausted. Gazing at the stranger's freckled face, he could see the worry on her brow. Achingly, he moved his lips. 'Mike … my name is Mike Fletcher.' And then he passed out again.

CHAPTER 7: A RUDE AWAKENING

The angry ringing of the telephone downstairs cut through Nathen Turner's cosy slumber. Bounding down the three flights of stairs to the kitchen, he grabbed the handset.

'Hello, Nathen here,' he mumbled sleepily, shivering in the cool morning air.

'Nathen, it's Hulk.' The burly voice of the fisherman sounded urgent on the line.

'Hulk, what the hell? What's happened … something wrong? What time is it?'

'About seven-thirty,' Hulk said, glancing down at his watch. Turner could hear birds twittering merrily in the background, enjoying the morning. Wherever Hulk was, he was outside. The voice of the giant pressed on. 'You know that guy I told you about last night – the one who found the coin and witch symbol thingy? I went over, soon as it was light this morning, to tell him what you said about being careful and stuff – he's gone. Simply disappeared.' Hulk's words came tumbling out quickly, his voice full of concern for the missing photographer.

'What do you mean, gone? He can't have gone far, surely – why the big panic?' Turner was not a morning person. He felt irritated and cold, wanting nothing more than to climb back into his warm bed.

'I'm not sure what's happened, Nathen, but it doesn't feel right somehow. Listen …' the superstitious Hulk pleaded with him down the phone. Not wanting to leave anything out, he described each detail of his visit to the croft that morning. Shortly after dawn, he'd motored across the bay to call on Mike Fletcher. With Turner's words ringing in his head, he'd had a sleepless night, wanting to get over as soon as possible with the satellite phone so that the holiday visitor could talk directly to the psychic. He'd found the door to the croft and byre wide open with no sign of its guest, an oil lamp still burning on the windowsill. Inside the house, all Fletcher's things were still there, with the bed neatly laid out and no trace that it had been slept in. A thick waterproof outdoor coat hung carelessly from a spike above the mattress. Wherever Fletcher had gone, he certainly hadn't intended to be out for long in the chilly weather. Plates and cutlery from the night before were neatly cleaned and stacked next to the sink, and the stove was ice cold. He'd guessed it hadn't been attended to since the previous evening. Outside in the byre, it looked like he'd moved both slabs off the top of the granite workbench for some reason, and the outline of scattered footprints lay in the dirt. The thing that had caused Hulk such panic was the object he'd found lying next to one of the slabs. It was a human forefinger. Brown and wrinkled like old tissue paper, with a grotesque pointed yellowing fingernail. It looked incredibly decrepit; whatever blood had run through its withered veins had dried up long ago.

'You sure about the human finger part?' asked Turner urgently, alert and attentive to Hulk's story. The fisherman said he was. 'You still at the croft?' Again another 'yes' in reply from the giant. 'OK, go back in the byre and look at the pentagram sign behind the door. Take your time; check it over closely. Does it look any different from yesterday?' The line went quiet, picking up soft footsteps and the creaking of the panelled door.

'Oh my God! Nathen, it's definitely bleeding. I swear the thing is dripping blood and it's still wet.' Hulk had sunk to his knees behind the door, wiping the dirty crimson ooze that had leached down the panels and onto his hand. 'Arghh … bloody hell, it's burning my hand …' The skin was already blistering angrily on the fisherman's callus fingertips.

'Get out of there! Wash your hand in the sea, get in the boat and get away from there as fast as you can. Call me when you're back on the other side of the bay. Now, move NOW!' Turner was almost shrieking down the line in an attempt to get his friend to act quickly. The line went dead with an urgent grunted acknowledgement and the sound of frantic scrabbling as the boat motor roared into life.

By the time Hulk called back, Turner was already on the road heading north. He sensed something otherworldly was going on at this remote spot, and his psychic sixth sense was never wrong. With the pentagram now dripping and oozing, Turner felt certain that something unnatural, some ancient evil, had been let loose and was roaming the moor. The thought that his father's old partner could be in real danger from something supernatural was enough for him to move. Psychic coaching would have to wait – in Turner's world, friends and family always came first.

After hastily packing a small olive canvas weekender bag with essentials, he'd thrown on his clothes and bundled his sleepy dog, Kyle, into the back of his silver VW Golf. After grabbing a few old books and occult-looking items from the bedroom shelf, he'd taken a small brown leather Gladstone briefcase from a locked side cupboard. After a quick check of the contents, he'd been satisfied and had headed downstairs to set up the service that diverted all incoming phone calls to his mobile, before climbing in his car.

Pulling in to Durham Services, he parked and took the return call from Hulk. This time Turner was the one speaking anxiously, his words cascading out without a pause. 'Do not let anyone go over to the croft. Do you understand me? Whatever is going on there is not going to take too kindly to being disturbed. I've no idea what it is, but I'm on my way north to you. The slight problem is, I haven't got a clue where you are, other than Scotland.'

Hulk had to smile at the man's impulsiveness. Turner's father had been the same, always wanting to get on with things. One of his favourite sayings, after a few ales at their local, had been, 'Thing wrong with problems is people. Won't do anything to solve them.' Hulk passed over the Benlogan address and a few waypoints along the route to look out for. In truth, Hulk would be glad of the company and was extremely grateful that Turner was heading up. The whole business was making him feel uneasy, and, although he was loath to admit it, a little afraid. Thanking him for coming, he ended the conversation with, 'Remember, if you think you've driven to the end of the known world, Nathen, you're probably in the right place.'

The rest of Turner's journey proved uneventful, but long. After six more hours of concentrated driving, he was three miles away before his satellite navigation system gave up. Whoever had programmed the map seemed to have forgotten about this particular stretch of remote countryside. Surrounded by the darkest night he'd ever experienced, he headed the car hopefully towards a small glimmer in the distance. With headlights on full beam, he eventually spotted an ancient stone cairn at the side of the road with 'Benlogan' scratched deeply in its upper rock. Luckily, his hunch had paid off, and he'd found the isolated community.

With a dozen properties in the village, it didn't take Turner long to find Hulk's house. It was a sprawling, L-shaped one-storey bungalow, with granite walls and a huge solid-wood front door. Stretching to relieve his stiff muscles as he got out of the car, he quickly headed over the gravel front drive and hammered on the door. The huge shape of his father's old friend blotted out the light from the hallway as he stood beaming on the threshold.

'Nathen Turner, as I live and breathe. It's been far too long, my friend.' Hulk grinned widely as he greeted Turner, patting him on the shoulder with his huge left paw. Turner buckled under the impact and smiled back, offering his hand. 'Can't shake it, I'm afraid – still not right after this morning,' Hulk said, holding up his right fingers wrapped tightly together in a neat crêpe bandage to illustrate the point. 'C'mon, I'll help you unload.'

'No!' shouted Turner, but it was too late. Hulk opened the car's back door and the shaggy muscular frame of Kyle bounded out in a desperate attempt to escape its steel prison. The dog leapt at him with a speed and power that would have knocked a normal-sized man flat on his back. Instead, Hulk deftly caught him in mid-air, laughing, and Kyle began enthusiastically licking his face. Hulk gently put the dog down and it ran around him in circles, wagging its long tail furiously.

'I think you've made a friend there. Feed him and he'll want to marry you,' Turner said laughing, watching the pair of them chase each other around the front porch like a couple of schoolchildren.

'No fear of that. I've escaped so far, and I'm too old to change my ways,' Hulk laughed back. The giant man had never been married. Had never wanted to be. He was one of those unique human beings that didn't crave human company, but accepted it gracefully if it was offered. The idea of sharing his personal space on a long-term basis had never held any attraction to him.

Inside, they dined on a delicious crab salad, followed by a huge bowl of steaming Scotch broth with homemade bread. Kyle feasted on hot lamb scraps from the broth and a mutton bone they'd found in the larder. Turner's appearance had caused his host much amusement. The flowery patterned black Hawaiian shirt, jeans and cowboy boots were as much out of place in the Highlands as they were back in Whitby. Throughout the meal, Turner sat shivering and rubbing his hands together, until Hulk threw him a brown Arran jumper, and insisted he put it on. It was so big on him that it looked like he was wearing a thick woollen mini dress, but it did keep him warm.

They made an odd pair, sitting around the roaring fire – the giant on one side and the cross-dressing psychic on the other – as they reminisced on old times and bawdy tales of his father's drinking exploits. Conversation flowed freely, as it does with old friends, even after years apart. It was over seven years since his father had passed away and his ex-business partner had moved north, but an outsider looking in would never have guessed.

'How's your mother, Nathen? Still a bingo demon, I assume?' Hulk was referring to her regular weekly appearance at the local bingo hall. She always used the same seat, and drank no more than four cups of tea during the evening. She believed that breaking any part of this ritual would bring her bad luck. One week, there had almost been a fight when a tourist inadvertently grabbed her favourite chair. Thankfully, Turner had been on hand to intervene before things went too far.

'Yes, I'm afraid so, but she doesn't go out much now. She moved into the care home down in Filey a couple of years ago. There are beautiful views of the sea and Coble Landing from her window. I think that looking out across the water soothes her – brings back memories of dad. Here, let me look at your hand.' Turner wanted to change the subject. Watching his mother grow older and weaker saddened him. She seemed like she was counting her days, longing to join Turner's father in whatever part of the afterlife he'd ended up. In his mind, he'd never thought his mother would age, imagining the boisterous lady of his youth continuing for an eternity. How many other sons and daughters had thought the same? he wondered, before pushing the darkening thoughts out of his head.

Pulling over the Gladstone briefcase, Turner removed the bandage from Hulk's damaged hand. The sheer sight of it made him wince. From the first joint up on each finger were white blisters bursting with milky fluid. Angry orange blotches spattered the rest of the digits all the way down to the knuckle. Using a small strangely shaped bottle of thick milky liquid, he soaked a triangular blue cloth illustrated with yellow alchemical symbols, and wrapped it around the hand.

'Keep the dressing on until morning. It will feel a lot better by then,' Turner said matter-of-factly, as if this was a regular occurrence in his daily existence.

'How do you know this stuff, Nathen? What the hell is going on at the croft? I don't mind telling you, this has got me jumpy. I'm imagining shapes in the shadows – last night I left a lamp burning all night, for goodness' sake!' Hulk seemed embarrassed by his confession and sat gazing at the floor, refusing to make eye contact.

Turner reached into his canvas bag and pulled out an old, thick book bound in cracked black leather. 'I don't know, but I do understand what burnt your hand. It's all in here. You won't believe what I'm about to tell you, and, in truth, I used to think it was all nonsense as well. That is, until something happened, and … well, let's just say I'm a believer now.' Turner opened the book and started to explain.

'This book is the first one ever written that exposed phoney witchcraft. Reginald Scot, a well-respected country gent, put it together after years of research. Scot was a credible man of means during the seventeenth century. He wanted to get his colleagues to see past superstition. In those Elizabethan times, not believing in witchcraft was like not believing in trees. Scot felt disgusted that many old crones and paganists were being persecuted and killed without proper evidence of any wrongdoing.' Turner opened the book to an illustrated page showing an array of strange torture devices used to draw confessions from alleged witches, and waved it at Hulk.

'Scot's book exposed the devious methods of the witch finders, and the simple conjuring tricks they used to demonstrate supposedly "supernatural" powers in their accused prisoners. I mean, don't forget, these witch finders got paid well for each witch they brought to justice. It was in their interests to find people guilty. Scot thought that, by publicly exposing the witch finders' deception, it would put an end to the killing of innocents. The problem for Scot came after Elizabeth I died and James I came to the throne – he was a huge believer in witchcraft and demonic powers. So much so that he published his own bloody book on the subject. I mean, can you believe that? A king writing about demonic powers and stuff, scaring the hell out of the population.' Hulk was nodding 'no' silently, enjoying the tale.

'James had all copies of Scot's book burnt when he became king of England in 1603. See, if what Scot wrote was true, and the witch trials were all faked, it made the king look like a fool. It wasn't until much later that it got reprinted, but some sections were missing. Copies of the entire first edition of the book were never found, and the later work was put together from salvaged fragments.'

Hulk bent forward for a closer look at the bound pages. The book was certainly ancient, with half the binding of the spine missing. Pale, yellowing pages jutted unevenly from the body of the closed book, as if cut haphazardly in the binding process. Hulk loved stuff like this, old stories and legends. It took him back to the fairy tales of his youth.

Now in full flow on his favourite subject, Turner said, 'This is a first edition. The only one I know of in existence. It was found hidden in the cellar of Oswin Hall, back home in Whitby. I used to do fake ghost hunts at the hall, in the older parts of the building, catering for the tourists and goths passing through. You remember me doing that, right? It was great fun.' Turner was smiling at the memory.

'Yes, and I remember Oswin Hall too, the old Tudor manor house up from the railway station. How's Juliet Armstrong? She was one foxy lady. I used to fancy her something rotten,' Hulk said enthusiastically, lost in lewd thoughts as he pictured the hall's owner in his head.

'She died about a year back. It's got new owners from down south.' Turner knew there was a lot more to her death than this, but going through what had happened to her with his old friend didn't seem appropriate. Changing back to his subject, he said, 'Oswin Hall had a water leak in the cellar, and one of the walls was replaced. This book was hidden behind the original brickwork, wrapped in sacking – they gave it to me, totally unaware of its significance, knowing I'm into this kind of thing.'

Hulk looked downtrodden at the news of Juliet Armstrong's passing. It seemed like everyone from his old world was leaving him, and he felt lonely and empty somehow. Turner could see he was hurting, so he decided it was best to leave any more talking until later. 'Look, let's talk about this in the morning. We've both had a long day.'

Hulk pulled himself upright and shook his head as if to

wipe away the melancholy. 'No, Nathen, please go on. Feeling sorry for myself, that's all. Daft old bugger.'

Turner shrugged an 'OK' and opened the crusty volume near the back. 'This has all the missing sections. Look – see this section on things Scot couldn't explain and mysterious curses?' Hulk was gazing wide-eyed at an image similar to the pentagram behind the byre door. 'What you found is mentioned here, the bleeding symbol. Some were drawn in animal blood, but the one at the croft can't be; it would have dried up long ago. Others used a special red ochre pigment, mixed up with the sap from a giant hogweed to discourage people from touching it. That's what I think we've got here. What you've got is nothing more than a burn from the sap. When you washed it in the sea, the salt helped draw out the poison, and the poultice I've put on should do the rest. The recipe is in here.' Turner pointed enthusiastically at the crumpled page. There was a printed list of ingredients written in old English and a description of the method needed to produce a curative elixir. 'Modern science has lost all this. There are so many things the alchemists knew that have disappeared with the passing of time.'

Subconsciously, Hulk flexed his damaged fingers. The burning pain was certainly a lot better, and any scepticism he may have had in the ability of his psychic friend disappeared. Curious, Hulk asked, 'So, why is the symbol bleeding? I mean, the stuff was pooling on the floor.'

'I don't know. Apparently the paint, mixed with the hogweed sap, is runny when it's applied and creates the dripping impression you saw first.' Turner pointed at the description in the book to back up his words. 'But I've no idea what has triggered it to run and streak – like you found it this morning. We need to get over there as soon as we can tomorrow so I can take a look. You OK with that?'

The giant nodded back. All this macabre talk was making Hulk feel uneasy and he wanted to lighten the subject in the gloomy room.

'So, are you really psychic, Nathen? I mean, can you show me something?' Hulk sounded like someone challenging a magician to demonstrate his favourite party trick. It was the best he could think of to change the conversation.

'Not really – I don't do shows and stuff anymore. Now I help people develop their gifts, if they think they have them. Not much of a living compared to before, but I hope it will keep me in the black. When you rang me about this, it scared and fascinated me at the same time – I thought maybe I could help. You know, I definitely feel something supernatural here – can't tell you how, but I can sense it.' Turner was deadly serious and stared straight back at the fisherman.

Hulk met Turner's gaze, shivering a little at the thought of something supernatural roaming about the Highlands. Now he'd started the conversation, he felt compelled to know more, so he asked, 'What do you mean, you can sense it? How is that possible?'

Turner looked down at the floor briefly, remembering back to dark days when a real avenging spirit had sought him out for help. 'Look, I know it's difficult to believe but, trust me, I absolutely know there is a realm – call it spirit, afterlife, whatever – that exists beyond what we know. I've seen it; I've experienced it. It nearly killed me. After seeing things like that, it changes you. Now I find I can sense things.'

'So what do we do – I mean, how does it work?' Hulk shifted uncomfortably in his seat, leaning forward a little for Turner's answer.

'Being a psychic is like going into a dark room with an elephant in it, but you can only touch the toenail. Then you have to guess what it is. You know it could be a rhino, a hippo, a mammoth, or whatever, and you have to figure it out. Like this situation – we know there is a pagan symbol painted on the door that was meant to ward off evil somehow. But what that evil is, and why the symbol's changed, we have no idea.' Turner was desperately trying to explain the unexplainable and this was the best analogy he could think of.

Hulk thought for a moment, wondering how to rid the superstitious thoughts clouding his mind. 'Well, if it turns out to be a bloody elephant, you'll be the one picking up the poo! Man, those buggers can crap for England – I remember seeing them at Whipsnade Zoo as a kid. Piles of the steaming stuff, I tell you – hell of a lot more than the Andrex puppy can cope with …'

Turner nearly fell off the little couch laughing, and the dog rose from his slumber by the fire, wondering what all the fuss was about. Holding their sides, chuckling hysterically, their worries over the past twenty-four hours evaporated into the night.

CHAPTER 8: HEALING AND DREAMS

On the other side of the bay to the two friends, Mike Fletcher found himself alone on the mossy bank outside the estate lodge. He remembered falling asleep, but had no memory of how he had come to be outside in the chill night air. His bare feet sunk into the spongy lichen as he tried the wide front door. To his surprise, it was locked.

The outline of the white pony was just visible, standing motionless, with one of its rear hooves resting on its toe, the head drooped and the ears flat. Fletcher guessed it was dozing, so, rather than disturb it, he headed round the other side of the building. With cloud cover blocking out the moon and stars, the grounds had become an unfamiliar panorama of grey and black. As he cautiously tracked through the foreign landscape, he noticed the skeletal arms of the trees on the ridgeline picking up a faint glow from a light in one of the bedrooms. Fletcher inched his way carefully towards the bright window.

Inside the bedroom, he recognised the figure of a freckle-faced girl – somehow she seemed familiar. Lying motionless on the bed, she'd carelessly fallen asleep with her oil lamp still burning. Stuttering shadows from the flame flickered across her face and a mess of crimson hair nestled deep in a mound of pillows. The overall effect was unnatural, the dark hollows of her cheeks giving her features a cruel, skull-like appearance.

Risking her wrath, he tapped gently on the leaded windowpane in an attempt to wake her so that she could let him in. Louder and louder he tried, until eventually she responded to the noise and gazed sleepily over at him. Fletcher smiled reassuringly, a little embarrassed at the situation he found himself in. The response was not what he expected. Her head bobbed strangely back and forth, eyes wide in fear, and she was trying to scream. Confused by her reaction, he raised his hand against the window to signal her to come out. Her shrieking was intense, rising and falling between hoarse gasping breaths.

The room light caught his hand on the windowpane, and he looked down in horror to see four withered brown digits, with a gap where his forefinger should be. Fletcher began screaming, shrieking and wailing into the night ...

'Wake up!' Someone was shaking him roughly by the shoulders. The freckle-faced girl leant over him; her round features were a mask of concern. 'Wake up – you've been dreaming. You're safe here. Can you hear me? Can you remember? My name's Maggie Douglas. You're in my house. You've had an accident.'

The pain in Fletcher's left leg was excruciating as he tried to sit up. Looking around, he could see he was in a small bedroom, identical to the one in his dream. Quickly, he glanced down at his hand to find it perfectly normal with all fingers in place and some minor scratching on his palm.

'How did I get here? What's happened to me?' Fletcher

tried desperately to get off the hard mattress and push to his feet.

'You need to stay still. You've been badly hurt. I found you in the ravine. I think you must have fallen down the bank.' Maggie talked quickly, trying to give Fletcher as much information as possible in the hope it would calm him down. 'Look, your leg is in a bad way – you shouldn't be trying to move.' She pushed him gently back onto the bed and made him sip at a glass of water. 'I don't know anything about you – where are you from? I've never seen you around here before.' Maggie cradled his head as he drank.

Fletcher gasped from the pain in his leg. 'I'm on holiday … staying at Lanner's Point Croft … arrived yesterday, or maybe it was the day before. How long have I been here?'

'I found you this morning and brought you here. This is the estate lodge – your croft is easily a couple of miles east from here, through the woodland. How come you're so far out?' Maggie was genuinely curious; visitors were rare in these wild parts.

Then Fletcher remembered and began to shake uncontrollably. 'There was something in the byre. It was horrible, ancient … like from an old corpse. But it moved … it moved towards me. I ran … out into the forest to get away. That's all I can remember.'

Maggie leant back, wondering whether this strange man had some form of mental illness. His story sounded more like one of the tall tales her neighbour, Julian Etienne, was fond of telling. Slightly concerned he might be unstable, Maggie left him briefly to fetch Callum from his work butchering the venison. The sight of the craggy-faced man entering the room with blood on his hands made Fletcher jump and he vainly tried to get off the bed again.

'Steady, son, steady,' Callum said calmly, looking down and realising how he must appear to the stranger. 'It's deer blood, son, that's all. Let me go clean up.' With that, he was off to the kitchen.

Returning with the odd brown stain on his tweed trousers, he sat on the bed next to Fletcher. 'Look, son, you've had a fright. We've patched up your leg as best we can – I don't think it's broken but, if it is, we're going to have to move you to a hospital. We'll see how you go in the next couple of days. I'm Callum – I'm in charge of the estate.' Maggie raised her eyebrows at his self-promotion from head keeper, but let it go.

'You were in a bad way when Maggie found you. Likely, you'd be dead by now if she hadn't got the presence of mind to get you back here.' Callum looked across at Maggie, who seemed genuinely pleased by the recognition. She whispered quietly to him that Fletcher said he'd seen something ancient and horrible in the byre at Lanner's Point Croft. Callum suppressed a chuckle and mumbled under his breath, 'If you ask me, the whole bloody place is ancient and horrible.'

Fletcher noticed the two of them whispering and, in his fragile state of mind, imagined they were deciding what to do with his body and which part to eat first. Feeling he desperately needed to get away for his own safety, he pushed to his feet and promptly fainted.

By the time Fletcher woke up, it was late evening. Callum sat quietly puffing on a pipe, reading a book under the soft glow of an oil lamp. A large glass of single malt whisky sat at his elbow, and, judging by the half-empty bottle next to it, this was not his first drink of the evening. 'I've sent Maggie to bed,' he said simply when he saw Fletcher wriggling about on the mattress.

The sweet smell of the Cavendish pipe tobacco was not unpleasant and Fletcher found himself inhaling deeply, savouring the scent. His father had been a pipe smoker and the fruity vapours that filled the room brought back the simpler memories of his childhood.

'You hungry?' Callum asked, and pushed a tray of ham and pickle sandwiches over to his wounded guest. Fletcher accepted gratefully, hungrily munching through the first sandwich like it was a speed-eating contest. The tweed-clad keeper poured him a glass of lukewarm beer that was equally well accepted and downed with relish. 'So, do you want to tell me what brings a city boy like you out here?' It was obvious to Callum from the softness of Fletcher's hands that he wasn't a manual worker, and the clothes were new, not battered like his own.

Fletcher opened up and poured out the story of his multiple sclerosis diagnosis and the impact it'd had on his life. How he hoped that time away would help him decide what to do, how to shape his life. Callum didn't do sympathy, so grunted in response, 'So, what's next? Sounds to me like you're running away.'

In truth, Fletcher was running away, and his gruff host had hit the nail on the head. 'I don't know – everything is so new. Trying to cope ...'

'Cope! Try living out here, son, and then you'll know

everything you need to know about coping. In this world, you either do or you don't do. Everything in the middle is a load of excuses for weak men. If you ask me, you need to decide what you want, then get on with it. Simple as that.' Callum topped up his whisky, having stated what he saw as the blindingly obvious.

Ever since Fletcher's diagnosis, all his family and friends had given him soft words of sympathy. The frank and brutal directness of his host, rather than upsetting, was incredibly invigorating. Callum was right, of course; he did need to decide what to do, and then get on with it. For the past few months he'd been doing nothing except wallowing at his sister's, feeling sorry for himself. Fletcher took an instant shine to the keeper, impressed by his straightforward and honest view of the world as he saw it.

Callum Benvie, like his father before him, had lived off the land all his life. After a brief and, to his mind, unnecessary schooling at Fort William, he'd lived solely in the lonely expanses of hill and glen. In a life filled with dangers and difficulties, Callum put his trust completely in wild nature. After watching the Presbyterian and Catholic sides of his family tear themselves apart, over when and what they should worship, he had no time for church dogma. The religion of the land was his simple faith. It wasn't that he was an atheist; rather, out in the wild he had no need to think about it. Callum's world involved living by tooth and claw, protecting game and controlling vermin with lethal force.

Fletcher munched hungrily through another sandwich, and for the first time realised that he owed his life to this man and his friends. 'Is it OK if I stay here for a while? I don't think

I'll be able to cope at the croft on my own like this,' he mumbled with a mouthful of sandwich, and pointed down at the tightly bound leg.

Callum puffed deeply on his briar pipe and flooded the room with more aromatic smoke. Looking the broken photographer up and down, he shrugged his shoulders in a gesture meant to say 'maybe', but what he actually said was, 'We all figured you'd be staying for a while anyway. But don't pull the "poor me" card. I've got no time for that. You want to get better, right? Well you're going to have to work at it. Once your leg starts healing, you need to get moving and keep the circulation flowing. It's going to hurt like hell, and you're going to have to get on with it. Strongest painkillers we've got won't help you.'

'Agreed,' Fletcher nodded, feeling revitalised by Callum's straight-to-the-point approach. He knew, if he tried his best, that this pipe-puffing mountain man would be firmly in his corner, pushing him to do more. That was precisely what he needed; he just hadn't known it up until now.

'I'll ask Maggie if she can get your stuff from Lanner's Point Croft tomorrow, after she's checked on the sheep. You got much with you?' Callum thought the city boy probably had about fifteen suitcases and all the Bear Grylls accessories he could carry.

Fletcher assured him that he only had a couple of bags and a camera rucksack, plus food supplies, and they were welcome to collect the latter if it would come in useful.

Callum lifted his empty glass up optimistically. 'No whisky in that lot, is there?'

'Bottle of Laphroaig I bought on the way up – a guy at

the petrol station in Pitlochry recommended it to me. I've never tried it before. Is it any good?' Fletcher bent forward, looking hopefully over for the keeper's approval.

'It's better than good, son. It's perfect!' Callum eased back in his chair, thinking contentedly about the peaty nectar he'd be helping himself to the following evening, courtesy of his unexpected houseguest. Perhaps having Fletcher around wasn't such a bad thing after all, he thought, topping up his glass and raising a toast to the photographer.

CHAPTER 9: NO ONE AT HOME

'Told you he'd gone …' Hulk paced restlessly up and down inside Lanner's Point Croft, looking for any signs of Mike Fletcher. Turner and Hulk had headed over by first light, the psychic clad in a hotchpotch assortment of warmer clothing Hulk had scrounged from his friends, leaving the dog, Kyle, with his neighbour. Zipping up his borrowed black fleece jacket against the cold, Turner headed into the bedroom.

'I see what you mean – his coat's still here. If he were planning a trip in this weather he'd be a fool not to take it with him. I think we'd better look outside for tracks, try and pick up where he went.' Turner motioned Hulk out the door and began searching for any clues.

They spent an hour combing the grounds around the house and the byre, but nothing made any sense. Leading from the middle of the broken-down byre wall, in the thick mud from the rain, were bare footprints. Small and not well defined, like those of a child. These faded against the mossy canopy that carpeted the rest of the front of the croft, making it impossible to pick up a trail. Heavier cut Vibram-soled boot prints were scattered around the byre entrance. The prints overlapped in a muddy mess, giving no clue as to where, or in what direction, Mike Fletcher had headed.

Turner grabbed an oil lamp from the croft and started exploring the inside of the byre. Sure enough, the pentagram on the door was a dripping mess of red, huge globules of the bloody ooze pooling on the floor.

'Keep away from that, Hulk, and watch your step around here,' Turner said, waving his hand to cover the entire floor area around the door. Hulk flexed his injured fingers and nodded.

Turner quickly made his way to the broken sandstone slabs sitting haphazardly either side of the granite bench. Scanning in the dirt, he found no sign of the decrepit finger Hulk had described to him so vividly the night before, and said so.

'I swear it was there, Nathen. Down where your foot is now. I didn't want to touch it – gave me the shivers.' Hulk rooted around on the floor, scraping back the thick dust, searching for the gnarled digit.

Turner spotted the exposed carvings on the underside of the sandstone slabs and cursed under his breath. 'Look at these,' he called over, gesturing Hulk to look, waving the oil lamp so he could see. 'This is not good … this is really not good …' With fingers probing across the lettering, Turner was translating and mumbling quietly. 'It says in Latin: As above, so below. Then there are some other characters that look like planetary symbols. These are old. Whoever made it was trying to hide or protect something, I'm sure of that.'

'Protect what? This place is not exactly on the top-ten list for places to rob,' Hulk said, slightly confused, turning to examine the strangely carved figures in the stone, worried by the psychic's intense expression. Nathen Turner was normally a pretty easy-going, fun-loving guy, but none of that was evident as he sat mumbling to himself in the lamplight.

Turner didn't answer. Springing to his feet, he started pacing around the granite base, dipping the lamp into its hollow centre. He jumped over the lip, dragging his lanky legs behind him awkwardly as he climbed inside. Hulk couldn't see him anymore.

'Nathen, you OK? Come on, man, you're scaring me.' Hulk clambered heavily to his feet to find the psychic on his knees, scraping furiously at the dirt floor inside the granite base.

'Is there any rope around here?' Turner said, twisting clumsily in the confined space to peer up at the giant. Hulk looked at him like he'd gone completely mad. Shrugging his shoulders and cursing silently, Hulk grabbed a short length of hemp off the wall and threw it down. Turner was digging away at something and threading the hairy twine through it. After about five minutes of panting effort, the psychic jumped out with the end of the rope in his hand.

'Right, with me, pull. Hard as you can,' Turner commanded rather than asked. The rope snapped, hurling them both backwards. Another five minutes and more scrabbling later, they were trying again. This time it worked. Slowly and steadily they were lifting a slate slab, levering it on its edge against the side of the hollow base. Telling Hulk to carry the weight, Turner let go and peered down inside.

The light from the oil lamp cast deep shadows down into the hole. Underneath the slab was a square black opening about two feet across. Turner bent over for a closer look, lowering the light onto the shallow shelf around one side.

Smooth rock walls headed down deep underground, carved here and there with weird shapes and symbols.

'I'm going in,' Turner said without a look back, and lowered himself into the small opening.

'Stop, for God's sake, stop! You don't know how deep it is. I can't follow you in there – I'll never fit through.' Hulk reached down with one hand to grab Turner, pulling back hard with the other on the rope. The hairy twine was cutting into his injured hand, but Hulk was used to pain from a lifetime of hard labour spent at sea.

Turner ignored him and disappeared down the hole, dragging the oil lamp after him. Spreading his long legs out against each wall, he pushed his back against the cold granite and slowly slid down. After about ten feet, his boots hit a hard surface, and he was able to crouch down and look around. More strange symbols littered the walls, and a squat tunnel headed off, at a right angle, to the west. The air was cold and damp, soft drips of icy water leaching through the tunnel roof. Much like the granite base above, whoever had built the thing had cut directly through the solid rock. The workmanship was superb, the walls as smooth as polished marble.

Turner shouted upwards, his voice echoing loudly off the walls. 'There's a tunnel – I'm going to take a look and see where it leads. Maybe Mike Fletcher has got himself trapped down here. If I'm not back in twenty minutes, call for help, OK?'

'OK, but I think you're bloody crazy. You have no idea what's down there,' Hulk bellowed back, nervous sweat beading his forehead.

Turner ignored him and headed off quickly down the tunnel, his body bent double under the low roof. The path ahead was straight and clear so he made quick progress as he followed its gentle slope deeper underground. Turner could sense the air changing, from damp and musty to dry, tasting almost metallic in his mouth. For some reason, he felt no fear; somehow his senses knew he was not in any danger. But he also felt that there was something supernatural, or spiritual, about this place. This was his psychic radar kicking into gear, and he trusted his life to it after the experiences he'd had in the past.

Pushing the oil lamp ahead, he could see the squat tunnel opening into a chamber of some sort. Moving ahead too briskly, his leather-soled cowboy boots skidded on the damp rock and he flew forward, tumbling into the gloom. By the time he'd recovered his senses, he was lying flat out on a pile of cracking brown bones. Panting cloudy breath into the air, he lay there and looked around. The chamber was cool and dry, about fifteen feet long and ten feet wide. Carved into each side of the long walls were two rock shelves equidistant from each other. The thing holding his attention was what lay on three of the four rock shelves. All except one of the stony slabs held a robed figure, clothed in black. Levering himself up off the pile of bones, he scanned his light over the nearest figure. The dusty black cloth looked like a hooded monk's robe that had been pulled tight around its contents. Carefully he pulled open the robe, worried it might disintegrate in his hands, but the cloth held firm. A year ago he would have run away in dread, but now he simply peered in with the curiosity of an archaeologist. The soft light picked up the brown frame of a human skeleton, both arms crossed peacefully across its chest. In the mouth of the skull, and in each eye socket, lay a coin. Rather than disturb the dead, Turner leant forward to closely examine each one. All the coins were the same, bearing the image of St Benedict and the phrase *Vade retro satana.* The other two robed figures on the slabs had the exact same coins, arms-crossed pose and identical black robes. Turner respectfully pulled the robes back around the skeletal remains and knelt down to examine the bone pile he'd landed on.

With some relief, he realised they were all animal bones. Piles of the things, heaped carelessly, one on top of another, as if discarded after a large feast. Making no sense of it, Turner scanned round for any signs that Mike Fletcher had been down here. Nothing at all – the empty rock shelf looked exactly the same as the other three. If anything, it appeared cleaner and less dusty. At the far end of the room, a granite frame surrounded a wide oaken door of regular height. The design was old, Turner guessed medieval, maybe from the thirteenth or fourteenth century. The door was either wedged or locked; he couldn't move it at all. With nothing else to see, and no other way out, he headed back up the tunnel to find Hulk leaning down anxiously, listening for any sign of him.

'You are one crazy guy, Nathen. You scared the hell out of me. I had visions of you being eaten alive, or dragged to hell by some godforsaken creature. What's down there?' Hulk asked, not sure he wanted the answer. He had removed the slate slab completely using his immense brute force, and reached down an arm to help Turner climb back up again. After much grunting and cursing, the pair reunited in the byre, Turner dusting himself down and telling the giant about his underground adventure.

'Looks like a crypt to me. There are three bodies.'

Hulk grabbed Turner, staring straight at him, eyes wide. 'What do you mean, bodies? Murdered, you mean? Was Mike Fletcher one of them?' Hulk was visibly sweating and trembling as he spoke. He was not prepared for Turner's reaction – he laughed.

'No, you daft bugger. These bodies are more use to fossil hunters. I don't know how old they are, but I'm guessing at least a couple of hundred years. They look like they were monks, or something like that, from the way they've been laid out. There's no sign I can see that anyone has been down there in living memory. The room has another way out, but it's locked or blocked on the other side.' Turner still chuckled as he spoke. Hulk was amazed at Turner's calmness, like this was an everyday thing. Maybe, he thought, in his weird psychic world, it was.

In need of refreshment, and a change to a less forbidding environment, the pair headed to the croft and lit the wood stove, warming their chilling bodies in the amber glow. Sitting propped on the fish crates, mugs of tea and biscuits in hand, they were starting to relax again.

The front door slammed open hard, and in stepped a fiery-haired lady with fury in her eyes. 'Who the hell are you and what are you doing here?' shouted Fiery Hair from the doorway, raising a large stick that she'd picked up outside.

The two house invaders jumped, spilling their tea, and turned to face the doorway. Hulk recognised the woman immediately, burst out laughing, and said, 'Hey, Maggie. Is this how you greet all your men?'

'Hulk, what the hell are you doing here?' Maggie's mouth dropped open in surprise at the sight of the giant man, who stood up quickly and hugged her warmly in an over-enthusiastic bear hug.

'Nice to see you too, Maggie. This is an old friend, Nathen Turner, from back home in Whitby. His dad and me go back a long way. Nathen, meet Maggie Douglas, or stick-wielding psycho lady as you know her now.' Turner smiled and nodded meekly from across the room, his heart still racing after the redhead's dramatic entrance. 'We're looking for a guy called Mike Fletcher – he's renting the place. Went missing yesterday. You seen him?'

'Seen him? I found him next to dead in the ravine.' Maggie went on to explain how she'd found the injured Fletcher and taken him back to the estate lodge. That morning, she'd headed down in the Argocat to get Fletcher's stuff. The forest path had become too narrow for the multi-wheeled vehicle, so she was forced to travel the last half-mile on foot. Fletcher had told Maggie he'd seen something in the byre that frightened him, and he'd fled in a panic. So, suspecting some horror or danger from the voices she'd heard inside the croft, she'd grabbed a stick and made her dramatic entrance.

Turner watched Maggie as she talked to the giant towering above her. He guessed she was probably mid-thirties, her freckled features glowing red from her time spent outdoors on the hills. It was hard to say whether he'd call her attractive. The loose work jeans, baggy wool jumper and wax jacket gave little clue as to her actual body shape. Maggie stomped over in her green wellies and shook Turner's hand. Close up, she smelt of peat and wood fires, a scent he thought Chanel were unlikely to favour in their next collection. Her clear blue eyes examined him, boring through him as if to decide whether he was a trustworthy type.

'Hi Nathen. Sorry if I scared you. Can you help me get Mike's stuff together in here, while me and Hulk clear the bedroom?' Maggie's voice was calm but firm, suggesting an answer in the negative would not be well received. The psychic nodded and said he'd be delighted, then busied himself grabbing what he could see, and stuffing it in a rucksack left in the corner.

Between the three of them, they'd packed up the essentials within twenty minutes. Turner offered to help carry the load back to her vehicle, a kindly gesture that resulted in much unexpected hilarity. Looking at his snakeskin cowboy boots with the burnt toes, Maggie had pointed and laughed. 'Are you kidding me? In those things you'll be a liability in this mud. I'll give you about ten yards before you fall flat on your backside.' Turner was a little embarrassed, but she was right. In truth, he was more a beach and city guy, not used to coping with this type of environment. With a nod saying he wouldn't be long, Hulk grabbed a couple of bags and headed with Maggie out the door.

Alone, Turner had time to reflect. Nothing he'd sensed so far had made him feel like he was in any danger and he felt foolish at overreacting to Hulk's call. Turner was enjoying this small *Boy's Own* adventure in the wilderness. Things were certainly more interesting than coaching a few potential psychics back home. Why someone had made a hidden entrance into an old crypt was a complete mystery. Perhaps the pentagram symbol in the byre marked the secret entrance to the crypt, but it seemed more than that. Turner had no idea what the carvings and symbols on the sandstone slabs meant. Were they a warning of some kind, or something less sinister, and he was letting his imagination run away with itself? It seemed Hulk had done exactly that when he'd believed he'd found a dried-out human finger on the floor. It certainly wasn't there today. The skeletons in the crypt were exactly that – skeletons with no human tissue left on any of them, covered in musty old robes. Plus, Turner had checked – none of them had any missing digits. Apparently Mike Fletcher had seen something that had scared him. But, like Turner, he was a city boy, not used to the wild and its night predators. Crunching his way down to the water's edge, he fished out his Gladstone briefcase from Hulk's boat. Turner had repacked it this morning with the witchcraft book he'd shown Hulk, plus a few other things he'd thought would prove useful. Maybe the book would provide some answers. A good read and a nice cup of tea sounded like just the thing to clear his thoughts.

On his way back, he spotted a swift flash of brown hair darting past the byre, and then bounding into the croft. Intrigued, he quickly made his way back up the bank to find a huge brown tabby cat with a bobtail sitting calmly on one of the fish crates near the wood stove. Green eyes gazed easily back at Turner, as the enormous feline gently licked its paw and began to groom its face. There was something about the animal that felt primordial, something not of this world. One thing was for sure, it was like no cat he'd ever seen before – it looked like a stray housecat that had been on a steroid diet.

'Hello there. Mind if I join you?' Turner asked politely, not sure why. He had no idea he was talking to the most ferocious wild predator left in Britain. The Scottish wildcat simply stared back in response. Scrabbling through what little food Hulk and Maggie had left behind, he found a tin of sardines and offered it to the furry guest. Large sharp claws speared the tasty treat and the cat greedily gulped it down.

There they sat, at home in each other's company, the cat languishing comfortably on top of one crate, Turner on another, drying his muddy boots by the stove as he dozed off into a dreamless sleep.

CHAPTER 10: THE FLY FISHERMAN

Hulk was amazed. Nathen Turner sat snoring away by the wood stove next to the biggest Scottish wildcat he'd ever seen. Slowly, the cat opened an eye and glanced across at the huge man in the doorway. Immediately springing to its feet, it darted past him and out the door.

Turner stretched lazily and yawned, woken by the noise. 'Oh, hey Hulk. I meant to do some reading but must have nodded off. Everything OK? You look a bit shocked.'

'You know you had a wildcat in here, right? Next to you – there …' Hulk pointed at the vacated fish crate.

'Oh yeah, gave it some sardines. Nice cat, beautiful markings, must be a stray.' Turner nonchalantly put another pot of water on the stove so he could make a brew.

'It's not a stray; it's a wild animal. They're rarer than tigers – only about a hundred pure bloods left in the wild. Bloody vicious things.' Hulk looked the psychic up and down for scratches and limbs hanging off, amazed at his coolness. 'One nearly had my mate's hand off when he disturbed it scavenging on fish scraps. You're not hurt, are you?'

'Don't be daft; I'm fine. I think it likes me.' Turner smiled, dropped a couple of teabags in a pot, and motioned Hulk to join him.

The pair sat and talked through what Maggie Douglas had told them. At least Mike Fletcher was alive and safe, and in good hands up at the estate lodge. Hulk filled him in on the head keeper, Callum Benvie, describing him as a loyal friend but not somebody you'd want to get on the wrong side of. Callum had had a reputation as a regular Casanova in his youth, bedding most of the single ladies in a ten-mile radius before he was forty. When Turner whistled at this, Hulk reminded him that this amounted to only around twelve women in this remote wilderness. He told Turner that Maggie had never been married, just the odd boyfriend or two from Benlogan, but none had ever lasted past a week or so. Maggie seemed like she had no need for any long-term romantic relationship with a man. Callum and Maggie lived off the land, their lifelong platonic friendship a thing of local legend (and frequent gossip).

Turner warmed his hands around a mug of steaming tea, lost in thought. 'Do you think Mike Fletcher did see something that scared him, Hulk?'

'I don't know. Places like these can creep tourists out. When you live here, you get used to the night noises. It's usually no more than the wildlife going about their business; we don't have any crime up here.' Turner nodded as Hulk was talking, then seemed to make a decision.

'You don't mind if I stay here for a couple of days, do you? The sleeping bag's still in the bedroom and there is more than enough food left. Be nice to experience it before I go back to Whitby. I reckon two nights will give me enough time to explore. Plus, I can catch up on my reading.' Turner patted the *Discoverie of Witchcraft* book at his feet. 'What do you think? That OK? Will you be alright with the dog?'

Hulk was a lot more relaxed about the croft now that Mike Fletcher had been found. Going over it in his head, he'd come to the conclusion that maybe, yesterday, what he'd thought was a decrepit finger could easily have been a weirdly shaped twig, and his imagination had done the rest. Besides, it was two nights – Turner didn't have a lot of time to get himself into trouble. 'Sure, no problem. It is beautiful out here; I think you'll enjoy it. Be careful, and promise no more diving down holes in the ground. It will help me anyway – with all this back and forward I'm not getting any fishing done. No fishing means no money, and I'm not exactly flush with cash.' Hulk said his goodbyes and motored back across the bay.

Turner set about searching the croft to see what he could scavenge for his brief stay. No problem with the remaining food supply, and the sleeping bag should prove cosy enough. Maggie had left Fletcher's spare pair of walking boots near the bed, enclosed in a zipped plastic carrier. Turner pulled them out and checked the thick rubber sole. They certainly looked expensive, but he didn't recognise the brand. On a whim, he placed one of the shoes against his battered cowboy boots to check the size. They looked about the same, so he pulled them on and trotted in and out of the two rooms, checking the fit. Good enough, he thought. Certainly much better grip than the sheer leather of his boots.

Borrowed shoes and a flask of water in hand, Turner headed west out of the croft into the forest, loving the feel of the fresh mountain air on his face. The trees filled the woodland path with a sweet smell that reminded Turner of rosemary and bath salts. Ancient Scots pines pushed their spiny tentacles together over his head, cocooning him in the green blanket of nature. Heading high up the trail carving its way around the hillside, Turner felt relaxed, soothed by the unspoilt environment. Later, over a nice supper, he could read up on the symbols covering the slabs and the door, but for now he wanted to enjoy his unexpected holiday in the wilderness.

Panting as he climbed higher, Turner pushed on until the forest broke into a wooded clearing surrounding a small inland loch. Knee-high reeds guarded the sides of the mirrored surface, the loch glowing bluely in the afternoon light. Flickering dragonflies darted above his head, chasing each other like flying matchsticks across the water. Turner sat down on a mossy tree stump, breathing in the majestic beauty of the place.

On the other side of the loch, something was moving. Keeping still and quiet, Turner watched in fascination as the figure of a medium-sized man waded out from the shore and flicked a fishing line expertly into the water. Cast after cast, the figure moved along the shoreline, hunting for his quarry. After a few minutes the line went taut, the light rod bending deeply with the strain. Turner watched the figure skilfully play the fish, giving line when it tried to speed away or go deeper, and shortening it as it tired and finally gave up the fight. Three minutes of pulling and splashing later, a shimmering fish had been safely landed and hauled to the shore. Whoever this man was, he was certainly a virtuoso fly fisherman. Back out wading and covering the water with his deft flicks, it wasn't long before another gleaming fish made its way into his waiting net. As Turner stood to continue his walk, the man spotted him and waved him over.

'Hi, I haven't seen you before – you on holiday?' the man asked cheerily, puffing slightly as he transferred his latest catch into an oilskin bag lying on the shore.

'Sort of. I'm only around here for a couple of nights. I'm Nathen, Nathen Turner. You certainly know what you're doing with that thing.' Turner pointed to the man's fishing rod. The shaft of the rod was made of a thin wood, possibly bamboo, with a rusted iron reel bound to the handle. It looked incredibly old and Turner had never seen one like it before.

'A couple of nights, eh? Seems a strange place to come for such a short time. I'm Julian Etienne. I live about half a mile that way.' Julian pointed over the hilltop to the north. 'Just catching something for tea. Want to join me? I don't get many visitors – it would be nice to catch up on news from the outside world.' Julian smiled hopefully at the psychic.

Turner took an instant liking to Julian Etienne. He seemed comfortable with himself and his world, like the two were intrinsically bound in a beautiful marriage. It was difficult for Turner to guess the man's age; he had one of those faces that could put him anywhere from mid-forties to late seventies. Flecks of grey and black hair surrounded his bald crown in a pattern reminiscent of a badger's fur. His green waistcoat was littered with tiny flecks of feather, the fly patterns hooked in randomly to the thick fabric. There was something about him that was different. Whether it was Turner's spiritual sixth sense, or a gut feeling, something about him seemed special and unique.

Gladly accepting the generous invitation from such a charming character, Turner trotted behind his wader-clad host across the hilltop and through the heather slopes below. Julian's house was built from square granite bricks surrounded by raised beds full to the brim with an assortment of vegetables. Looking over the low slate roof, Turner could see several beehives and another granite outbuilding some distance from the main house. Inside proved cosy, with three rooms lined floor to ceiling with bookcases. Amidst this library-cum-dwelling, one of the rooms carried a simple double bed with a wooden cross above it. The others were laid out as living areas, with a stove, table and several wooden chairs scattered in the kitchen area. While his host busied himself preparing the fish, Turner scanned the huge book collection. Every one of them was a work of some scientific nature, but that was not what caught Turner's eye. Three long shelves were overflowing with ancient scientific texts, none later than around 1900. Turner recognised the names of some of the authors – Roger Bacon, Dom Pernety and the father of modern medicine, Paracelsus, amongst many others.

Julian noticed Turner scanning through the books. 'Are you interested in science? As you can see, I have somewhat of a passion for the subject. I've been collecting for a very long time.' When Julian said 'long' he emphasised the word and smiled slightly to himself, as if remembering a happy memory of his first acquisitions as a young boy.

'These are incredible; it's the best collection I've ever seen. I love old books on subjects we've forgotten existed. Please don't laugh, but I specialise in anything supernatural, old rituals, that kind of thing,' Turner said, making his excitement at discovering the old texts obvious to his fly-fishing acquaintance.

Julian walked over and removed one of the dusty volumes. 'You see this?' He opened the large book to show Turner finely crafted script and intricate drawings. 'People thought the writing in here was supernatural when it came out. That's simply because they couldn't understand it at the time.' He turned a page to show Turner an elaborate diagram of a chemical distillation process, decorated with eagles, snakes and lions. 'There is much more to our world than we know – we just don't know how to look for it yet.'

Turner held the book and examined the images. 'I've seen this type of picture before. Well sort of – without all the chemical apparatus on. Down at Lanner's Point Croft, carved on a slab in the byre. What does it mean?'

'It's alchemy – a mix of science, spiritual philosophy and psychology all rolled into one. When these were written, there was no such thing as copyright or patents. So, if the scientists, or should I say alchemists, discovered something, they wrote it down in coded diagrams like this. All the images mean something to the initiated.' Julian talked almost like a teacher to a pupil as he pointed out the various animals and weird figures to his interested guest.

Finally, thought Turner, a kindred spirit, his affection for his host growing by the minute. All his life, the psychic had been studying obscure and bizarre texts on the supernatural; now he'd finally found someone with the same passion for ancient knowledge, albeit in a different subject. Quickly, Turner described what he'd discovered at the croft, the pentagram and the crypt. 'It fascinates me, Julian. You know, trying to understand who would do these things and why.'

Turner thought for a moment, decided he could trust Julian, then continued, 'I know you won't believe me, but I've been face-to-face with a ghost. The experience nearly killed me, but it wasn't the spirit's fault. Look ...' Turner lifted up his shirt and fleece to show a white mark around his heart in the shape of an open palm. 'The spirit touched me, healed me. I owe it my life.' Reflecting afterwards, Turner had no idea why he did this to a relative stranger, but somehow he felt Julian would understand.

Julian did, and simply nodded as Turner re-arranged his clothing. 'I do believe you. Out here I've seen many things I don't understand. But, hey, it keeps life interesting, don't you think?' With that, Julian headed back to the stove, leaving Turner scanning his book collection. Turner had never seen anyone take his admission of being touched by the supernatural so much in his stride. It was like he'd told Julian some everyday fact, like it was raining outside. More intrigued by his host, he joined him at the kitchen table.

Over a delicious meal of brown trout, potatoes and carrots, the two sat and chatted like old friends about ancient beliefs and things long lost to the passing of time. Turner didn't have anyone back home he could talk to like this, not with this level of knowledge. Jade often lost interest in some of his more bizarre ideas, even though she was a firm believer in the supernatural herself. Julian talked well, explaining how he believed the universe was a strange and wonderful place, full of ancient mysteries. For Turner, the reality of his psychic experiences had always surpassed his wildest imagination, making it difficult for him to fit into a closed-minded society.

Julian accepted his tales of the supernatural without judging him as a delusional lunatic with an afterlife fetish. Turner felt relaxed and at home with his genial host, relishing the conversation. He asked Julian again whether he had any ideas about the strange carvings on the sandstone slabs in the byre and the hidden crypt.

'There was an old Benedictine monastery here many years ago – maybe what you found is part of that. Sometimes you see remains of the old abbey walls if the water in the loch gets low,' Julian said, meaning the inland loch where he'd caught their meal. 'Like most of its kind, the building was destroyed not long after the Reformation in England finished.' Julian looked a little sad as he spoke, as if somehow sharing the pain of the many souls uprooted in King Henry VIII's religious upheaval. 'I'd be interested to see these carvings and the crypt – do you mind if I pay you a visit tomorrow?'

'Of course, be my guest. Allow me to return the favour of the meal – I haven't got much, I'm afraid, but it should be more than enough for the two of us.' Turner hoped his assessment of the meagre rations left at the croft were correct.

'Yes, I'd like that. I can bring venison if you like it. The taste is a little gamey if you're not used to it, but very nice. Freshly brought over the hill yesterday – I help the head keeper on his stalks, and he pays me in meat. I don't have much use for money out here.' Julian was in good spirits at the thought of visiting Turner; it was so rare for him to meet new people these days. He'd met two strangers in as many days, and this one was uninjured and a great conversationalist.

Julian had no idea who Mike Fletcher was or where he'd

come from – Fletcher had still been unconscious when Julian had left the estate lodge. The thought that Turner and Fletcher might be connected in some way never occurred to him.

In his enthusiasm to discuss the carvings and the crypt, Turner had never thought to mention Fletcher either.

After a mug of strong tea and more philosophical conversation, Turner was on his way back down the hill, picking up the forest trail to Lanner's Point Croft in the fading light. The time with Julian had proved fascinating, and Turner thanked his good fortune of running in to him that afternoon. Opening the croft door, he found the Scottish wildcat waiting impatiently for him on a crate beside the unlit stove. Smiling at the clandestine feline's burglary skills, he opened another tin of sardines and lit the wood burner. There they sat for the rest of the evening like an old couple, Turner reading his book, and the cat snoozing quietly in the warm glow from the fire.

CHAPTER 11: AN UNWELCOME VISITOR

While Turner and his furry companion warmed by the stove, Callum Benvie was chugging back his third neat Scotch of the evening up at the estate lodge. Helping himself to the bottle of Laphroaig that Maggie had rescued from the croft, he was toasting Mike Fletcher's health around a bristling fire in the lounge.

In clean clothes, and with a bellyful of venison, Fletcher sat awkwardly propped in a tatty lounge chair opposite the keeper. Maggie busied herself tidying up from their evening feast, clanging pots in the small kitchen next door. Fletcher's damaged leg had been raised onto a leather footstool and he kept repositioning himself as waves of pain periodically washed over him.

'You look a lot better today, son,' Callum said, breaking the silence between the pair, his compliment taking the photographer by surprise. Whether it was the whisky or the warmth of the roaring fire, Callum was in a much more genial mood than the previous evening. 'How's it feel?'

Fletcher rubbed his bound thigh over the top of a pair of clean cargo pants retrieved from the croft. 'Better than yesterday, thanks. Sounds silly, but it aches inside. Can't describe it. I really appreciate what you've both done for me.'

'Oh, hush, don't be silly. We'd do the same for a wounded

dog.' Callum meant what he said, but the comment wasn't exactly a boost to Fletcher's ego. 'You know this multiple sclerosis thing you've got? Is that why you fell down the ravine?' Callum took another pull on his whisky and gazed curiously over at the prone figure.

'No, nothing like that yet, thankfully. I feel a little embarrassed – something scared me and I ran into the forest. Somehow I lost my footing, and next thing I knew I was here, looking up at Maggie.'

As if on cue, the red-haired shepherdess headed into the room and flopped down on the settee next to Callum. Pouring a small whisky, she raised her glass and said, 'Slainte,' before taking a generous sip.

'Sorry, what did you say?' Fletcher asked, leaning forward, bemused by the strange word.

Maggie had forgotten Fletcher was a southerner, unfamiliar with the local dialect. He'd settled in so well in the short time he'd been at the lodge that she was already accepting him as part of her Highland family. 'Slainte – it's a Gaelic word,' Maggie said, smiling across at Fletcher. 'It means "health", same way you'd say "cheers".' Maggie raised her glass and took another sip, saying 'slainte' again, and then snuggled herself down into the seat, enjoying the warmth of the whisky as it glided down her throat.

'Oh, I see. Sorry. Well, same to you … slanty!' Fletcher took a drink, savouring the strong peaty taste.

Maggie cracked up laughing at his attempt to speak Gaelic. She'd got changed from her regular dowdy hill attire into snug-fitting jeans and a tight plain T-shirt. The mop of wild red hair was combed and tidy, and a splash of makeup smoothed her freckled complexion. Fletcher noted the changes with approval; he'd been watching her for most of the night.

Maggie Douglas spotted the photographer's admiring gaze and went slightly pink in the cheek. It was rare for her to have male company of a similar age at the estate lodge, and Fletcher was such an easy guy to talk to. All of her boyfriends up to now had been rugged hill types, married to the land. They approached courting in the same rough way they'd shear a sheep. Fletcher was different. He was polite, interested in what she did, and didn't seem to take himself too seriously. Callum noticed the changing atmosphere between the pair, decided to make himself scarce and headed off to bed.

'Don't you get lonely out here? Or are you and Callum partners, if you know what I mean?' Fletcher asked when they were alone, feeling a little embarrassed as he fished to find out whether Maggie had a boyfriend.

Maggie giggled at the obvious way Fletcher was attempting to unearth her private life. 'We're good friends, always have been. Callum's like a father to me. My family have been on this land for hundreds of years, one way or another. I've got an older brother in Benlogan who helps on the boats. At least he says he does – I've never seen him do a day's work in his life when I've been visiting. He reckons it's too remote over here.' Maggie sipped on her whisky, thinking about her bone-idle sibling and sighing unconsciously before continuing.

'My parents are long gone. They worked with Callum, and I stayed on, looking after the sheep and helping where I could. Suits me fine. I like the fresh air and the independence.

Anyway, what about you? Where's Mrs Fletcher?' Maggie started doing her own not-so-covert investigation into her unexpected houseguest's private life.

'There was someone I thought I'd spend my life with. Turns out I was wrong. When my health went, I lost her as well.' Fletcher hung his head, reliving the emotional rollercoaster after his multiple sclerosis diagnosis.

For the first time, Maggie felt sorry for Fletcher. Here was a man whose life had been completely turned upside down through no fault of his own. She had seen his inner strength in the past twenty-four hours, fighting to use the rough crutches Callum had made for him to hobble around the house. In truth, she didn't know much about his diagnosis other than he'd gone blind in one eye, and his future health prospects remained uncertain. From the outside, he looked like a regular guy, but she knew on the inside that his nervous system was gradually being destroyed by the disease. Maggie moved over and knelt next to him, holding his hand gently in hers.

'Well, you're here now and that's what matters, eh?' she said softly, stroking the back of his hand. 'You can stay here as long as you like and heal. You know, I'm a big believer that everything happens for a reason. Maybe this was meant to be, and you were supposed to come here.' Maggie looked up at Fletcher. Tears of sadness were beginning to trickle down his cheeks and he self-consciously rubbed them away with his sleeve.

Taking a deep breath, Fletcher tried, and failed, to get rid of the dark thoughts flooding through his mind. Looking mournfully at his kneeling companion, he sobbed, 'It's so unfair, you know? I mean, what's all this about? How come nobody knows why you get this disease and how to cure it? I wake up every day wondering whether something else on my body has stopped working … it's doing my head in. Coping with the uncertainty.' Fletcher started sobbing openly, gasping in huge gulps of air as his thoughts drifted ever darker.

Slowly, Fletcher tried to pull himself together and put a brave face on things after his emotional outburst, wiping tears clumsily from his face. What must she think of him? he thought. She'd saved his life, and now he felt like he was using her as a counsellor for his inner demons. 'Look, Maggie, I'm sorry,' he said, squeezing her hand lightly, feeling the warmth of her flesh on his. 'Ignore me. I don't mean to burden you with this. Thanks for being so kind to me – it means a lot.'

Maggie stood and kissed him gently on the forehead, wrapping her arms around his seated frame and hugging him warmly. 'Come on,' she said, 'let's get you to bed. You'll feel better in the morning.' Fletcher nodded an 'OK' gesture back, and Maggie gradually pulled him to his feet and passed him the homemade crutches.

The pair hobbled down the short corridor to Fletcher's room and manoeuvred him carefully onto his mattress. With a last kiss on his forehead, Maggie gently closed the door and then headed to her room.

Outside, the pale light of the full moon picked out the front of the lodge, painting it in a soft silvery glow. From the fringe of the trees, a dark shadow slithered slowly across the mossy ground. It moved around the house, skirting through the blackness, making deliberately for somewhere. The oil lamp from Maggie's room burnt amber rays across the lawn, and carefully the shadow edged its way towards them. Making no sound, the hunched black shape eased slowly to Maggie's window.

Inside, Maggie was sitting at a small dressing table, removing her makeup and combing through her hair, thinking about Fletcher. Over her shoulder she could see the leaded window reflected in the small vanity mirror. She sensed a movement outside. Something crossed behind the panes. Curious, Maggie picked up the lamp and peered through the leaded glass. Nothing; the light of the moon flooded the empty lawn. Shrugging her shoulders, she sat back down.

Scratch, scratch, scratch. Something clawed at one of the panes. Irritated this time, she whirled round to see a hideous brown face with gleaming eyes glaring in at her. She recoiled to the bed, trying to shout for help, but no sound came out, her voice paralysed with fear. Her room was the old pantry and the window didn't open, so at least, she thought, whatever it was couldn't get in. The scratching sound stopped and a pecking sound took its place. To her horror, she realised that whatever this dreadful creature was, it was unpicking the lead from the panes. The noise continued and a diamond-shaped piece of glass fell into the room. Long bony fingers reached in and tugged viciously until, one after the other, the panes crashed down.

Maggie froze in terror as a wraith-like figure clambered into the room. Quickly, it twisted its long bony fingers into her hair and dragged her head over to the side of the bed. In one terrifying motion it bit her violently in the throat. Maggie screamed. A long guttural shriek filled with fear and pain.

Callum, already woken by the sound of the breaking glass, burst through the bedroom door to see a hooded shrivelled figure holding Maggie down while she struggled bravely to get free. The crumpled brown face of the wraith turned to Callum and hissed, fresh blood dripping from its mouth. Then the barefoot creature was up and out of the shattered window into the night.

Thinking quickly, Callum picked Maggie up like a rag doll and ran with her to the kitchen. Pushing her shoulders into the sink, he ran cold water through the bleeding wound, soaking her T-shirt. There was a short semi-circular cut over the top of her left shoulder. Three inches to the right and Maggie would have been dead. Somehow in the struggle she'd managed to deflect the bite away from her neck.

The first-aid kit had been left on the shelf above after tending Fletcher's wounds. Grabbing the iodine, Callum poured it liberally through the wound. Maggie screamed in pain from the stinging of the brown antiseptic. Carefully, he sutured the cut and then bandaged it with a thick dressing and surgical tape. By the time he was done, Fletcher had managed to hobble his way from the bedroom, looking terrified after hearing the screaming.

Fletcher stared in horror at the blood covering Maggie's T-shirt. 'My God, what the hell is going on?'

'Can you handle a gun?' Callum asked bluntly, wanting action not explanations.

'Not really. I've never been around them.' The bizarre scene was getting stranger, and more frightening, to the photographer.

Callum pulled a revolver out of the bureau drawer,

loaded it and released the safety. 'Right, take this.' Callum passed the gun roughly to Fletcher. 'All you have to do is point and pull the trigger. You've got six shots, that's all, so don't waste them.' He ushered Fletcher into the living room and sat Maggie down next to him as he was talking. 'You look after her. She's been attacked and will likely go into shock. Keep her warm and get her a drink if she wants it. You got all that?'

Fletcher nodded, handling the gun gingerly, as if he expected it to go off at any time. Callum ran down the corridor and Fletcher could hear doors and cabinets being furiously flung open and closed. When Callum returned, he was holding a shotgun and wearing a head torch, a squat bag of spare cartridges slung carelessly over his shoulder.

'You stay here,' Callum ordered Fletcher. 'Anything comes in you don't recognise – shoot it. Make sure you shoot to kill – aim for the chest or head.' With that, Callum headed out the front door at a run.

'Wh … where are you going,' Fletcher called after him. Maggie lay pale, barely breathing, next to him.

'I'm going to kill, son. I'm going to find the creature that attacked Maggie and kill it.' Callum's voice disappeared into the night as he slammed the front door behind him.

Amidst the fear, above all else, one thing stayed in Fletcher's mind. Callum didn't say he was going to kill a burglar, a poacher, or a man. He was going to kill a creature. Fletcher pulled the gun close to his body, fingering the trigger, darting anxious glances around the room.

CHAPTER 12: STALKING BY MOONLIGHT

Years of experience had made Callum an expert tracker. Picking up signs of barefoot prints outside Maggie's window, he pushed on east following the trail. The light of the full moon cast long shadows across the landscape and he darted from one to the other, hiding from his prey.

The tracks headed along the muddy road, deep with vehicle tracks, before turning up onto the heather moor above the treeline. Callum moved slowly and steadily forward, placing each foot with a rolling motion so as not to make a sound. He cut the light from his head torch, crouched down and listened carefully. Gradually, he allowed his senses to tune in to his environment, filtering out the gentle roar from the ravine waterfall in the distance.

The swathe of low heather provided no hiding place for something the size of the creature he'd seen in Maggie's room. Callum closed his eyes to allow his vision to adjust to the gloom quicker. When he opened them again, things were a lot clearer, the moonlight positively flooding the hill slopes. Lying flat allowed him to look across the heather line, searching for any movement in the distance. Minute after minute ticked slowly by before he spotted what he was searching for.

Below the grey crags of Bean-nighe, a shadow was bounding forward, springing through the heather. Callum began to move quickly in a low crouch, covering the distance as quietly as he could. The shadow stopped at a thin stream gargling its way down the slopes. From this distance it was difficult to see, but it seemed that the shadow was drinking deeply from the stream. Crawling, he inched forward, sliding his body through the coarse foliage.

Callum watched as the figure tossed back its hood and scanned the landscape with eyes glinting in the moonlight. The soft illumination spread across the shrivelled features of a woman, an incredibly old woman. Her withered skin was pulled taut over hollow cheeks, her matted grey hair a tangled mess down her back. Shooting some feral creature was one thing, but the thought of shooting a woman made him pause. Whoever she was, he needed to stop her, but this would be cold-blooded murder.

Callum shouted towards the figure as he jumped to his feet. 'You there, stand up where I can see you. I'm armed and not afraid to shoot.'

The parchment-like face spun towards him and glared. For the first time in his life, Callum felt afraid. Whoever she was, there was something unnatural about her. The shrunken frame jumped to its feet and ran towards the crag. Stunned by the vigorous movement of the scrawny crone, Callum aimed his shotgun and fired. The shot caught her in the leg, but she kept going, desperately limping up the steep crag side. Then she simply disappeared, gone into the night.

Callum wiped his brow, his heart pounding. Cautiously, he made his way forward. The hard stone of the crag left no tracks; it was impossible to make out which direction she'd headed. He needed to think. Sitting down by the stream, Callum weighed up his options: follow her up the steep slope – impossible as he was running blind with no tracks; sit and wait here until morning – that left Fletcher and Maggie alone all night; or come back in the morning when it was light. The latter would be his best option, he thought. Callum knew he'd wounded her, but not how badly. He didn't think the withered crone could make her way back to the lodge tonight, but, in case she did, he wanted to be there. Whoever she was, she was obviously deranged, and he had no idea what she might be capable of.

Running back, he followed his tracks easily in the moonlight and burst back into the lodge, panting. Fletcher had the revolver trained on Callum's chest with a quivering hand; Maggie was asleep on his lap.

'Callum! You scared the life out of me! You OK?' Fletcher gasped, putting the revolver down gingerly on the side table.

Callum didn't answer, striding purposefully to the table and pouring a large whisky. Looking affectionately at Maggie, he simply said, 'She been alright?'

Fletcher could see the hurt and concern in the keeper's eyes, almost as if he was blaming himself for not protecting her. 'Sleeping mostly. All she's told me is that some withered brown creature came in through the window and attacked her. She hasn't been making much sense, to be honest.' Fletcher ran his fingers gently through Maggie's hair as she dozed.

Callum pictured the wrinkled face of the hooded woman in the moonlight. 'It wasn't a creature, son; it was a woman.

Some decrepit old crone I tracked across the moor.'

'Have you … killed her?' Fletcher asked nervously, not sure he wanted an answer.

Callum downed his whisky and poured another 'No, clipped her though. I lost her in the crags. Don't worry, I'll find her in the morning. How the hell the woman is still alive – I mean, her skin is all cracked and withered. Her hands would look just as at home on a bloody skeleton, but she moves like a young 'un. Unbelievable.'

Visions of his terrifying night in the byre came flooding back to Fletcher. 'Oh God! I may have seen her! She was outside the croft, in the byre. That's what I was running away from when I fell.' Fletcher leant forward to grab a glass and help himself to a whisky.

Callum sat and listened intently as Fletcher told him about the lightning strike on the byre, finding the St Benedict coin, and then a decrepit human finger on the floor. As he described the bony hand and black shape that had come crawling over the broken-down wall on the night he fled, the keeper nodded. From Callum's view, this was definitely the same woman he'd seen that evening. With a lifetime on the hills, the keeper believed he knew every rock, branch and living creature in the area intimately. This wraith-like woman, dressed in some sort of black robe, was new to him – it must be the same person, he thought.

Fletcher wasn't so sure it was simply an old woman, convinced there could be a more occult explanation after his discovery of the pentagram symbol on the byre door, and the strange carvings underneath the sandstone slabs. He said as much to Callum, who snorted in derision.

'Tell me, son, do you believe in ghosts?' Callum asked, back in direct questioning mode.

Fletcher thought for a while. 'No … but I'm afraid of them.'

'Well, I bloody don't believe, and I'm not afraid. Load of old cobblers made up by people with nothing better to do. Simply because some weirdo artist from ages ago draws a funny symbol on a door, everybody goes about muttering and crossing themselves. Load of old bollocks.' Callum's language was getting worse as the effects of the whisky kicked in.

Fletcher pressed the point. 'You know Hulk, I guess? One of the fishermen from Benlogan?' Callum nodded 'yes' at Fletcher. 'Well, he brought my stuff over. Said he has an old friend who specialises in these types of pentagram symbols. I was supposed to talk to him, but never got a chance. Called him Nathen Turner, I think. Something like that. I still think the symbol and carvings are linked with the old woman somehow.'

'Superstitious nonsense, son. Complete waste of time.' Callum said, as ever, talking straight to the point. 'This Turner character will probably make it up anyway if he thinks there's a profit in it. Met his type before, believe me. What I saw tonight was a living, breathing, vicious old woman. The only thing for certain is that I'm going to get her tomorrow, and that'll be the end of it. You can watch things here when I'm gone, OK?' It was a statement rather than a question.

Fletcher gave up trying to argue and looked affectionately at Maggie's sleeping figure. She was lying on her uninjured side, facing into the room with her back snuggled into the couch. Fletcher had put a small pillow under her head and it rested gently on his uninjured leg.

'Do you think you'll be alright sleeping there for tonight?' Callum asked Fletcher hopefully, feeling a little worse for wear from the alcohol. He needed sleep, and he needed it now. 'I'd rather not disturb her. We've some blankets to keep off the chill, and I can stoke up the fire.'

Fletcher willingly agreed, enjoying the closeness of the shepherdess. Within a few minutes they'd improvised a more comfortable position for Fletcher and propped his injured leg on a few blankets. Callum weaved his way down the hall and Fletcher could hear loud snoring almost as soon as he'd shut his bedroom door.

As Fletcher closed his eyes to rest, all he could see in his mind was the vision of the withered hand climbing over the byre wall, coming directly at him. Easing more upright, he laid one hand on the revolver, the other on Maggie, and spent a sleepless night imagining terrifying shapes forming in the shadows, straining his ears for the slightest sound.

CHAPTER 13: VISIONS AND CONVERSATION

Unaware of the frightening visitor at the estate lodge, Nathen Turner was dozing peacefully at the croft, lost in his dreams. He dreamt he was sitting reading in a large library, stacked high with all shapes and sizes of books. The oak-lined walls glowed in candlelight that flickered gently, casting soft shadows across the ceiling. A noise disturbed his reading, and Turner glanced up to watch a hooded monk enter the room. The cloaked figure was a man of medium stature, his features concealed by a large hood. One of the St Benedict coins he'd seen on the bodies in the crypt hung centrally on a silvery chain around his neck.

The monk moved quietly across the room and started combing the bookshelves, as if searching for something. Turner could hear himself asking the man what he was looking for. Swinging around to face him, the monk smiled, glad that someone had spoken to him, explaining he had taken a vow of silence and dared not speak to anybody before being spoken to.

'I'm Father Sebastian. This is my home,' the monk said, his voice sounding empty and distant. 'I have come seeking help for a friend, my dearest friend.' The robed figure appeared to glide towards Turner. 'She is so pale and ill. Please, can you help me?'

The monk's smiling face shone bright in the candlelight. Turner felt like he recognised the man somehow, but he couldn't place where he'd seen him before.

Slowly the vision of the library faded and he was in a dark room surrounded by chemical apparatus. Thick fumes clung to the ceiling and the whole place smelt acrid and stale. In the centre stood a huge teardrop-shaped furnace, with glass tubes releasing steamy vapours out the top. Inside, flames licked upwards across the base of two blackened brass pots, hung centrally below the point of the tear shape. Drops of pale yellow and red liquor dripped slowly from the tubes, mixing into a waiting glass bottle that was already half full. Stoking the furnace was a beautiful young lady in a long brown dress and stained apron. Muttering to herself, she was prodding and poking at the apparatus as if checking for leaks.

Then the vision faded again and Turner was standing over a bed containing the frail figure of the same woman close to death. Her rattled breathing caused her body to convulse with pain; the monk he'd seen in the library knelt next to her, sobbing. The woman's figure was little more than a skeleton, her bony fingers grasping the monk's hand.

'Father … Father … can you hear me? What is wrong with her?' Turner asked the hooded figure quietly. Slowly the monk's face turned to face him, the soft smiling features replaced by a ghastly skull with hollow dead eyes and yellowing teeth …

Turner woke with a start. Maybe staying alone in the wilderness had not been such a great idea after all, he thought. The dawn light was already pushing through the bedroom window, so he unzipped the sleeping bag and headed into the front room. His furry feline friend had disappeared when he'd headed off to bed the previous night; how the hell it got in and out so easily, he had no idea.

After a light breakfast, Turner went back to his reading, trying to interpret the meaning of the symbols in the byre. The strange-shaped letters inside the pentagram on the byre door certainly looked occult in nature, he thought, feeling slightly unnerved by the idea. Turner opened the *Discoverie of Witchcraft* volume on his knee to a section entitled 'Occult Writings and Their Hidden Meanings'. This part of the book had never been published, all trace of it thought lost when James I had burnt all known first editions.

After scanning page after page, he found the letters transcribed in a section called 'The Enochian Alphabet'. Turner read slowly, moving his index finger under each word so that he didn't miss anything. The section described how the sixteenth-century royal astrologer, John Dee, claimed to have been told about the Enochian language by angels. These divine spirits had apparently communicated directly with Dee through his trusted spirit medium, Edward Kelly. This was during the reign of Elizabeth I, when witchcraft was classed as a crime punishable by death. Turner knew, from his own research, that Dee firmly positioned his studies as scientific and astrological in nature, and had never fallen foul of the witchcraft laws. He assumed, rightly, that Dee's Enochian text had been accepted as divine, rather than occult, in origin by his court companions. Looking at the strange writing still made Turner feel uneasy; it was like no script he'd ever seen.

Carrying the book outside, Turner compared the transcribed alphabet in the book with the markings inside the still dripping pentagram. Reading clockwise it spelt 'HANDAL' when translated into modern English. The psychic wondered whether the symbol was a symbolic doorway and HANDAL meant exactly what it sounded like – 'handle' when spelt in its modern form. This seemed silly to Turner – what self-respecting paganist would write something as plain as 'handle' on such a thing. He dug deeper into his book. After four more pages, he found what he was looking for. 'Enochian words,' he read, 'are written backwards and must be read right to left.'

The word became 'LADNAH', and Turner was no further forward. He kept reading. Finally, at the end of the long appendix, there was a translation of Enochian words and phrases into their English meaning, like a bizarre foreign dictionary. Scanning down to the middle of the page, he found LADNAH translated as 'Ark of Knowledge'. Finally, he was getting somewhere. The text went on to explain that Ark of Knowledge literally meant a store of information somewhere – ancient knowledge somehow codified for use by future generations. Turner knew that this idea of ancient secrets hidden away for generations was not unique; many such things had been created throughout the ages, and provided the foundation of many wild adventure tales he'd read in his youth. He also knew that some believed that the tarot hid the secrets of the ancient Egyptians within its bizarre artwork. Turner guessed that the pentagram symbol, painted deliberately behind the door, was a signpost to this particular Ark of Knowledge's location; it was somewhere in the byre.

Glancing around, Turner spotted the overturned sandstone blocks with their strange illustrations, figuring that this might be what it meant. If he could decode the drawings on the slabs, maybe he could finally understand the ancient knowledge the carvers had meant to pass on.

'Hellooo … anybody at home?' the clear voice of Julian Etienne called from outside. In his enthusiasm to discover the mystery of the symbol, Turner had completely forgotten about inviting Julian for lunch.

'I'm in here, Julian. Watch your step by the door and don't touch any of the red pigment,' Turner shouted back from inside the byre.

Julian trotted in cautiously, holding a small bag filled with venison steaks. 'Lunch,' he said, holding up the bag with a grin.

'Perfect timing. I've just finished figuring out what the symbol on the door means. Come inside. I'll tell you as we eat.' Turner motioned Julian into the croft and set about preparing the steaks.

After scrabbling through his food rations, Turner found tins of new potatoes, mushy peas and green beans. Apologising for the slightly odd food combination, the pair sat down and munched happily through their meal as Turner passed on what he'd discovered.

An hour later, they were peering over the carvings on the sandstone slabs in the byre like schoolboys looking at a difficult exam question. Levering the two blocks together had taken them over half an hour, using wood to gradually push and shove the giant slabs across the dirt floor. Viewing the entire carving, Julian identified the central figure of a monk holding a cross as St Benedict. The eagle and lion sitting either side of the figure, he believed, were illustrating some form of transformation process. Apparently, in ancient chemical texts, symbolically the eagle represented some volatile process, and the lion a stable one. Combining them together was traditionally meant to illustrate some type of transformation, physical or spiritual. The Latin text, 'As above, so below', carved above the figures, also supported Julian's transformation theory – he told Turner this was an alchemical saying, dating back to the time of the Hermetic philosophers. The alchemists were all about transformation, he explained, constantly striving to refine things to their purist form. Three smaller symbols at the base of the carving were unclear, eroded with the passing of time. Turner marvelled at the man's grasp of esoteric knowledge, gathered, no doubt, from Julian's reading of the ancient texts in his unusual library. Once again, Turner felt a strange bond of friendship between them, as though they were bound together like members of some strange club hell bent on unearthing long-lost knowledge.

'I think these three faded symbols at the bottom are meant to represent the fundamental essences of all things – sulphur, quicksilver and salt,' Julian said in a matter-of-fact way, running his fingers over the faded outlines as he spoke.

'What do you mean, fundamental essences?' Turner asked curiously. 'I thought the old beliefs described the world as made up of four elements. Earth, fire, water, air – that type of thing. I've seen those types of symbols before on tarot cards.' So far, that was the only thing Turner was familiar with.

His head was starting to hurt as he tried to absorb what Julian was saying.

'Well, yes and no. The alchemists believed that everything was alive; everything has a soul. That's what sulphur represents here, the spirit of life not the chemical element.' Julian moved his finger to the centre symbol as he continued. 'This one is quicksilver – we call it mercury nowadays. Again, this symbolises that everything is connected – high to low, day to night, above and below. This last one, salt, means base matter, like earth if you like.' Julian looked up to see whether Turner was following him. He wasn't.

'OK, look, think of it this way. Basically this carving illustrates a method to carry out some type of transformation. It could be physical, like changing one thing into another, or spiritual, maybe a religious awakening of some kind. I can't tell, and I don't think we'll ever know for sure.' Julian looked up from the slab to see whether this made more sense to the psychic.

'So this is an instruction sheet on how to change something into something else?' Turner beamed back, thinking he'd finally grasped the idea, hoping, for the sake of his growing headache, that Julian would stop explaining. His head was starting to pound dully inside, like someone was trying to get out by banging on his skull with a particularly heavy hammer.

'Yes! You've got it!' Julian seemed pleased he was finally getting through.

Turner breathed a sigh of relief, and unconsciously shook his head, trying to clear it. He thought for a while, glad of the brief silence, the pain in his brain easing slightly. Looking again carefully at the slab, his nose almost touching the stone near the oil lamp they'd brought with them, he said, 'I don't see any occult or pagan symbols here. And I know it sounds crazy, but I can't feel any sense of evil about the thing.' Turner felt a little embarrassed bringing his psychic sixth sense into the conversation.

Julian nodded in agreement, then set about examining the granite base the slab used to sit on. 'Is this the entrance to the crypt you told me about? Down here?' he asked, pointing into the open base, the hole still uncovered after Turner's exploration.

'Yes. You won't be able to see it without the light.' Turner grabbed the oil lamp from the sandstone slab and passed it over. Julian manoeuvred his way into the hollow base of the granite slab. The access to the crypt was down a fairly deep vertical shaft, meaning they both couldn't go inside – one needed to remain in the byre to help the other back up. Agreeing Julian could explore on his own, Turner was amazed at the man's agility. Expertly, he braced himself against the sides of the shaft, and then literally hopped his way down quickly to the bottom by flexing his legs. If this was what country living did for your fitness, Turner thought, he'd better start thinking of relocating. Even with walking his dog, and the odd day out hiking with Jade, Turner couldn't compare with the sprightliness of his new friend, who must be at least thirty years his elder.

Inside, Julian crouched, making his way along the smooth tunnel like a mole in familiar territory. Out of sight of Turner, he was a changed man, totally at home in this underground lair. Crunching through the pile of animal bones at the tunnel's end, he stepped easily into the larger space of the crypt, waving the oil lamp in front of him. Swiftly, he scanned the two rock shelves in either wall and then stopped dead. As with Turner's visit, three remained occupied with the skeletal remains of monks, lying at peace within their musty black robes, and one was empty. Frantically, his hands darted over the empty shelf, feeling into every corner, muttering 'Oh God, no' under his breath over and over again.

Practically running, he crossed to the large oak door at the end of the room, the one Turner hadn't been able to move. Reaching high on the lintel, he pressed on two of the rocks, one after the other, then again, and the door eased open. Pulling hard against the rusted hinges, he squeezed through to the other side. Julian held the light high and scanned the interior, keeping his back firmly against the door.

As with the tunnel, the chamber behind the door was hewn directly into the granite, but it was much larger than the crypt. Rough-sawn timber tables lined the edges of the room, surrounding a central tear-shaped furnace. Row upon row of chemical bottles with cork stoppers filled the shelving on the far wall, each with a neat handwritten label. The nearest table was scattered with parchment covered in Latin text with scribbled chemical formulae.

Julian swiftly searched the room, looking for something, flinging papers desperately across the floor, tumbling empty flasks in his haste. He grabbed a small vial and silver spatula from the far wall, and then carefully began scraping a fine red powder from inside one of the distillation tubes poking out of the top of the furnace. After carefully recovering every small grain of the deposit into the vial, he seemed satisfied. Wrapping it carefully in his handkerchief, he pushed the small bottle securely into his pocket. Realising that Turner might be wondering what was taking him so long, Julian quickly closed the door and headed back through the crypt.

'There you are. I was starting to get worried,' Turner said, peering at the top of Julian's shiny head down the hole. 'What do you make of it?' Julian was already above ground before he'd finished the sentence, not needing Turner's outstretched hand to help him up. The psychic marvelled again at his new friend's gymnastic ability.

'Well, it's definitely interesting, I'll give you that.' Julian wasn't even out of breath from climbing up the entrance shaft. 'The bodies are definitely Benedictine monks, though. They must have been left there hundreds of years ago.' In truth, Julian had not examined the skeletal remains. He already knew what they were, and when they were put in the crypt.

Julian dusted himself off and smiled. 'Well, that was fun! Thanks for letting me look at your discovery.' Julian reached out his hand and Turner shook it warmly, feeling the strength in the fingers. 'I'd better get back home. Bad forecast for tonight and I want to beat the weather.'

Turner thought the pair would sit and chat about the contents of the crypt, but his fly-fishing acquaintance would have none of it. Politely excusing himself, he made his way back up the forest track, wishing the psychic a safe trip home the next day. The speed of Julian's exit seemed strange to Turner after his geniality of the previous day. Maybe the skeletons had freaked him out a little, he thought, and he wanted to get away from the place as fast as possible.

As Julian had predicted, later that day the weather turned with a fury like hell itself. Huge hailstones battered the roof of the croft, causing Turner to cower by the wood stove, hugging a mug of tea like his life depended on it. The Scottish wildcat came bounding in from behind the fireplace and jumped, trembling, onto a fish crate. The psychic crawled around the back of the stove to find a small hole dug through the brickwork. Somehow, his feline friend had either tunnelled through the brick, or exploited the gap, to make its swift entry and exit to and from the croft. Hoping the cat would come back, Turner had kept some of his delicious venison to one side, and the soggy moggy was gratefully wolfing it down.

Hour after hour the storm rumbled down the mountainside, blasting the building with more huge hailstones. As they hammered on the glass panes, Turner began to worry that the windows would shatter, exploding a torrent of lethal glass fragments into the room. Mike Fletcher's outdoor coat was still hanging over the bed, so he wrapped it tightly around himself and headed outside to close the shutters. As soon as he opened the door he regretted his decision. The freezing hail prickled his face like he'd walked into an explosion in a needle factory. Sliding his body down the wall, he reached out a shivering hand to release the shutter catch. The wood panel slammed hard against the croft, and he managed to secure it in place before slipping down to his knees on the greasy ground.

What he saw when he stood up made his blood freeze. At the entrance to the forest path, a hooded figure was watching him. A bony, withered figure, black hood pulled tight around the head. Turner wiped his eyes, thinking he was seeing things. The figure remained still, unmoved by the hailstones battering its small frame.

CHAPTER 14: STORMY TRAILS

Turner stood with his back braced against the croft wall, staring over at the hooded figure. For some reason, an overwhelming sense of pity filled his senses as he tried to get a better view through the scything hail. He felt in no danger, despite the macabre appearance of the withered frame. Whatever this person was doing here, somehow he felt it didn't seem to involve him.

'Hi there,' Turner called, trying to sound friendly and unafraid. His voice was either lost in the storm or ignored.

Slowly, the robed figure moved forward across the mossy lawn towards the byre, dragging one leg limply behind. Awkwardly, it climbed over the broken wall and slid inside. Turner pulled his coat tighter and pushed his way against the wind to peer into the byre. The only signs he could see were bare childlike footprints in the dirt, and a wet trail leading to the granite slab. Cupping his hands to his ears, he listened intently for any sounds of movement down below in the crypt. He thought he could hear creaking, like the hinges of an old door protesting at being opened after a long sleep. Then a shrill scream echoed down the tunnel, its wailing despair filling the air like a thick fog. A thin weak voice was crying, 'No … it can't be … no …' And then deep wrenching sobs rattled from below.

'Hello … hello … are you OK?' Turner called out. He had walked with revenging ghosts and lived. This was nothing like that; he knew whatever, or whoever, this was had been a full-blooded human at some point. If the figure were truly supernatural, it wouldn't have struggled to get over the wall, but would have glided through it. This thing was alive, breathing and living in the mortal plane. Mortals didn't scare Turner.

The sobs had stopped abruptly when he'd called out. He heard a limping shuffle heading back down the underground tunnel towards the entrance shaft and then a robed figure scrabbled up the sheer walls, back into the byre, with the ease of a spider climbing a wall. A bony hand grasped the top of the granite base and hauled up the frail body, shining eyes peering cautiously over at Turner. With an awkward heave the full frame of the robed figure stood up.

'You not afraid of me, boy?' a woman's voice said from beneath the hood.

'No.' One simple word, no more, from the psychic.

A withered hand with a missing forefinger reached up slowly and pulled back the hood. The brown shrivelled face of an incredibly old woman glared at Turner. 'How about now?'

Turner peered at the hollow cheeks and cracking skin, lank grey hair a tangled mess down her back. Dried blood flaked around her mouth, and she was grinning horribly over at him.

'No,' Turner said, meeting her gaze head-on.

The woman laughed, a soft tinkling laugh of a girl, the frail body convulsing as she chortled on and on. Turner laughed with her, the bizarre pair dripping wet from the storm.

Turner looked at the awkward way she was holding her weight. 'Can I help you? You're limping.'

Her laughter stopped abruptly. 'No one can help me, boy, no one. I'm as good as dead. You may think I look dead already, eh? Well, I'm not.' With that, she pulled up the hood again, and bypassed Turner by walking straight out of the byre door. As she grasped the wooden frame, she looked down at the dripping pentagram. 'How'd you find me – was it that?' she said, pointing at the symbol.

'No, well maybe yes. I'm not sure.' Turner was trying to rethink his reading of the symbols and whether he'd misinterpreted their meaning. When he looked up she'd gone, vanished out of the door and into the forest. He felt compelled to follow her, find out who she was, and what she was doing here. So much for a couple of relaxing days in the wilderness, he thought. In truth, he was thoroughly enjoying himself; the bizarre nature of it all suited Turner down to the ground.

In the fading light he could make out her bare footprints heading west into the forest. Step by step he followed, losing the trail occasionally on the mossy ground. After about an hour, Turner stood at the top of a deep ravine, sounds of a waterfall cascading at its head. The woodland canopy shielded the worst of the weather as he pressed on, following the ridgeline.

Thirty minutes of steady climbing later, the ground gave way to heather moor, dominated by a huge grey crag in the far distance. Darkness seeped across the landscape quickly, and Turner began to stumble over unseen rocks and roots.

Pausing to catch his breath, he sat and let his eyes grow accustomed to the evening gloom. Across the line of the heather, he could see the hooded figure of the woman limping towards the granite base of the overhanging crag. Thankfully, the weather was easing, the hailstone barrage now a light misty rain. Picking up speed, Turner crunched his way through the coarse ground, gaining rapidly.

Then he heard something – the sound of a child singing a gentle lullaby somewhere off to his left. Breaking off his pursuit to investigate the noise, he made his way slowly towards its source. Sitting calmly on a rock was a young girl dressed in white, washing clothes in a deep rock pool fed by the babbling brook running off the crag. She sat gently singing to herself, the lilting, sad tones washing over Turner. In time with the singing, she was beating and wringing out damp clothing, concentrating hard on her work. The thing that caught his attention was the nature of her laundry. Every single item was soaked in blood. No matter how hard the child tried, she could not remove the frightening stains.

He knew immediately that she was some sort of apparition of the mountains; he could sense the trappings of the spirit world surrounding her like a comforting shroud. The sense of loss and loneliness he felt from the singing tugged at his soul, making him feel sorry for the girl. He stepped closer so that he was standing with his boots almost in the water. 'Hello, little one. Why are you out here?' Turner stepped to the bank of the stream opposite the girl.

A soft beautiful face with round eyes looked up, as if noticing him for the first time. 'Hello, Nathen Turner. What is it you want to know from me?' the girl's lilting voice asked, the tones soft. The hair on the back of Turner's neck stood up, prickling the back of his head uncomfortably. The realisation that this sad figure already knew who he was confirmed his assumption that she was a spiritual being. Something tugged at Turner's memories as he desperately tried to remember the many legends and folk tales he'd read about haunting figures of the mountains.

Finally, he thought he had it. 'You're the "Bean-nighe" spirit – the washing woman of legend?' he asked, his voice quavering a little.

The girl sat smiling at him. 'Yes. You also walk with the spirits – I can see that.'

Things like this, that would normally totally throw the average person, were simply a part of Turner's daily life. Seeing a spirit, any spirit, was as normal to him as meeting an old friend. Turner tried to remember the detail of the washing woman legend; this girl might be able to help him uncover the mystery of his hooded lady.

'Do you know the old lady in the hooded robe and what has happened to her?' Turner sat perched on a low rock opposite the young girl, wobbling slightly as he tried to keep his balance.

The spirit looked across at him, her wide eyes gleaming in the reflected moonlight from the stream. 'Yes, but I can only tell you what is to come, not what has been. If you wish to know, you must realise that you cannot change what is to be. Nothing you can do will alter what I tell you. Do you wish to know about your own future?'

Turner thought this over. He'd rather not know if something horrible was going to happen to him and there was nothing he could do about it. 'No, I only wish to know about the hooded lady.'

The girl opened her arms and looked to the sky, rolling her eyes back in her head. Gently her body rocked backwards and forwards as she sang her tender lament across the water. The singing stopped and the smooth tones of the girl spoke again, more forcibly this time. 'She will die tonight, but not by your hand. Someone will weep for her. Tears of love … and loss. A love long hidden from the world. She will die.' The soft singing started again.

Gradually her singing began to fade. As it did, the figure of the girl and her bizarre laundry vanished into mist, blown across the heather by the wind. Turner called after her, but she was gone, leaving no sign behind. Scanning the heather moor across to the crag, Turner realised that this spiritual diversion had caused him to lose sight of the hooded lady. Travelling as fast as he could, he headed for the base of the crag, where he'd last seen the limping figure.

After about ten minutes of crunching as fast as he could across the heather, he stared up at the huge rock face, glancing about desperately for any signs of her. Nothing. Somehow he felt he should warn her, even though the ghostly girl had told him that nothing could be done to prevent her fate. Clambering up the shingle slope, his feet slipping on the loose stone, he made his way to a narrow rock ledge some twenty feet off the ground. Skirting the rock face, he sidestepped his way along until the ledge opened to a narrow path. Ahead, he could see the opening of a small cave and he walked cautiously towards it, watching his footing. With no light to guide him, he called inside the cave mouth. No answer except the echo of his own voice. He tried again but still no answer.

Turner pressed on along the path and realised he had no idea how to get back to the croft. In his enthusiasm, he'd completely lost his bearings. Sitting down on a huge boulder, Turner looked back across the moor, trying to figure out where he'd left the forest. If he could spot the entrance to the forest trail he'd walked along, then, hopefully, he'd be able to follow it back along the ravine and down again to the croft. His thoughts were interrupted by a gruff Scottish voice from behind him.

'Stay right there, son, and don't do anything stupid.' Turner jumped at the sound of the rough voice breaking the stillness of the night and felt the barrel of a gun pushing hard into his neck. 'Who the hell are you, and what are you doing up here? Poaching maybe? Well, you've picked the wrong bloody place to do it.' Turner was too frightened to answer and stood rooted to the spot.

'Who are you? I said! Turn around so I can see you, and put your bloody hands up.' Turner turned slowly to see the snarling face of Callum Benvie pointing a shotgun at his head. Callum had been on the hill all day looking for the withered old woman who had attacked Maggie Douglas the previous evening. Little did he know, he and Turner were both searching for the same person.

CHAPTER 15: A COLD WELCOME

Turner looked apprehensively at his tweed-clad aggressor, taking in the heavy boots and the relaxed way he was holding the shotgun. Whoever this was, he was a man of the land, totally at home in this wild environment. The snarling face was angry, but Turner sensed more than that. This man was furious about something, like he'd been wronged in some way and wanted revenge at any cost. Deciding that confronting the man head-on would be stupid and dangerous, he tried lightening the mood.

'Hi, I'm Nathen Turner. At your service.' Turner offered a slight bow that was met by an angry grimace from Callum as he took a half step closer to his Highland interloper. Turner could smell the earthy musk of the man and the waft of burnt peat, as if he'd been sitting too close to a fire. Undeterred, Turner pressed on. 'This must be the traditional Highland welcome I've heard so much about.' Turner smiled broadly at the furious face.

'Don't get smart with me, son. What're you doing here?' Callum Benvie growled, pushing the shotgun an inch closer to the end of Turner's nose.

Turner needed to think. How could he say he was following a strange hooded woman across the moor because he sensed she was in danger? The best reply he could muster was, 'I'm staying down at Lanner's Point Croft for a couple of days. I've been out for a walk – got lost when the weather turned bad.' He hoped this excuse was good enough to calm the fuming mountain man flexing his finger worryingly over the trigger.

'So, you know Mike Fletcher?' Callum said, less hostile than before, taking a step back and lowering his gun. He vaguely remembered Fletcher had mentioned some guy called Turner back at the estate lodge.

Turner jumped on the opportunity. 'Yes, of course,' he lied, breathing in the sweet night air that had replaced the heavy scent of the man as he stepped back. Turner was good at lying, having built a previous career as a fake psychic medium on his prowess. Turner certainly knew of Mike Fletcher from Hulk, but he'd never met him. Trying to back up his claim, he tugged on the green jacket and tried to sound confident. 'Look – this is his coat; my wardrobe is not exactly designed for this environment.'

Callum narrowed his eyes and glanced over the ill-fitting garment. The sleeves rode about three inches too short on the lanky figure of the psychic. 'You seen anybody else out here?'

'No,' Turner lied again. 'I think I'm in need of a clean pair of trousers – you scared me to death.'

Callum grunted. 'Sorry, son. I'm a bit edgy. I've been trying to track something out here all day. Mike Fletcher's staying with me.'

'Are you the head keeper? Maggie was down at the croft yesterday, getting some of Mike's stuff. She said he's been hurt quite badly.' Turner hoped that throwing a few truths amongst his lies might help this man to trust him a little.

'Yes, that's me. Callum, just call me Callum.' Mentioning Maggie's name seemed to have had a calming effect on the keeper and he pushed the shotgun inside a holster on his back. 'You say you're lost? You'd better come back with me until we can sort something out. There's not much light left, and that storm's coming back in.' Callum gestured at the blackening clouds swirling menacingly above the crag.

The ill-suited companions made their way back across the moor to the dirt road leading to the estate lodge. Callum was a man of few words, so Turner gave up trying to talk to him in the end, bounding behind, desperately trying to keep up. Soaking wet, puffed and red in the cheek, Turner followed the dour figure into the house.

Mike Fletcher and Maggie Douglas sat comfortably in the living room, drinking tea in front of a roaring peat fire. Maggie looked a lot better, the colour back in her cheeks as she chatted gaily. Fletcher looked relaxed and at home, his injured leg supported on a mound of pillows. At the entrance of the dripping pair, the conversation stopped abruptly.

'Who's he and why is he wearing my coat?' Fletcher said, looking confused, taking in the tall blond figure with the goatee beard wearing his clothing. Callum spun on the spot and pulled his gralloch knife from his belt, holding it tight against Turner's throat.

'Whoa there, killer! That's the second time you've tried to murder me in the past hour.' Turner took a step backwards, hoping he was close enough to the door to make a run for it. This guy was way too unstable. It seemed like he wanted nothing better than the psychic's head stuffed and mounted next to the deer horns proudly displayed on the walls.

'Callum! Put the knife down!' Maggie jumped to her feet and pulled Callum's arm away in case he didn't follow her instructions. 'That's Hulk's friend, the psychic guy. I met him yesterday. Sorry, I can't remember your name.' Grunting and swearing under his breath, the keeper re-sheathed the knife and sulked off to the kitchen.

Turner rubbed his throat and twisted his head side to side, checking it was still attached. 'Is he always like this? Good grief.'

Maggie led a trembling Turner into the room, pulling him gently by the sleeve. 'We've had a shock, that's all – there was an incident yesterday. We're a little on edge,' she said, as she offered him a chair by the fire and pushed a cup of tea into his hand.

Turner re-introduced himself and repeated his lie; he'd gone for a walk and got lost in the weather, again omitting the part about the hooded woman. Apologising to Fletcher for borrowing his jacket without permission, he found the photographer a pleasant companion and easy to talk to. When Maggie offered dry clothing to change into, they'd all laughed hysterically at Turner's loud Hawaiian shirt hidden underneath his layers of borrowed mountain wear. Due to the lateness of the hour, and the impossibility of Turner finding his way back to the croft in the dark, Maggie offered him the couch for the night. When he'd gladly accepted, Callum had reappeared, grunted in disapproval and then stomped off again towards his bedroom. Following the scare of the previous evening, Callum intended to keep watch all night after he'd grabbed a few hours' sleep. Maggie headed for the kitchen to prepare supper, leaving Fletcher and Turner alone, warming by the fire.

The two men sat like old friends, swapping stories of their experience in the wilderness, and, in particular, the regular reappearance of the Scottish wildcat. Neither had seen an animal like it before, and Fletcher was amazed to find it had dozed comfortably next to the psychic. Turner explained how he'd headed up to the croft after Hulk had called him, so he could see what was going on, first hand.

'So, do you have powers and stuff, like Hulk told me? I mean, can you see into the future, that kind of thing?' Fletcher felt a little silly asking the question but his slim fireside friend intrigued him.

Turner was happy to talk about his spiritual experiences. 'Well, not really. It's just that stuff happens to me that others find weird. Look, I know the psychic business is littered with smooth operators with a convincing chatter, but we're not all like that.' Again, he omitted to add that he had been one of the smooth operators once, and continued, 'Do you believe in fixed fate? You know, like maybe free will is a myth and everything has been decided for us already?'

Fletcher rubbed at his bandaged limb and readjusted it to a more comfortable position. 'No, I don't think so. I mean, I'd have to believe it was my destiny to fall down the ravine and injure my leg.'

'Right – so no one can say for sure what the future holds, yes? See, I believe the person we are creates the future we make for ourselves. So, when people have a psychic reading, by someone who knows what they're doing, it can give them insights – a new understanding of their situation, if you will.

That's basically what I do and teach others to develop.' Fletcher looked lost in his own thoughts as Turner said, 'The whole fixed fate thing is a hangover from a medieval life view. You know, we all have power to change our own lives if we take some responsibility for it.'

'Not true,' Fletcher muttered under his breath and looked away.

Turner glanced across at the forlorn figure cradling his empty teacup, wondering why he'd touched a nerve with his new friend. He tried a different approach. 'I find I can often sense things about people,' he said, scanning the photographer sitting in his chair. 'For example, I know you're troubled from the way you're holding yourself. I don't mean the leg. It's something deeper; something has changed your whole view on life.'

'I have multiple sclerosis,' Fletcher said, and looked down to the floor as if he was admitting a guilty secret.

Turner now understood Fletcher's reaction to his free-will line and sat silent, not sure what to say next. Eventually, he said, 'I'm sorry. I didn't mean to pry.'

Fletcher refilled both of their cups from the teapot. 'It's OK, honestly. Does me good to talk about it. I've not got my head around it myself. Like, one day I was fine, then boom, that's it, mate, your life's over. That's why I came here, trying to figure out what to do next.'

Fletcher explained what had happened to him at some length, covering every dark turn of his emotional rollercoaster. To his surprise, he found Turner an enthusiastic listener, eager to understand what the diagnosis could mean and what options the photographer thought he had for his life.

Fletcher leant forward, speaking earnestly, holding the psychic's gaze. 'It's like living a lie, you know? People look at me on the outside and don't see anything wrong. You did, but everyone else doesn't. They don't notice that I'm partially blind – the constant pain in my face feels like I'm being stabbed all the time. And I get so tired, you know? It's like having a bad flu without the runny nose and cough. I'm sure my friends think I'm making it up.'

'Then maybe you need different friends,' Turner said simply.

Maggie returned to the serious pair, carrying a tray filled with bowls of steaming broth and crusty bread. Turner noticed that she sat deliberately close to Fletcher and was diligently helping him balance the soup bowl on his lap, ripping off a portion of the bread for him. Perhaps, Turner thought, the photographer had already found a new friend. With Maggie in the room, the atmosphere changed and the conversation moved to lighter, more tongue-in-cheek matters, like why Callum was such a miserable old so-and-so. When Maggie said that he was more at home talking to their pony than people, Turner chuckled and spilt some of his soup. After Turner had helped Maggie clean up, she made her excuses and headed to bed, still feeling the after-effects of the night before.

Fletcher reached over for the whisky and offered a glass to Turner. The photographer appeared a little nervous as he downed his drink in one, then poured another. This second one followed the first; it looked like he was trying to build up courage to tell Turner something. As he sat with his third in so many minutes, he'd made up his mind.

'I saw a ghost down at the croft.' Fletcher sat back, relieved at his admission. He went on quickly to describe the decrepit finger and the withered hand he'd seen climbing over the byre wall, unable to stop now that he'd started.

Rather than react with shock or scorn, Turner matter-of-factly said, 'Was it wearing a hooded monk's robe?'

'You know, don't you? … You must do. You've seen it too!' Fletcher almost jumped for joy at the realisation that he hadn't gone crazy the night he'd fled for his life through the forest.

Turner didn't want to lie anymore. Whether it was the whisky or the pleasant company, lying felt wrong to him. 'Yes, I've seen it, or rather her. It's not a ghost; it's an old woman. I've no idea where she's from, where she lives, or how old she is, but she's human just like you and me.' This time Turner downed his whisky and poured another large measure.

'That's impossible – the hand, it was old brown skin and bone. How could such a thing be alive? Callum's seen it too – he said it was just a woman, but I didn't believe him. He chased her across the moor.' Fletcher was not coming to terms with the fact that he'd run from an old lady very well at all.

'I spoke to her.' Turner gazed unblinking, looking over at his agitated confederate.

Turner told the whole story, leaving out the part where he'd met the mysterious spirit girl washing her bloody laundry in the stream. He thought, rightly, that this would be stretching Fletcher's belief system a little too far in one night.

'It … she … attacked Maggie last night. At least I think so. They won't talk about it. All they've said is that some withered old woman broke through the window and bit her.

That's why Maggie's got the bandage on her shoulder and Callum is in Wild West shoot-out mode.' Fletcher mimed loading a pump-action shotgun as he mentioned the antics of the head keeper.

Turner smiled at the gesture. 'I think they've got it wrong. She looked harmless to me. How the hell can an old lady break a window, climb in and bite somebody, for goodness' sake. What on earth would be the point? It was probably some stray farmer's dog gone feral, or something like that. Sounds like a case of mistaken identity. She probably happened to be walking on the moor, and Callum put two and two together to get eight.'

Fletcher had to agree, and felt foolish that he'd run away from an old lady. He visualised explaining to his sister how he'd injured his leg running away from an aged crone. This one, he was never going to live down. After another quick drink, Turner helped Fletcher hobble down the corridor to his bedroom, before grabbing a couple of blankets and improvising a snugly bed on the couch.

Within minutes, both of them were sleeping soundly, the alcohol and the fresh mountain air having had their sedative effects on the pair of city boys. Outside, the second storm of the day had passed by, leaving a chill cloudless sky littered with glittering stars. From the outbuilding, the pony whinnied and started pacing around in circles, sensing that something was wrong. Behind it, a black shadow slithered around the building, heading straight across the lawn to Maggie's window. In the gloom of the night, it was just possible to make out a decrepit hand with a missing forefinger reaching up quietly onto the sill.

CHAPTER 16: NIGHTMARE BY STARLIGHT

Maggie lay uncomfortably on her back, dozing lightly, her head nestled amongst the pillows. The room was exactly as it had been the previous evening, except for the hessian sacking Callum had temporarily taped in place over the broken window, gently swaying in the night breeze. For the past hour, Maggie had kept rolling onto her injured shoulder and waking up with a little cry of pain. She could hear Turner and Fletcher still swapping stories in the living room and, judging by the odd outburst of laughter, they were enjoying each other's company. Trying again to sleep, she rolled onto her uninjured side, facing the wall.

Inch by slow inch, the window covering was being silently peeled back from the outside. A bony finger poked underneath, blindly searching for the end of the securing tape. Long yellowing nails pecked at the fibres of the straw-coloured material, pinching and pushing to get a hold. The fabric was soaked from the storm and the brown tape was gradually losing its grip. Grabbing a curling corner, two withered digits pulled back slowly and steadily, then stopped. The hooded figure outside was listening. Then the withered fingers started probing and pulling again, until a small corner of the window was exposed.

The hooded face peered through the gap, squinting into

the bedroom to see whether the vandalism had gone unnoticed. Maggie still lay on her side, facing the wall, her chest rising and falling in a slow rhythmical pattern. The silvery rays of the waning moon smeared dark shadows across the sill, highlighting the withered hands picking at the tape. A huge burst of light scanned the lawn as Callum appeared from the front of the croft. Shotgun in one hand, searchlight in the other, he was certainly not trying to hide his presence. Every few paces he paused, listening, and moved the wide beam from side to side. Callum had slipped quietly out the back door about an hour ago, determined no harm would come to anyone at the lodge tonight. Not being able to stop the attack on Maggie lay heavy on his conscience. He felt responsible and vowed to himself that it would never happen again. Waiting for an opportunity to hide, the hooded figure crouched against the wall, spreading the monk's robe out like a giant shadow. As Callum turned to scan the beam over the pony and the outbuilding, the wraith-like shape darted out of sight and waited.

Ten minutes became an hour, as Callum relentlessly paced around the lodge, poking his light into the darkest corners, checking and rechecking his path. The sound of the two men inside saying their goodnight farewells drifted out into the night, causing the keeper to stop and head back inside. Callum wasn't used to houseguests and preferred his privacy. At least now he could make himself a strong coffee without having to talk to any of them, he thought. The hooded figure watched him disappear and then slid from its hiding place, amongst the heather, to resume peeling away the window covering.

Working more quickly, the withered fingers pulled hard to free the last of the remaining tape before, finally, the hessian sacking came free. Turning to check for Callum's reappearance, the wrinkled features under the hood shone palely in the moonlight. The old woman's hollow face was twisted in malice, the eyes gleaming brightly, mouth open in anticipation. Had Turner seen this side of his hooded visitor in the byre, he would most definitely have been afraid.

Carrying the window covering, the hooded crone slid inside, her injured leg causing her bare bony feet to slap wetly on the sill. Crouching and barely moving, she checked the bedroom again. Maggie hadn't moved, her slow, measured breathing filling the small space. Quickly, the old woman pushed the hessian back over the window, so that all would look well to a casual observer outside. This time, she didn't want to be disturbed in her work.

Scouring the room, she threw back her hood and listened for any signs that she'd been heard entering the estate lodge. Sounds of gentle snoring came from the room next door and also down the corridor from the living room. There must be at least another two people in the house, she thought; she'd need to be careful. Callum's searchlight briefly flicked past the window, spearing a sudden beam of light through the hessian-covered gap. Instinctively she ducked, then smiled menacingly to herself as the sound of the keeper's footsteps moved on around the building. So he was back outside and she was inside – perfect, she thought.

This time she needed to do it right. This time the sleeping frame of Maggie Douglas must never wake up. Licking her dry lips, she remembered her previous attempt at biting

Maggie's neck. Stupidly, her bloodlust had got the better of her; this mustn't happen again. Pushed underneath the bed were a couple of thick blankets and an extra pillow. Limping softly across the floor, she gently slid out the fluffy pillow and then paused again, checking that she hadn't disturbed her sleeping victim.

Rising high on her withered toes, the old woman held the pillow almost to the roof and directly above Maggie's head. She stood still, savouring the moment. Then the pillow came down with a slam over the sleeping figure. Maggie never knew what hit her, struggling on her back as the cotton filled her mouth, blocking her air supply. The old woman was smiling, almost laughing, as Maggie struggled underneath the withered limbs that pushed the pillow ever harder onto her face. Then Maggie's body went limp.

Light flooded the room, outlining someone standing silhouetted in the doorway. 'Stop – you don't want to do this,' a man's voice said calmly, without any malice. The snarling figure of the old woman dropped the pillow and raised her arms to defend herself from the intruder, thinking it was Callum with the shotgun.

The figure in the doorway didn't move. 'You will get no harm from me, but you must stop this.' The shadowed figure took a pace forward towards the snarling crone.

The old woman spat back, 'What do you know? She's poison, all her kind. Treacherous scum, every one of them.' A withered hand reached back down to pick up the pillow.

Outside, Callum paused. He could hear voices inside Maggie's bedroom. Cautiously, Callum poked his head through the hessian covering on the window and looked inside. When he saw the old crone towering above Maggie's still and lifeless body, he snapped. Diving headfirst into the room, he smashed the robed figure hard in the gut with the butt of the shotgun. Wincing in pain, she fell to the floor, her monk's robe spreading out around the frail frame. Callum quickly levelled the shotgun at the wrinkled face glaring back at him.

'No, Callum, no! She doesn't know what she's doing.'

Callum spun to face the familiar voice coming from the open doorway. From his window vantage point, he'd been unable to see anyone else in the room. The beam from his dropped searchlight shone bright and clear on the bald head of the man. It was Julian Etienne.

'What the … Julian?' As Callum turned in surprise, the shotgun moved with him, away from the shrivelled figure on the floor. The old woman leapt to her feet, pushed past Julian, and sprinted down the corridor as fast as her good leg could carry her.

Determined that this murderous hag would not escape him this time, Callum followed at a run. Explanations from Julian could come later – now he wanted revenge. Kicking the sleeping Turner on the couch, he shouted at him, 'Wake up, psychic boy, and put your boots on. Maggie's been attacked – we've got a murderer to catch.' Turner was the only able-bodied man left to help him. For some reason, Julian wanted to protect this evil old crone. Callum didn't want to protect her; he wanted to kill her.

Turner woke from his deep, alcohol-fuelled sleep to see Callum glaring, as if daring him to refuse to help. Not understanding, but following orders, Turner pushed on his borrowed walking boots and ran after the retreating figure of the keeper. Out on the moor, Callum was already hundreds of yards ahead, chasing the robed figure that limped frantically between shadows, looking for cover. Julian caught up with Turner as he stood panting and flustered, trying to regain his breath.

'Julian? What are you doing here? What the hell is going on?' Turner started running again, talking between huge gulps of air.

Julian was a lot fitter than he looked and was coping with the pursuit much better than Turner. 'Isobel attacked Maggie. I think she's killed her.'

'Isobel? Who the hell's Isobel?' Turner said, even more confused than before.

'There,' Julian said, and pointed at the robed figure limping desperately ahead. 'She's my wife.'

CHAPTER 17: SORROW IN THE SHADOWS

This was madness, thought Turner. How could the old crone he'd seen in the byre be married to Julian? She was ancient, decrepit, more corpse than bride. If the withered hag was so evil, why had she left Turner without a look back, and not tried to attack him? He'd spotted no sign of her at Julian's house when he'd visited. And why on earth would she want to attack Maggie? Turner's mind racing, he panted after the retreating figure of Julian.

Ahead, Callum was shouting at the woman, screaming obscenities into the night as he chased after her across the moor. The two figures seemed close together up on the ridgeline below the looming crag. Bright beams from Callum's searchlight were frantically darting side to side as the torch bounced carelessly on the strap over his shoulder. That could mean only one thing. The keeper was close enough – he didn't need to hold the light anymore. Then a shotgun blast boomed out into the night and Turner heard a huge splash, like a boulder falling heavily into water.

The searchlight was still, searching in one particular place. Julian was stumbling forward, racing, trying to reach Callum and grab his gun. Behind, Turner fell hard, tripping over a heather root and landing headfirst in the twiggy foliage. Scratched and bleeding, Turner scrambled on, desperate to catch up with the men. He could hear Julian and Callum arguing furiously, the keeper's gun twitching dangerously near his old friend. The keeper sounded like he was threatening him, pushing angrily at Julian's small frame.

Turner pulled up quickly and listened. A soft girl's voice began singing a sorrowful lament, the melancholy tune filling his head. Turner felt heartbroken, an overwhelming sadness filling him to the core. Confused, he looked around for the source of the noise, blotting out the raging voices up ahead. Maybe the spirit he'd seen on the moor had returned, or perhaps she was trying to get his attention. Slowly, as if walking in a dream, Turner moved away from the men and walked further towards the crag, following the noise. The sorrowful singing grew louder as he found the stream and rock pool where he'd seen the mountain spirit sitting the night before. There was no sign of the young girl washing her bloody linen, just the singing, crying gently into the night. Bubbling waters, swelled by the rain, cascaded down through a deep channel cutting through the heather, draining into the pool below. Turner's boots were squishing along the damp peaty banks, as the voice in his head grew louder with every step. Peering down into the deep pool, all he saw was blackness, the glassy surface reflecting the pale light of the moon. There he stood, silent and alone, drawn to the spot by the ghostly singing in his head.

Julian spotted the hunched figure of the psychic over Callum's shoulder, his angry words trailing off in mid-sentence as he felt the sadness surrounding the man. Turner was standing still, head bowed, as if in prayer. Pushing past Callum, Julian trudged towards Turner, ignoring the shouting of the gun-toting keeper behind his back.

Julian tugged at Turner's sleeve, trying to get his attention. 'What is it?'

No response. Turner stood gazing into the inky depths of the pool.

'What is it? What's wrong with you?' Julian said, more urgently this time, pulling harder on the sleeve.

Turner was crying, weeping openly, his tears dripping gently onto the mirrored surface of the pool. 'Can you hear that? Can you hear the singing? Saddest thing I've ever heard.'

Callum had caught up and was peering into Turner's distraught face, trying to understand what had come over him. 'Hear what? I can't hear anything. What's wrong with you, man?'

The swinging glow from Callum's light shattered the darkness, the piercing yellow beam flooding the rock pool. Julian looked down into the icy waters and fell to his knees in grief. There, bobbing in the depths, was the figure of the old woman. Tangled grey hair spread like a spider's web around her wrinkled features, eyes wide in fear staring back at him. The sodden black monk's robe sank away behind her into the deep, exposing a frail skeletal frame wrapped in withered skin. Her thin arms reached desperately upwards, as if searching for the surface in the last moments of her life.

Julian wrapped his arms across his chest, hugging himself, and fell to the ground. 'No … no … this is my fault. I'm so sorry.' Rocking back and forwards on his knees, he looked into the pool, hoping the figure he'd seen in the water wasn't there.

'What? What is it?' the gruff voice of Callum asked the

pair, still pointing his shotgun forward as if expecting an attack at any moment.

Julian sobbed between breaths, not taking his eyes from the pool. 'She's dead … drowned … in here …'

'Well, good bloody riddance. She can stay there and rot.' Callum turned his back on the grieving pair and stomped off back to the estate lodge, his job done. As far as he was concerned, this wicked woman had killed his best friend, and drowning was far too good for her. Even better if he'd shot her, he thought; she deserved it in his eyes. Callum kept his own version of the law out here, as many who'd tried to cross him had found out to their cost.

Turner knelt down to Julian and held him. He could feel the man's grief trembling through his body. The lament continued its sorry dirge in Turner's head as the pair sat cradled in the darkness, eyes fixed on the murky pool. Slowly the singing faded, the silence acting to wake Turner as if he'd been in a dream. Julian sensed a change in the psychic.

'You understand, don't you? I can feel it somehow, you know?' Julian said, almost pleading with Turner.

Turner stood up and brushed off the remains of the heather roots clinging to his clothing from his fall. 'In truth, I don't know what I understand, Julian. I met this old woman yesterday at the byre outside Lanner's Point Croft. It's just … well … I didn't feel afraid of her. She came up here and I followed her. I got lost in the storm – Callum found me. He's one scary guy.'

'Callum is Callum. He has a simple way of looking at things – right and wrong, nothing in between. Don't judge him too harshly – he's a good man at heart.' Julian stood and started looking about for a large stick.

Turner watched Julian pace up and down the bankside, thinking things were getting stranger and stranger by the minute. 'What are you doing?'

'I need to get her out – bury her properly.' Julian stopped as if thinking. 'Will you help me? Bury her, I mean.'

Turner certainly didn't like the idea of the old lady slowly rotting away in her watery grave. The thought of it made him shudder. Still, he felt this woman, whoever she was, could not be truly evil. Turner couldn't explain why exactly, but he had learnt to trust his instincts. Without replying, Turner started helping Julian find something long enough to reach the old lady and bring her back to dry land. Struggling in the dark, the pair eventually managed to hook a jagged fallen branch into the sodden robe sinking in the rock pool, and pull the withered body out. Other than the grazing on her leg from her previous encounter with the keeper, there was no sign that she'd been shot – Callum's blast must have missed. Somehow she'd lost her footing and fallen into the freezing water. Turner felt that Callum wouldn't care either way, the mood he was in – as long as she was dead, and no longer a threat, that would suit Callum's bloodlust just fine, he thought. Respectfully, Julian closed the eyes of the corpse and wrapped the body tightly in the robe, before lifting her lightweight frame easily into his cradled arms.

As the two half walked, half stumbled back through the heather, Turner followed along unsure where they were heading. He could sense that his grieving companion was lost in his thoughts, so he kept all the questions rattling around in his confused brain to himself. Expertly, Julian navigated a path through the forest, down the hill that butted on to the heather moor. Turner realised where they were going – back to Lanner's Point Croft. They walked on in silence; Turner couldn't say for how long. His mind raced, going over and over the events of the past day.

Finally, they passed through the treeline again into the familiar open glade around the croft. Without asking, Julian grabbed an oil lamp from inside, then headed straight to the byre, passing the broken-down walls glimmering palely in the moonlight. Creaking open the door, Julian headed quickly to the hollowed granite slab and summoned Turner to help him lower the body down into the opening of the crypt. Just as before, Julian easily hopped down the entrance shaft, then reached up to help the psychic lower the frail corpse, before helping Turner climb down. Underground, the two men ducked through the short stone corridor into the noiseless space of the crypt, carrying the body between them. What memories would drip from these ancient walls, thought Turner, as he scanned the swathed bodies of the monks, lying silent, their voices unheard. Julian seemed comfortable in this granite grave, like he'd been inside it thousands of times before. He'd told Turner that he had no knowledge of the place, that his first visit had been after their venison meal. Turner now realised that this must have been a lie. Julian had the air of a man at home, comfortable and confident in this macabre setting.

Feeling uneasy at discovering there was more to Julian than met the eye, Turner remained quiet and helped him place the lifeless figure on the vacant stone shelf cut into the wall. The sodden robe clung to the scrawny frame, dripping wet trails down the walls and forming shallow pools of water on the floor. Pausing, head bowed, Julian looked down at the corpse forlornly, as if all hope had been drained from him.

Turner couldn't contain himself any longer. When he finally spoke it made Julian jump. 'Who was she, Julian? How could she be your wife?'

'Your answer is in there,' Julian said, and pointed to the large wooden door at the end of the room. Turner had been unable to open it on his previous exploration of the crypt and now he felt worried about what hidden horrors might lurk inside. Julian pressed a couple of granite blocks in the frame above the door, and it sprung open slightly, allowing him to heave it open. He stepped inside and beckoned Turner to follow.

Julian sat calmly on the edge of one of the rough-sawn timber tables lining the edge of the room, and waited for the psychic to take it all in. Turner was picking up and reading the labels on the myriad chemical bottles, and walking around and sniffing at the acrid smell coming from the teardrop-shaped furnace in the centre of the room. Shocked to find such a place behind a door he'd thought long locked and disused, Turner stared in amazement at the sheer antiquity of the place. In truth, he was also more than a little relieved to find no further hooded bodies in it, living or dead.

Julian's voice broke the silence. 'If you truly want answers from me, what I tell you must remain a secret. You cannot tell another living soul. Within this room are things beyond your wildest imagination, way beyond modern science's understanding of our world. Can you swear to take what you learn to the grave? Can you promise me that, Nathen Turner?'

CHAPTER 18: ALCHEMY OF THE SOUL

Turner had come too far to stop, and gave Julian his solemn vow. He needed answers; the thought of all the strange events rattling around in his head, unresolved, for the rest of his life, was not a comfortable one.

Julian ushered Turner to a small stool tucked underneath one of the tables, motioned him to sit, and then sat down facing him.

Holding the psychic's gaze, Julian said, 'I have not been completely open with you, and for that I am truly sorry. I know this place – I helped create it. I own Lanner's Point Croft – the letting agents handle all the bookings. I never get involved with who stays, or when. If I'd thought that anyone would ever discover its secret, I would never have let anyone come. What I tell you is the truth – I promise you on my life.'

Turner took in the unflinching gaze and the earnestness of the man. Hopefully he'd finally find out what was going on, leaving his troubled mind in peace. Not wanting to interrupt, he simple nodded back an 'OK' as Julian continued.

'You remember we talked of alchemy? Not something from a fairy tale, I mean real alchemy from the books you saw at my house.' Turner remembered, but his knowledge of the subject was still next to nil.

Julian pulled over some of the sheets from one of the

tables and pushed them under Turner's nose. They were large-format pages of curling vellum, filled with handwritten drawings, strange symbols scrawled across the page. Turner respectfully leafed through them, one at a time. None of it meant anything to him, and he said so.

'Alchemy is not understood easily. These papers were written long before patent law or copyright. They are coded, as I told you when we looked at the markings on the sandstone slab.' Turner looked again, and, sure enough, some of the symbols from the carved slab were on the ancient pages.

'Many fools believe that alchemy is the process of turning lead into gold. It is not.' Julian wanted Turner to understand the importance of what he was saying, and kept looking up from the papers to make sure he was listening. 'It is purely and simply the process of bringing things to their purest form. Their highest state, if you like. Gold has always been seen as the purest form of metal, and that is where the confusion has arisen in all the old texts. The true purpose of alchemy is to bring us, human beings, to our highest, purest state of life.'

Turner kept quiet, fascinated by the imagery on the pages and now feeling excited at the discovery of the hidden chamber. Enthralled, he looked over at his seated companion with new eyes, listening intently to every word.

Satisfied that he had Turner's full attention, Julian said, 'Alchemical knowledge has always been hidden, passed down from master to master for generations. Some called these people the "cunning folk", the "wise men" or the "healer" of the village. Normally they were blacksmiths by trade, or had some skill working with furnaces and such like. Isobel – my wife – the old lady you met here yesterday, the one we've laid to rest next door, was one of these healers. Never a blacksmith, you understand – she was too frail – but a healer dealing in potions and remedies.' Julian gestured sadly to the withered body they'd fished from the pool, dripping wetly on the stone shelf in the crypt behind him. 'When I first met Isobel I was ill, almost at my last breath. She cured me – saved my life.'

Turner had seen many unusual things, but the thought of the withered crone healing anybody seemed odd to him. Given her appearance, it hadn't looked like she could heal herself. His confused expression said as much to Julian.

Sensing Turner's internal dialogue, Julian said, 'I know it seems hard to understand. We met many, many years ago. She wasn't always as she appears now. Look around you. How old do you think this place is? How long have the monks' bodies been at rest in the crypt? I swear to you, what I say is the truth. Isobel and I met in the year of 1560. I am over four hundred years old, Mr Turner.'

Silence. The dim crypt echoed with the dripping of the water from Isobel's robe, the ancestral chamber of death flickering eerily in the light from the lamp. Turner simply didn't know what to say. Slowly, he looked again at the man sitting calmly in front of him, trying to judge the truth in his words. Julian knew all about this place, it seemed, and the secret way to open the door to the chamber in which they sat. So why hadn't he come clean before? What was he trying to hide? How could such a fantastic claim be true?

Julian hadn't moved, and sat staring down at the floor, talking quietly, as if to himself. 'You know, people would think it's a blessing living so long, but it's not; it's a curse. A long life means watching all those you care about die before you. When I fled from persecution, I left people dying behind me. Their faces still haunt me to this day. I'll never forget the smells of the rotting corpses in the streets. The death, the poverty. People were desperate. I thought I could escape it all but it followed me. Death clung to me like an old friend.' Julian kept gazing at the floor, refusing to meet Turner's gaze. 'It was a different life, a different world. They called me Father Sebastian then.'

Turner jumped a little in surprise at the name, remembering his dream from the croft. A little hesitantly he said, 'I saw you. At least I think I did. In a dream I had – you were in a library, looking for a way to cure a sick lady.' Turner examined the features of the seated figure, and recognition set in. They were definitely the same basic shape as the monk he'd seen in his dream, although somewhat older and more haggard. Turner had learnt to trust things he saw in his dreams. He still felt that Julian was holding back, as if hiding a guilty secret. 'Who are you, Julian? Tell me the truth … what happened to you?'

Julian looked up at Turner with relief in his eyes. He had never expected a person wrapped in the trappings of a modern culture, where cold science ruled the thought processes, to take him seriously. Turner was different somehow, like he'd seen many things that couldn't be explained, and accepted them. Remembering that Turner had told him he'd studied the supernatural, Julian moved to the other side of the room and removed a sliding panel from the top of one of the wooden tables. Reaching in blindly, he removed a dusty velvet bag about the size of a large grapefruit. Heading back to the table nearest Turner, he beckoned him over to watch. Slowly, he pulled a small wooden base from the bag, then a round quartz crystal that gleamed in the light from the oil lamp. It was the most beautiful crystal ball Turner had ever seen, and much larger than the ones in his own collection back home. Inside the quartz, tiny inclusions streaked across the centre, like fiery arrows shooting through the light. Miniature rainbows bloomed in several different places, changing shape and size in the soft illumination.

Julian saw Turner's expression change when he looked at the crystal, the psychic leaning in, fascinated by the stone. He handed the heavy sphere over to Turner's cupped hands, as he said, 'This belonged to a friend of Isobel's. She was a healer and a diviner as well, but she was also labelled as a witch. She'd spent time with a coven in North Berwick, as one of the "cunning folk", and often used to stay here with us. She had real power, some way of making nature turn to her bidding, but she never used her skills for evil. Her magic, if you want to call it that, was always used for good, and she worked with us to help the poor and destitute.'

Buckling slightly under the weight, Turner rolled the shimmering ball in his hands, feeling its power and energy seeping into him. In a way he couldn't explain, he felt an instant connection to it, like it was calling to him from the depths of time.

Julian watched the psychic rolling the crystal ball in his

hands. Shadows glinted across his face as he moved it in the light from the lamp. Julian moved closer, and said, 'The owner of this crystal was called Caitlin … Caitlin Smith. I'm not sure whether that was her real name – she was orphaned as a child and never knew her parents. I think she took the name because it is fairly common-sounding. Or it was back then. The last thing she wanted was to stand out from the crowd. Far too dangerous in those times – witches did not have a long life expectancy when we first met.'

Turner remained silent, briefly closed his eyes and concentrated. Back in familiar territory, Turner allowed his mind to empty as he connected with the crystal. Gradually, he could feel its power flooding his body with a strange energy that made his palms tingle. When Turner had first started doing crystal-ball readings, he'd simply made the whole thing up as he talked softly to his clients. After he'd begun to feel more confident in his spiritual abilities, things had started to change. Images came to him, like figures and shapes rolling through a mist in his thoughts. Truly, if they appeared in the crystal, or in his head, he wasn't sure. He reverently placed the crystal back onto the wooden stand. Finally, he looked back at Julian and said, 'This crystal feels different. There is something special about the quartz. I can feel it. Almost like it's alive.'

'Yes, you are right, it is alive – in a way. I have only ever seen Caitlin use this before. She used to place it in one of the mountain streams when there was a waxing moon. She said it cleansed the crystal and re-energised it. At least I think that is what she said – it was a very long time ago. Have I remembered correctly?' This area of knowledge was not

Julian's expertise and he looked a little embarrassed as he spoke.

Turner could feel the power of the ancient quartz calling out to him as he peered into its sparkling depths. 'Yes, that is a common way people use to refresh the stone. Others use things like sea salt, and I knew one person who used to bury her crystal in the ground. It depends on the diviner. They know what works for them.'

Happy he'd remembered correctly and that the psychic was taking him at his word, Julian started to explain further. 'Caitlin put an enchantment on this crystal. It can show images in its depths to those that have the power to use it. I have never been able to use it alone; I've always needed Caitlin to help. But she can't do it anymore …' Julian's voice trailed off as if he was about to say something else, then stopped himself. Looking back at Turner, he said, 'Do you think you can use it to see visions of the past? It can only tell the truth to those who can tap into its power.' Julian had sensed that there was something different about the psychic from the first time they'd met. He hoped he was right, and that they'd be able to resurrect the power of the crystal so that Turner could see, first hand, scenes from his long life manifested inside the stone.

'I'll try, Julian, but nothing is certain. Please, take the crystal and cup it in your hands, like this.' Turner placed one hand cradling the stone and one above. Picking up the heavy object with amazing dexterity, Julian did as he was asked. 'Don't try and think of anything in particular. Feel your energy connecting and soaking into the clear depths of the quartz.'

Closing his eyes to block out any distractions, Julian breathed slowly and deeply, allowing his mind to flow freely. Gently, the psychic took the glittering crystal and placed it carefully on the stand, muttering something in Latin under his breath. As Turner stared deep into the crystal, strange shapes were forming. He could see pictures emerging, like he was watching some sort of ethereal television set.

CHAPTER 19: CRYSTAL VISIONS

Julian gazed in wonder at the familiar patterns forming inside the stone, in awe of the psychic's ability to use it. Turner felt delighted. If he was being honest with himself, he'd never thought anything would happen. The two men sat silently, peering intently into its depths, almost holding their breath as recognisable shapes moved and shifted inside the iridescent quartz.

Slowly, Turner saw the outline of an abbey appear, set in the meander of a wide river. It was a beautiful and tranquil scene with four monks busily going about their chores. Julian was the tallest of the four, standing on a stool, gathering apples from a tree bursting with ripe fruit.

Tears dripped wetly down Julian's cheeks as he gazed into the crystal, seeing the images emerge and change, like cloud formations taking on familiar shapes. 'That is Finchale Priory in the North East of England,' Julian said, providing commentary to the story unveiling in front of Turner's eyes. 'We had an idyllic life then, giving half our day to God and the other half to heavy physical work, labouring in the gardens and orchards surrounding the abbey. I trained as a carpenter; working with wood always seemed to relax me. Three weeks every year, other monks from Durham would come to stay for respite. It was from one of these that I learnt about the terrible events that would lead to the destruction of all I held dear.'

The images changed to the monks rapidly gathering clothes and basic belongings into rough sacks, before heading out across the fields as though fleeing an invisible foe.

'The Reformation had arrived with force, and Henry VIII's troops were flooding the land, reclaiming monasteries for the new Christian faith, with Henry as head of the church. Many monks were put to death, the buildings and lands seized in the most brutal fashion. My brothers and I fled, but the prior refused to leave and run in fear from the armed men. Over two years we travelled north, living from hand to mouth, sleeping rough most of the time. By the time we reached North Berwick, I was seriously ill; the toll of the journey had been too much for me.'

Turner looked up, away from the images. 'You're making the Reformation sound like genocide, Julian. That's not my understanding. I thought it was mainly an administration task and that all the monks were rehomed peacefully.' Turner didn't know much about things like alchemy, but he'd certainly spent many hours studying various religions from around the world.

'History is written by the winners. Not all you read is the truth; it is the version the conquerors wish you to know to justify their actions,' Julian said, the memories of his past suffering pushing through his mind, causing him to slump forlornly, resting his head heavily in his hands.

Turner moved his gaze back to the quartz, a little unsettled by this particular version of history. Nuns in white robes were leaning over a man sweating and shaking in a makeshift wooden cot. Fallen plaster littered the floor in the squalid room, and one of the company knelt on the floor in prayer, as if administering the last rites.

Julian looked fondly at the white robes of the sisters, swinging and bustling as they went about their daily tasks. 'Cistercian nuns took us in when we got to North Berwick. Their building was not in the best of repair, having been ravaged by many battles between the English and Scots through the years. But they were kind, friendly people. Despite all their care, I got steadily worse. Then she arrived, my Isobel … beautiful, loving and tender. She was a healer in the village. Well, I say village – it was no more than a row of houses back then.'

The images showed Julian propped in bed, being fed soup slowly, spoon by spoon, by an attractive blonde lady dressed in a simple green linen dress. Turner was struggling to reconcile the woman in the dress with the wrinkled old crone lying in the crypt, so he leaned in closer to try to get a better view. It was definitely her, the withered features plump and glowing with life. She was looking tenderly at her patient, eyes gleaming, mopping his brow and talking happily with him.

Julian smiled at the memory. 'We fell in love. A happiness I'd never felt before overwhelmed me. Have you ever had that? A person you know is the one for you?'

Turner nodded, his thoughts flitting to Jade and where she'd be. Loneliness swept through his body and he felt a yearning to hold her in his arms again.

'Then it happened again.' Julian's voice brought Turner's thoughts back into the room. 'I'd walked from one disaster to another. The Scottish Protestants were on the march, determined to rid Scotland of the French Catholic influences, as they saw it. Anyone not part of this new, Scottish, Reformation was being trampled underfoot, so we fled north again. This time, we needed to find a place so remote that we'd be left in peace. That's how I ended up here.' Julian raised his arms and swept them around the room as he said 'here'.

Turner looked around the granite chamber and, without thinking, stood up and began walking around the assorted wooden benches crammed with archaic objects. The place was certainly ancient and he was struggling to find something in Julian's words that didn't ring true. The rough wooden tables, full of discarded pages littered with alchemical symbols, and the centrally placed, strangely shaped furnace made him feel like he'd stepped back in history.

Julian joined him in the centre of the room. 'When we arrived, the site of the old Benedictine monastery was still standing and the entrance to this crypt was through there.' Julian gestured to the far corner of the room, past the teardrop furnace, at a pile of broken stones piled up high, in what Turner could roughly make out was an old archway. 'This room was an area for prayer and preparing the bodies, before we converted it as you see now, with the furnace. The crypt was empty; all the bodies had been taken away by whoever cleared the place. In the graveyard above, we found the headstone you saw in the byre – the sandstone slab on the granite bench, cracked in two by the lightning. We'd never seen drawings like that before and began to study their meanings, visiting church libraries, buying texts where we could. Caitlin joined us from North Berwick, and offered her own, more occult, interpretations of them. That's how we discovered the secrets of alchemy.'

Turner thought of the old books he'd seen at Julian's house, the many ancient alchemical works he'd never heard of, let alone seen before. Julian went on to tell him how they'd built the laboratory in which they sat, piece by painstaking piece, based on the knowledge hidden in the texts. They wanted to use alchemy to create medicines, heal people and help the local community. Witchcraft was still a capital offence at that time, so, in case their work was misunderstood, they'd toiled in secret, opening up a hidden entrance in the byre and closing the existing one. Slowly, they established a small monastic community in the abbey, but lived in constant fear of persecution. Wanting to preserve their knowledge for use by future generations, they'd marked the hidden entrance to the alchemical laboratory with a pentagram, mixing the ochre paint with poisonous sap to discourage anyone who tried to remove it. Then, at least if they were taken away or killed, some adept would hopefully stumble across the mark and unearth the secrets below. The significance of the symbol would be clear to other initiates, and hopefully their work could benefit future generations.

This didn't add up to Turner. 'But the symbol on the door in the byre looks fresh, and wouldn't the pentagram make the place more associated with witchcraft, the exact thing you were trying to avoid? I don't understand. If the symbol has been there for hundreds of years, surely it would be too faint to read by now.' Turner was puzzled, trying to reconcile what he'd seen with what he was being told.

Julian nodded, understanding why his companion was

confused. 'Back in those times, people feared anything supernatural. Using the pentagram meant that they stayed away, believing the place cursed or a meeting place for devil worshippers. It was the coded words inside the symbol that were important. Only other alchemists would be able to interpret them – it marked a place of hidden knowledge.'

Turner understood this from his decoding of the Enochian text, secretly glad of the success of his detective work.

'But, truthfully, I don't know why the paint has started to run and drip. It was, as you say, dirty and barely noticeable before. All I can think is that the lightning strike triggered a reaction in the paint somehow. But I'm guessing.' Julian shrugged his shoulders, and looked back at the psychic, sharing his bewilderment about the dripping paint.

Turner felt foolish. He'd headed north on a desperate plea to save a complete stranger and his father's old friend from what he'd assumed was something supernatural or deadly witchcraft. In actual fact, the symbol he'd misinterpreted over the phone simply marked a hidden alchemical laboratory, whose sole goal of existence had been to help people. Feeling it was not the right time to admit his mistake while Julian was in full flow, he kept quiet and continued listening.

Julian began talking excitedly, living in his memories. 'After years of trying and failing, we finally produced a fine red powder that we believed would cure all ills. Obviously, we couldn't use this on the villagers until we'd tried it on ourselves – I mean, what if it killed instead of cured? So we each made a drink from the powder and swallowed it down, unsure whether we'd taken our last breath. It worked! We stopped aging and simply didn't get sick. We were also much stronger than before and able to take on much more arduous physical work.'

At least that explained Julian's remarkable ability to climb in and out of the crypt unaided, Turner thought, and his ability to chase across the moor without missing a step, while he had panted behind him.

Julian was positively beaming, taking pride in his past achievements. 'It did wonders for our spiritual studies. The villagers saw what, they believed, the power of prayer did for us. We had many converts and held regular services privately in people's homes, my fellow monks and I acting as father confessors to whoever needed us. Caitlin and Isobel became renowned healers, saving many lives and offering comfort to those in the most need. We reduced the dose and mixed the powder with other tonics so that it had the power to heal, but not prolong life as it did for us. The village was thriving. People thought that the location, and the sea air, was the backbone of their healthy constitution. But, of course, we knew otherwise.' Julian nodded knowingly to himself. 'All was well until the Douglas family arrived.'

Julian motioned Turner to look again into the crystal. A large man on a horse was thundering through the moorland, followed by an array of angry villagers carrying flaming torches and spiked wooden staves. They hunted for something, or someone. The large rider pulled up short, and dragged a blonde woman by the hair from behind a gorse bush, her eyes wide in fear. Turner recognised the woman immediately; it was Isobel.

'Oh my God! What are they doing to her?' Turner said

in horror, as the woman was pushed into a small cell, her head clamped into a strange iron frame with four sharp prongs, two against the tongue, two against the cheeks. She was fastened to the wall, held upright by her bonds, as the large man shouted at her, pushing a sharp bodkin into her arm. Blood dripped redly onto the floor, forming dirty pools at her feet, the spikes in her mouth biting into her tongue as she tried to scream.

Looking at the images in the crystal pushed all the happiness from Julian's voice. Almost spitting out his words with a mix of disgust and anger, he said, 'The man on the horse is Donald Douglas, head of a landowning family from Inverness – strict Presbyterian and God-fearing people. What he couldn't buy, he took by force, and the Benedictine abbey sat square in the middle of prime grazing land. We refused to move this time, not the least of our worries being the discovery of the underground laboratory. You recognise the woman?' Turner nodded 'yes' as he'd recognised the figure immediately as Isobel.

Julian looked into the crystal, tears welling in his eyes. 'Needing to find a way to get rid of us, he took my Isobel as a witch – the Douglas family had found out she was from North Berwick and were trying to capture Isobel and Caitlin. There was a huge witch hunt going on there at the time, supported by the king of Scotland, James VI – he later took over England and Scotland as James I of the combined territories. James thought that his ship had been almost sunk in a storm by witches from North Berwick, and he was determined to root them out. The witch hunt was the excuse the Douglas family needed to lock Isobel up and accuse her of being a witch on the run, hiding out here with us.' Julian started pacing the room, the injustice of the past burning in his mind. His wet tears dripped noiselessly onto the bare floor.

Turner couldn't shift his gaze from the horrific images emerging from the depths of the glimmering quartz. Isobel was being dragged to a large wooden stake, piled high with kindling at its base. Donald Douglas was smiling as he bound her hands roughly behind, and set a fire at her feet. 'This is too much, Julian. I can't watch this … please …'

Julian sat back down, wiping away the tears from his face and cupped his hands over the crystal, shading the view. 'After a week of torture and sleep deprivation, Isobel had broken and given them what they wanted, confessing to anything they asked. They made her implicate me, Caitlin and the other monks as co-conspirators, but by the time the soldiers came to get us, we'd hidden away in the crypt. Those were dark days, the worst of my life. Isobel was sentenced to death by fire, and all I could do was hide away down here. On the day of the burning, I hid and watched from over on the hill, powerless to help.' Julian was reliving every terrible second of the gruesome tale as if it was happening now, in front of his eyes.

'So how did she escape, Julian? I mean she must have, or she wouldn't be here.'

'Oh, she escaped, but at a cost. It was a windy day, and the flames licked about her body and lashed around the pyre, causing the crowd to keep back. By some cruel twist of fate, the bindings holding her to the stake burnt through while she was still alive. She ran screaming across the hillside, her skin a patchwork of burnt flesh. It was horrible, truly horrible. I found her next to dead up on the moor and carried her back here.'

Julian described how they'd lay hidden, he salving her burns as she clung onto life. At night, he told Turner, he would forage in the villagers' gardens, stealing vegetables and raiding larders for any meat scraps. Isobel's appearance was so ghastly to the human eye that Julian cloaked her in a monk's robe, the hood obscuring her face, and wrapped her singed hair in light linen underneath. After two months of hiding, Isobel had healed enough to be moved. The pair travelled to get away from the Douglas family, Julian as a carpenter and Isobel as a mysterious veiled healer, working in the backstreets of towns and cities, wherever they could find food, lodging and a friendly face. The other three monks decided to stay behind and stand their ground. It proved a fatal error of judgement. Donald Douglas persecuted them, one by one, on a variety of trumped-up charges, before having them publicly hanged. Julian had returned briefly to tend to the corpses, and laid them to rest in the crypt. It was dangerous work, but he refused to let them be food for the crows. 'He never caught Caitlin. She ... er ... disappeared ...' Julian said, seeming again to stop himself saying something about the owner of the crystal.

Julian took a deep breath to calm himself and regain his composure before continuing the story of his incredible life. 'I changed my name to Julian, as a play on the old Roman word for "youth", and ditched my robes for regular clothing. It was tough for us both at first, but, eventually, as the decades drifted by, the old superstitions of witchcraft passed, and the crimes and persecutions of the witch finders became public knowledge. Isobel's gaunt appearance shocked some, of course, but if there was any sign of trouble we moved again.'

Julian shifted in his chair, and removed his hands from the crystal. 'I was no longer recognised as a practising member of the church, so we were able to marry in a private ceremony, held by one of my old friends back in Durham. I won't bore you with our many adventures, over what would be several lifetimes' worth for everybody else. The main thing is, we survived it all, and came back here, to our old Scottish home, about thirty or so years ago. Isobel slept in the crypt most nights, comfortable in her own company. Resting with our old friends seemed to bring her some form of peace.'

Turner looked back into the crypt, wondering how sleeping amongst the monks' skeletal remains would have been restful for anybody. His expression must have given his private thoughts away.

'You must remember,' Julian said, 'the bodies in the crypt are the only family we've ever had; they hold no fear for us.'

Fair enough, thought Turner, they held no fear for him either, but the prospect of sleeping down amongst them still made him feel uncomfortable.

Julian began pacing again. 'We kept Isobel out of sight at her own request; she simply wanted a quiet life now that we were settled again. It worked well; keeping someone hidden in this remote area is not difficult. She would spend her days reading and tending the garden at my house when we didn't have visitors, or remain out of sight when there were lodgers at the croft.' Julian stopped, as if thinking about what he was going to say next and whether he could trust Turner with the information. After a long pause, he said, 'Then, a few months ago, Isobel began to change. Her behaviour became erratic – sometimes cheerful, sometimes in the blackest mood. What I didn't know was, she'd started working in the lab, trying to create some potion or medicine to restore her looks. I suppose being alone down here must have stirred up old memories, and she longed to be back to her old self and out in the world again.' Julian picked up a container holding a slick substance that resembled petroleum jelly.

'You see this? It's a compound of mercuric chloride mixed with lard, a medicine we used to treat syphilis sores last time we were here. This is one of the things she made to put on her skin – I know now that it can be lethal; the mercury is absorbed straight into the bloodstream. I think this has a lot to do with her mood swings; she was poisoning herself and didn't know it.' Julian put the dangerous mixture down with disgust.

'I don't know what other potions she tried, but they made her stronger and more deranged – it was frightening to watch. It was like some dark shadow had been opened in her soul, like she'd become possessed. Often I'd find her missing, or walking alone on the moor, muttering to herself. In the end, I just dropped the food off and left as fast as I could.' Julian pointed at the pile of animal bones littering the entrance to the crypt.

He motioned Turner to look again into the crystal and the psychic reluctantly resumed his gaze, wondering what other horrors would flow from its depths. Images were forming of Isobel inside the crypt, pacing up and down, waving her arms crazily in the air. From the tunnel entrance,

Julian emerged, carrying a small bag of supplies in front of him. Without warning, Isobel attacked him, punching and clawing at his face, screaming wildly like a frenzied animal. Julian was holding up his arms to protect himself, but she was hammering blows heavily against his forearms. He dropped to his knees, pleading with her, only to find that it made her more violent; she pounced on him, tearing at the flesh on his back. Julian was desperately pulling away, retreating rapidly back to the tunnel entrance. Turner couldn't take any more. He looked up into the crying face of Julian, feeling the torment of the man.

'She was so crazy last time that, God help me, I did a terrible thing. I covered the entrance to the crypt with the sandstone gravestone and blocked her inside. It took me an age to move it on my own, and I knew she wouldn't have the strength to lift the whole thing from below. I didn't have it in my heart to kill her but, you must understand, I feared for my life. Every day after, I came down and listened for any signs of movement, but I never heard a thing. That was three weeks ago, and I took some little comfort in the fact that finally she was at peace, amongst her oldest friends.' Julian was looking at Turner for some form of understanding, the guilt lying heavily on his conscience. Turner said nothing at first; he was thinking about everything he'd seen and heard.

After a long pause in silence, Turner said, 'So, you're saying she was dead? How could you know, Julian? Obviously she wasn't – she escaped your trap as soon as she could after the lightning strike, probably half-starved and more manic than ever. I hate to say it, but you've brought this horror on yourself.' Turner stood up and walked into the crypt, regretting how harsh his words sounded. Had he been faced with the same situation, what would he have done? Turner hoped he'd never find out. Respectfully, he pulled back the hood from Isobel's face and looked at the withered features. 'She didn't deserve to die like this, Julian. Why would she attack Maggie, and not come straight for you to seek revenge for imprisoning her?'

'Maggie is a Douglas. The blood of the criminal that tortured Isobel those long years ago runs through her veins. Isobel's desire for revenge on that cruel family is way above anything she could ever feel for me. As I've tried to explain, she became crazed.' Julian had joined Turner in the crypt and was looking down remorsefully at the figure of his dead wife on the stone shelf. 'That day I came to see you and climbed down here to the crypt, I found out she was missing and feared the worst.'

Turner remembered Julian's quick exit after their delicious venison meal. So that was why he'd rushed off, Turner thought. He'd been looking for Isobel.

Julian moved directly in front of Turner, holding his gaze. 'You remember? When I came down here? I was expecting to find her dead in the crypt, but there was no sign of her. I pretended I'd never seen this place before when you told me about it. I'm so sorry for deceiving you, but I didn't know what else to do.'

Everything was falling into place for Turner. Julian had lied to protect his secret, faced with the fear of a deranged Isobel let loose on the moor. The psychic didn't have it in his heart to add more guilt and pain to Julian's suffering, so he said, 'It's OK. I think I understand. You were in an impossible position. To be honest, I have no idea how I would react to such a horrific situation. So, how come you turned up at the estate lodge?'

Relief flooded Julian's face. He was an honest man of the church and the deception had been gnawing at him. He'd feared that his bond with the psychic would shatter when the truth was exposed. 'I've been tracking her ever since I found she was missing, figuring she might make her way to the estate lodge, and to Maggie. Tonight, I'd been waiting in the heather outside, hoping to spot her before anything happened. I thought I saw something clamber into Maggie's bedroom, so I ran inside, hoping I wasn't too late. Standing in the bedroom doorway, watching her towering over Maggie's limp body … I don't think she recognised me anymore.'

Images of the withered body bobbing in the depths of the pool flashed into Turner's mind, and he shook his head, unconsciously trying to clear them. Thinking back to the tragic scene, he said, 'Why didn't she climb out of the rock pool, Julian? She seemed strong enough to do it. I mean, she wasn't shot – Callum missed.'

Julian gently stroked the sopping wet hair of the corpse. 'She couldn't swim. None of us could. Swimming was not a common pastime in my youth. The water was so dirty in those days that it was a health hazard. We never learnt how to do it.'

Julian had lost everything he'd ever cared about and sadness overwhelmed him. He'd tried to live a good life, helping others in need, and giving as much of himself as he could. But now he felt it was all in vain as he looked down at the withered features of the creature that used to be his wife. He turned away, to shield his face from Turner, as more tears began to stream down his cheeks.

Impulsively, Turner put his arm around his shoulders. 'Look, I can't begin to understand what you've been through … living through so many lifetimes for it to end like this.' Turner thought of the love they must have shared, the love that had bound them together. Soul mates swimming against the tide of life; a long life; fraught with pain and suffering.

Julian gulped in air, trying to gain some control over his sorrow. 'I'll tell you what it's like. When you're young, you have hope and do so many things for the first time. I always remember the times of my youth as clearly as today. When I look back on those years, they seem to have lasted forever. Now I have so few new experiences that the days seem to slip by, like they all merge into one. I can't truly remember the last time I felt happy.'

Turner felt the same about his teenage years; the memories always seemed much more vivid and alive than any others. What that must be like for someone who had lived through so many changes in society – beliefs, values, rules – all shifting around him, Turner could not imagine. At heart, Julian remained a pious monk from an idyllic abbey, surrounded by his loyal friends. Now it was all gone, and only he remained. Lost for the right words to say, Turner gently covered Isobel's body and bowed his head in prayer. Silent in their own thoughts, Turner watched as Julian collected the crystal ball, pushing it back into the dusty velvet bag and putting it in his coat pocket, before the pair closed up the entrance to the laboratory. Julian helped Turner climb back into the byre, before following on himself. Between them, they replaced the black slate over the underground opening and manoeuvred the two parts of the sandstone slab over the granite base. Then they walked out into the cool of the night.

As they headed up towards the croft, Julian stopped and grabbed the psychic's hand, looking up seriously into his tired face. Slowly and deliberately he said, 'I promise you, Nathen Turner, I will do anything I can for Maggie and Callum.' He used Turner's full name as if making a solemn vow. 'Thank you for being a friend, and for listening to me. I will never forget you, and the help and understanding you've given me.' Julian pulled out the velvet bag with the crystal ball from his coat, and pushed it gently into Turner's open hand. 'Please accept this. It is of no use to me – I've never been able to use it on my own. Maybe it will help you in your work. Please take it.'

Too tired to argue, Turner accepted graciously, thankful it was covered in the cloth – he couldn't face any more visions that night. With a backward wave, Julian headed off up the forest trail, quickly out of sight, swallowed by the darkness of the night.

Finally, alone inside the croft, Turner flopped exhausted onto the bed and fell into a deep sleep. Soft footsteps padded in from the living area and green eyes gazed up curiously at the slumbering psychic. Gently, the Scottish wildcat hopped onto the bed and snuggled deeply between his arms.

CHAPTER 20: HOMEWARD-BOUND

Six hours later, Turner woke and sniffed, the sunlight blazing in through the bedroom window raising him from his slumber. A strong musky smell clung to the room, and the clothing on his chest was covered with mottled brown hair. Shaking himself down, he hungrily munched through the last of the bacon and eggs and made a strong pot of tea.

Sitting quietly, cradling his mug and perched on the edge of a fish crate, he was trying to make sense of his Highland journey. Thoughts tumbled through his tired mind. Hooded figures; skeletal remains; bleeding symbols; all cascading randomly in a blur of visual memories. How could good people, simply trying to help others, meet with such tragedy? he thought. He'd learnt a lot – certainly alchemy seemed to hold the same hidden truths he'd found with the supernatural. Somehow it was possible to create something, an essence perhaps, or an elixir, that could cure people and prolong life. Modern medicine prided itself on its ability to do exactly that. But at what cost? Current pharmaceuticals had their own myriad of unwanted side effects, but immortality was certainly not one of them. Not yet anyway. Plus, immortality was certainly not the blessing it appeared to be. In Turner's short lifetime he'd experienced pain and suffering, along with the joy of romance. How would he feel living through that cycle over and over again, watching all those he loved die around him? The bleak thoughts were making him depressed so he took a walk out into the morning air.

It was a beautiful day; light mist dusted the top of the mountains and the air was filled with the fresh scent of the pine trees. Back in his familiar cowboy boots, he felt more like himself and was longing to see his home again. To him, it felt like he'd been in Scotland for weeks, not days, and he was already homesick, missing Jade terribly. The love he'd seen in Julian for his estranged wife was having an effect on how he saw his own relationship. Perhaps he should commit once and for all to Jade and make a go of it. If he could achieve anything like the bond Julian had had with Isobel, that ability to stay together no matter what, perhaps he could truly find the love and sense of belonging he'd always craved. In his past, as a fake psychic medium, he'd always been an outsider, living on the fringes of society. Since he'd met Jade and changed his ways, he felt more accepted, more comfortable in his own skin. Jade had a way of bringing out the best in him, accepting his supernatural side and never taking him, or life, too seriously. With romantic thoughts filling his head, he took a last look around his Highland home.

The byre stood innocently protecting its secret, unfazed by the tragedy hidden below. On the inside of the door the pentagram symbol was a mess of red mush, totally unintelligible. Turner still couldn't figure out what had caused it to drip in the first place. Had Isobel thrown something on it, or had the sudden jolt of lightning activated some reaction? He'd probably never know for sure. For Turner, it still left the door open for a supernatural reason, and that suited him just fine. When he got home he'd have a chance to think it all through properly. Maybe the reason was hidden away somewhere in his bizarre book collection, and he relished the thought of uncovering more long-lost knowledge. Turner still felt there was something supernatural about the place, but he couldn't figure out what. Pushing the idea to the back of his mind, he headed down to the edge of the lapping waves frothing on the gravel beach.

Strolling on the rocky shoreline, Turner could see the scattered buildings of Benlogan across the water where Hulk would be getting ready to pick him up later in the day. The sheer beauty of the place captivated Turner. It seemed unspoilt, timeless even. How many other ancient mysteries could be buried in such places, he wondered, unseen for generations? Breathing in the cool, crisp air, with its slight tang of salt, he felt alive, invigorated by his short stay in this magical place.

'Nathen, where are you? Maggie's alive! She survived …' the voice of Julian called out, shattering his morning reverie. Julian was poking his nose around the croft and byre, hunting for the psychic. Spotting him on the shoreline, he came sprinting down, puffing heavily.

Turner watched his fly-fishing lunch companion running down the path to the shore. 'Thank God, Julian. Are you OK?' Turner feared his ancient friend might keel over with a heart attack judging by the redness of his face.

'I've … run … down … all … the … way,' Julian said, taking in huge gulps of air. Waiting a few moments to get his breath back, he panted, 'Mike Fletcher was already looking after her when I headed back up there last night. It was a close thing, apparently – she's been very lucky.'

Yes, she certainly had, thought Turner. But his flushed companion certainly seemed to have no luck at all. Feeling sorry for the man, he simply said, 'Come on, Julian, get inside. I'll make us a drink,' and they headed back into the croft.

Julian told Turner how he'd made his way back to the estate lodge the previous night and found Mike Fletcher painfully propped on Maggie's bed, watching her sleep. Apparently, Fletcher had woken up when he'd heard the commotion in Maggie's room, and got to her as quickly as he could. He'd found Maggie barely breathing, deathly pale and cold to the touch. It had taken the best part of an hour to revive her, Fletcher had told Julian, but then she kept screaming and grasping at her face. When Callum returned to find her alive and breathing, he'd supposedly hugged Mike Fletcher so hard that the cut on his leg started bleeding again.

Julian sat on a fish crate in the croft, next to Turner, gently sipping at his tea. 'I've left them drinking whisky together and singing bawdy songs in Maggie's room. She's enjoying watching the pair make fools of themselves.'

Turner laughed at the vision of the pair of complete opposites, mountain man and city boy, finding a common bond in their care for another.

Julian laughed along with him. 'I'm going straight back there. Another hour at the rate they're going and they won't be able to look after anybody.' Julian fished out a small, carved brown box from his pocket. 'I know you're going today. I just wanted to tell you, and also give you this.'

The box lid was decorated with a deeply etched Celtic knot design, the four sides covered with a variety of swirling patterns. Turner had seen one like this about a year ago with the exact same design, except it had been black. The discovery of that particular box had led to murder and tragedy, so he was less than pleased to see another one.

Turner looked at the box as if Julian was holding a live scorpion. 'Where'd you get that? I've seen those designs before and it didn't end well.'

Julian was confused. 'What do you mean? I made it – this is my design.'

Turner still refused to take the box from Julian, remembering the previous one he'd handled in an earlier ghostly adventure that had nearly got him killed. 'Your design? Has this one got a hidden compartment? Last one I came across had.'

Julian tried to push his gift into Turner's hand. 'Some I make have hidden compartments, but not this one. It's a simple box. It's how I make my living – I'm a carpenter, remember? I've sold them all over Scotland, but I'm surprised you've come across one before. What's wrong? I don't understand.'

'The last one I opened didn't bring me much luck, Julian. The hidden compartment ... well, let's just say it was hiding more than family treasures.' Small world, thought Turner, a little embarrassed at the way he'd spoken to Julian. Turner reluctantly took the box and opened it up to find a small vial containing red powder, nestled in hessian sacking. He held the vial up to the window, examining the contents. The powder looked like a fine red salt, but in the light it seemed to have a slight golden sheen.

Julian pointed to the vial and said, 'That's the last of the healing powder we made. I think Isobel was using it to keep herself alive in the crypt after I shut her in – that must be how she survived down there for the past few weeks. I want you to have it – I never want to see it again. Destroy it, use it, do what you will, and good luck with it. Lately, it has brought me nothing but misery.'

'Wow, Julian, that's one hell of a sales pitch! I can't accept this. I would never know what to do with it.' Turner handed the box and vial back to Julian.

Ignoring Turner's refusal, Julian said, 'The powder dissolves in water. The taste is a little bitter, but not extremely so. It does heal, I promise you. This small amount won't extend life too much – trust me. Please accept it. I still feel indebted to you after you were so kind last night. I'm leaving this place – there is nothing here for me now.' Julian stood to leave, putting the box on top of a fish crate.

Turner stood with him. 'Where will you go?'

'I don't know, maybe abroad, but I have no passport or documents fit for the modern age.' Julian turned and offered his hand to Turner, who shook it warmly. 'I doubt we'll ever meet again, but I hope that if you think of me, you will think kindly.'

In truth, Julian already had a clear plan of what he was going to do, but had no intention of sharing it with anyone else.

Julian waved his goodbyes from the forest path and disappeared into the trees. It was great news that Maggie had survived the attack, and Turner knew no further harm could come to her from Isobel's descent into madness. Isobel was no longer capable of hurting anyone, not anymore. But the harm had already been done to Julian, and Turner did not think those wounds would ever heal. How Julian would cope with the pain and suffering it had caused him, alone in the modern world, without the love of his life, Turner could only imagine. He still had Callum and Maggie, but Turner thought there would be some bad blood between Julian and the head keeper after the events of the past few days. Callum did not seem like the type of person who scored highly on the forgiveness scale. Julian had said he was 'leaving this place', but something about the way he had said it seemed strange. Pushing the musings from his mind, the psychic headed back to the croft to pack and get ready for his homeward journey.

Over the next hour, Turner made himself busy tidying the croft, washing dishes and hanging Mike Fletcher's outdoor coat back up. The last thing he wanted was for the photographer to return to a rubbish tip after he'd kindly been allowed to squat in his place. Finally, he packed away his book, the crystal ball and the wooden box into the small Gladstone briefcase, before taking a quick wash in the sink. The crisp cleanse did little to quell the musk of the cat that still clung to him, but it was the best he could do.

Mid-afternoon, the puttering of the small fishing craft boomed off the hills as Hulk pulled into shore and trudged up the bank, followed by Turner's dog, Kyle, bounding behind. At the sight, or rather smell, of Turner, the dog stopped in its tracks and raised the fur on its back, growling loudly.

'Don't be silly, Kyle. How can you be afraid of a little "eau de cat", you daft thing?' Before the words were out of Turner's mouth, the hairy brute flattened him to the ground, manically sniffing and licking at his chest.

Hulk watched the slobbery greeting, laughing hysterically, hands on hips. 'Well, Nathen. Had a relaxing time?'

Turner looked up, wiping dog drool from his top, and joined in the laughter.

CHAPTER 21: HUNTING IN THE DARK

Darkness flooded Lanner's Point Croft, seeping into every pore like a black fog. Now empty, the lifeless buildings looked derelict and alone amidst the grey shadows of the pine trees. Salty kelp imbued the air with a dry tang, the scent drifting in from the surf, bubbling in the bay. Amidst the silence of the night, a slinking furry shadow padded its way around the byre and slid inside.

Fumbling and scraping noises caused the cat to pause mid-stride, tense and prepare to pounce. Over by the granite table, a man was pushing hard at the sandstone slabs, heaving them ungracefully onto the floor. He was climbing over the lip of the base, disappearing briefly to strike a match and light the oil lamp at his feet. His face was gaunt and drawn, like an anaemic ghost of a man. A man who used to be. A man with nothing left to live for anymore.

Straining, he heaved on the slate slab covering the crypt opening, pushing his fingertips around the sides to get a better grip. The figure levered back hard, pivoting the slab on its short side and leaning it against the sidewall of the base. He'd done this same routine thousands of times, but it never got any easier. Sweat dripped wetly down his arms into the years of dust at his feet. Panting hard, he moved to sit on the edge of the exposed opening and took a final look around, as if remembering happier times; times of love, laughter and good friends.

Sitting there alone, calming his breathing, tasting the salty night air, he jumped as the huge green eyes of the Scottish wildcat appeared in the lamplight, peering down quizzically at him from the side of the granite base.

'Goodbye, old friend,' he said, smiling at the cat. His body dropped down the shaft, and he yanked the slate slab behind him so that it crashed back in place, covering the entrance. It didn't matter; he wasn't coming back.

Almost running down the entrance tunnel, he burst into the dry air of the crypt like a man reborn. Standing and smiling at the swathed skeletons of his oldest friends, he bowed his head in silent prayer before clambering onto the shelf where Isobel's body was still dripping, puddles of dirty water merging on the parched floor. Gently pulling back the hood from her withered face, he kissed her gently on the forehead and lovingly stroked the tangled mass of hair.

He hadn't lied to Nathen Turner; he was going away. Far away, where he could never return. What he hadn't told Turner about is what else his alchemical work had produced – gold of the purest form, worth a small fortune. Untold riches; hidden in plain sight around the crypt and laboratory. Together with his lifelong friends, he had cast it into shapes and then blackened the surface so that it looked like coloured iron, painting in the odd rust spot for effect. The hinges and handles on the door; the brackets that held up the shelving; anything and everything metallic. Piled carelessly under a table in the laboratory, an innocent-looking stack of dirty cannon balls, each about the size of an orange, made him the wealthiest man in Scotland. But wealth couldn't buy life.

The gold had come as a side effect, an accident of their myriad alchemical experiments in the search to find something that could heal and sustain life. As they produced it, they hid it, never spending any of it, living off the land exactly as they wanted to do. As he'd told Turner, producing gold was not the real goal of alchemy, and he knew that the scent of money changed a man. Letting his new acquaintance in on this particular secret was too dangerous, too tempting, for someone wrapped in the modern possession-obsessed culture. He had little time for those whose life ambition was to collect as many things as possible before they died. For him, life was about helping others, making a difference in the world. In some small way, he hoped he had.

Gently, he removed a small vial of liquid from his trouser pocket, carefully prepared at his house before he'd left, leaving a note for Callum nailed to his front door. Blowing out the lamp, he lay peacefully with the woman he'd loved for an eternity, their bodies swathed in a comforting cloak of blackness and pure silence. Smiling contentedly, he gulped the liquid down, feeling the sharp sting hit the back of his throat. And then he was gone.

After centuries of struggle, generations of hardship, Julian Etienne, the man who'd fled so long ago as Father Sebastian, was at peace in the arms of the woman he loved.

Prowling above, the wildcat was frustrated, flicking its bobbed tail angrily behind it. A few days earlier, it had found a crunchy brown treat lying on the floor of the byre.

Cylindrical, a little dry to taste and with a brittle nail at the end, it had nevertheless proved satisfying, and the furtive feline had felt invigorated after eating it. Somehow, it made the furry beast feel more alive, healthier even. Now it would have to hunt through the forest again, finding harder prey. Still frustrated, it slinked off into the night.

CHAPTER 22: MESSAGES FROM HOME

'Well, I'll say this about that dog of yours – he's one hell of a babe magnet.' Hulk sat with his giant legs stretched out in front of the fire in his bungalow. 'I've never had so much attention from the local ladies. All you've got to do is walk him down to the shoreline, then boom, in they come.' Hulk patted the snoozing hound lying between his feet.

Turner felt much more like himself again. After a steaming bath, he'd changed into his regular clothing of jeans and loud Hawaiian shirt, before tucking in to a huge meat and potato pie served up with fresh vegetables by Hulk. Sitting opposite the giant fisherman, Turner felt like he'd never been away.

'I mean, even Ruth down the road there, she won't normally give me the time of day. But with my furry friend here, she's all chat, chat, chat. I quite fancy her as well.' Hulk looked over at Turner for a response but got nothing. 'Nathen! Are you listening to me? Nathen …'

Nathen Turner, psychic medium, allegedly alert to all things others couldn't sense, was completely tuned out, lost in his own thoughts. Turner sat wondering where Julian would go and what life he'd create for himself. News of the attack on Maggie hadn't reached Benlogan yet, and hopefully he'd be long gone before it did. Hulk shook him roughly by the shoulder.

'Hey, come back to reality. I've been talking to you for the last half hour and you're sat there daydreaming.' Hulk headed for the kitchen, returning shortly with two brown bottles of beer and half-pint glasses. 'Here, thought you'd like one of these. Might loosen you up.'

Turner looked down at the colourful label on the bottle. It was Wildcat beer from the Cairngorms Brewery, a picture of a Scottish wildcat emblazoned on the front. Turner had to laugh at Hulk's little joke, assuming correctly that he'd got it especially after seeing him with the cat at the croft.

Hulk was delighted that his friend had picked up on the name of the beer. 'There you go,' Hulk said. 'That's more like the man I know. Just thought the sight of a little pussy might bring back some happy memories.'

Turner gagged on his drink, laughing hysterically, spraying beer and creamy foam across his clean shirt. 'You rotten sod, this was clean on. I've gone from smelling like an unwashed cat to a brewery in less than two hours.'

They were both laughing loudly. Kyle cocked open an eye from his slumber on the floor to see what all the fuss was about and then settled back down to sleep. For Hulk, the fishing had been good the past couple of days and he was in high spirits, wanting to share his success with a friend. Turner mentioned that he'd met the nearest neighbours on the peninsula and paid a short visit to the estate lodge. Rather than lie, he left out all the details about the hooded figure and the attack on Maggie.

'It has been a wild goose chase, I'm afraid. There's no hidden danger in that sign on the byre door; I got it completely wrong. Anyway, it's been great to see you, Hulk. Thanks for all your help.' Turner was enjoying the lukewarm taste of the smooth beer and downed his glass.

'I'll help you anytime. Let's not be strangers, eh? I've got your number and I can write if you like. At least send you a Christmas card – that'll be here before we know it.' Hulk grabbed some paper and a pen, and Turner wrote down his address in Whitby.

As Turner put down the paper next to his mobile, he swore under his breath. He had completely forgotten that he'd switched it off before leaving for the croft, thinking he'd be back later that day. He knew there was no point in taking it with him as the only place to get a signal was in Benlogan. Slightly nervous, Turner powered it back on again. After a long minute, as the screen kicked into life, the handset started ringing crazily. It was the automated voicemail service telling him he had new messages. More on edge, he dialled the service to find he had eight messages, three enquiries for psychic coaching help, and five from his girlfriend Jade.

Jade's first message was a polite 'Hi babe, just me seeing how you are. I'm flying back tomorrow. I've used up a bit of leave to finish early. Missing you like crazy. Should be back in Whitby early afternoon. Love you,' then building in intensity to the final frantic call. 'Where the hell are you? You're scaring me. Where's the dog? Please call me. I've been wandering the beach all day, looking for you.' And on it went for another minute or so.

Taking a deep breath in, he called Jade's mobile.

Jade was at the house in Whitby, pacing up and down the

kitchen. 'Nathen, that you? My God, where are you? Are you OK?'

'I'm so sorry, Jade, I really am. I'm in Scotland.'

Jade's pacing was getting faster. 'Scotland? What do you mean, Scotland? Don't make fun of me – where are you?'

'I'm in Scotland, honestly. I brought Kyle with me. I'm so sorry.'

As most lovers do when they're worried about their partner and then find out they're absolutely fine, she tore into him.

'How can you do this to me? I thought you were dead.' And on Jade went, chastising him for being so thoughtless.

It took over ten minutes for Turner to calm her down while Hulk made himself scarce in the kitchen. Promising to bring her the biggest bunch of flowers a man could carry when he returned tomorrow, the pair made friends again. Turner felt terrible – in his rush to get away, he'd completely forgotten to change his voicemail message, or leave a note at the house.

Hulk returned sheepishly with a fresh bottle of beer. 'You sorted it out?' he asked, hoping not to get a long sob story about the difficulties of being in a relationship.

Turner gratefully poured his beer, and raised his glass to the giant in appreciation. 'Yes – thanks. Completely my fault. I didn't think.'

For the rest of the night they swapped stories of the old times, over yet more beer, before Turner felt the exhaustion of the past couple of days creeping up on him. Not bothering to change, he fell sound asleep and spent a dreamless night with the dog dozing at his feet.

CHAPTER 23: REUNIONS

Nathen Turner knelt on the doorstep outside his small terraced house in Whitby, a huge bunch of flowers in his hand. He'd pushed a pink rose under the dog's collar; the furry companion sat patiently at his side, tail wagging slowly. Slightly nervously, he knocked on the door with his free hand.

The thick wooden door exploded open. When Jade saw him kneeling there with his puppy-dog 'please don't beat me up' eyes, she laughed and leapt down to hug him, half crushing the flowers in the process. Kyle bounded up excitedly, and started trotting round the pair as they hugged and kissed on the doorstep. Turner lifted Jade's small frame off the ground and carried her into the kitchen.

They sat for long minutes, holding each other and kissing, no need for words between the lovers. Turner had travelled down from Scotland at first light, leaving Hulk with his thanks and a promise to keep in touch. Throughout the journey, he'd worried about how Jade would react when he got home, a dozen different scenarios dashing through his mind. Finally, he'd settled on the kneeling approach, and prayed it would calm any remaining animosity she had for his disappearing act.

The kissing continued up the stairs as they headed to the bedroom. Jade pushed Turner back onto his double bed and guided the dog outside. Turner was about to object – he still smelt a little funky after the drive – but Jade was already undressing so he kept his mouth shut. They made love all morning, enjoying the feel of each other's tender embrace.

After showering together, and more passionate kissing, they were dressed, de-stressed and sitting holding hands in the kitchen. The beauty of Jade always overpowered Turner. She smelt of roses and lavender, long ebony hair framing a beautiful oval face. Although Japanese, she had green eyes, deep windows on her soul that Turner adored. Sitting barelegged in a short kimono top, Jade looked sexier than ever, and he said so, causing her to giggle and kiss him again. Turner was comfortable in a loud red Hawaiian shirt and jeans, his blond hair brushed back and goatee beard freshly trimmed.

As they drank green tea and nibbled on crispy toast, Turner explained why he'd dashed up to Scotland, fearing someone was in danger from witchcraft or something supernatural. Again, he kept his word to Julian about not mentioning any of their conversation in the crypt, but did explain about the hooded old woman roaming the moor. Dismissing her as someone with serious mental health issues, Turner described how she'd attacked Maggie before tragically drowning in the pursuit across the moor.

Turner crunched through more toast, scattering dry crumbs on the table, and said, 'So there was nothing supernatural to it, just some old lady with issues that caused her unfortunate end. It's sad rather than scary. The Highlands are a fantastic place, though. Most breathtaking scenery I've ever seen. Plus, I got to spend a little time with my father's old fishing buddy.'

Jade knew Turner well enough to know that, although he was explaining his trip matter-of-factly, the tragedy with the old woman would have affected him. Turner never wished harm on anyone, friend or foe, and didn't have an aggressive bone in his lanky body.

Turner reached down into his Gladstone briefcase and held up the brown box Julian had given him with the carved Celtic knot on the lid. 'Recognise this?'

Jade, eyes wide, mouth open, muttered, 'No, it can't be.'

'I met the carpenter who makes them – he gave me this. Weird, eh?' Turner opened the box to show her the small vial cocooned in the hessian sacking.

Quickly, Jade pulled out the vial and sacking and started poking the interior, twisting and turning the box in the light. Inch by inch, she felt over the smooth base and then shook it violently from side to side.

Turner smiled at her manic prodding. Jade had been involved last time, when a box like this had held a deadly secret that had nearly got them both killed. That box had a hidden compartment, released by tiny pegs concealed in the interior. Amused at Jade's hunt for a similar release mechanism on this one, he said, 'Don't worry, this one holds no secrets – it's only a box, I promise.'

Slightly embarrassed, Jade put the box down and picked up the vial, tipping the powdery contents back and forth. 'What's this? Looks like paprika, but there's a slight golden colour to it.'

'Some kind of health tonic. It's an old recipe, apparently – the carpenter and his friends made it for the locals.' Turner was pleased with himself. He was openly telling the truth without giving away the real secret and breaking his promise to Julian.

'Doesn't look healthy to me. Here ...' Jade gave it back to him, and Turner packed the box away in his briefcase.

That evening, the two lovers took a moonlit stroll along the sandy beach wrapping around the West Pier. It was a Friday night, so the locals and weekend tourists were out in force, the amusement arcades chirping and chiming away behind them on Pier Road. The aminic smell from the Fish Quay wafted down, mixing with the salt tang from the sea as they headed further out across Whitby Sands, the dog running ahead and diving in the spray. Turner kicked off his boots and paddled ankle-deep in the icy froth. Tripping and stumbling as she tried to balance on one leg, Jade levered off her tight sandals and joined him, playfully kicking water back at Turner. He seemed lost in his thoughts, silently mulling something over in his mind. The lifelong bond between Julian and Isobel had affected him, and he remembered the loneliness, the pure emptiness inside, he'd felt at being away from Jade in such an isolated spot. Again he thought of Julian, who had sacrificed everything for the one he loved, until the sadness of the past few weeks had finally driven them apart. He admired such love and commitment, and he knew, in his heart, that his only chance of finding it for himself was with the beautiful lady at his side.

'You know, Jade, I've been thinking. Maybe we should get married.'

Jade froze, wondering whether she'd heard him right. 'Wh ... what did you say?'

Turner looked into her gorgeous green eyes and said, 'I think we should get married.'

Whether it was shock, or sheer puzzlement, Turner couldn't tell, but Jade stared back at him nonplussed.

Impulsively, Turner dropped to his knees in the foaming spray and held her hand. 'My beautiful Jade, I love you so much. Will you marry me?' His trousers were soaked but he didn't care, nervously waiting for her response, any response in fact.

Jade's eyes welled up as she looked at the soaking figure kneeling in the surf. 'Yes,' she said, then paused as if thinking. 'Do it again – that was wonderful.'

Turner laughed. 'My beautiful Jade, will you marry me?'

'Yes!' Jade leapt down and hugged him passionately, causing the pair to lose balance and tumble into the shallow water. Laughing and dripping wet, they rolled over and over, hugging and kissing as the dog bounded around them, barking its congratulations into the night.

The soaked pair plodged off hand in hand across the beach, drawing amused looks from the tourists as they puddled down the street and across the swing bridge connecting the two sides of the town.

Back inside the house, Jade was ringing her family to break the news. She put the handset on speakerphone. 'Dad? Nathen's asked me to marry him,' she said excitedly down the line. There was a whoop of delight and muffled sounds that sounded like her father was doing a little jig on the other end of the phone. Jade had lost her mother in childhood. Her father had been her bedrock, and best friend, ever since.

Sounds of the muffled dancing came again. 'Oh, my

darling, I'm so happy for you. You must come down – we've got to celebrate. Woohoo!'

They were all laughing together, sharing this special moment in their lives. Turner needed to tell his mother, but it was way after her bedtime and the care home didn't like calls after they'd settled everyone down for the night. He'd have to wait until the morning. As Jade finished the call, they were both thinking the same thing. Somehow, they had to get word to their fellow housemates, Lee and Sandra, travelling in Australia.

'We've got to tell them. Lee's never going to believe you're finally settling down,' Jade said, hunting for a bottle of champagne in the cupboard. The best she could find was white wine, so there they sat, toasting each other with the slightly gamey, warm beverage. Neither of them cared, lost in the pure joy of the moment. The only way they'd be able to contact their Australian travellers was through email; the roaming pair made occasional contact when they came across an Internet café.

Turner sat down with his phone and tapped out a short message:

Lee and Sandra,
I'm making an honest woman of Jade. If you want an
invite to the wedding and free beer, please call.
Love,
Nathen (and Jade, the future Mrs Turner)

After more wine and giggling, the pair headed to bed. Turner lifted Jade over the threshold singing 'Here Comes the

Bride'. Jade moved sexily in time with his slightly drunken tones, doing a slow striptease provocatively near the bed. She'd got as far as unbuttoning her top before Turner lustfully jumped on her.

'Well, Mrs Turner to be, why don't we have a dry run of our wedding night?' he said, kissing Jade passionately and pulling her closer. Nathen Turner had never been so happy in his life.

CHAPTER 24: LONDON CALLING

Over two months later, the wedding plans were in full swing. With a couple of weeks to go until Christmas, Turner spent most of his time shopping, and it was driving him slowly crazy. They were heading to London to spend time with Jade's father, who'd promised them a night on the town and a mystery surprise. Turner secretly hoped the surprise was that all the wedding arrangements were finished, and he no longer needed to have detailed discussions about wedding cakes, wedding cars, or anything prefixed by the word wedding.

Pulling into the private car park behind the Docklands flat, Jade and Turner made their way up to the penthouse of the modern complex. Jade's father was a senior executive in the oil industry and, after travelling across the globe, he had done very well for himself. The apartment was a roomy three-bedroom affair, eclectically decorated in a blend of Japanese, American and British styles. Framed signed baseballs emblazoned with the Texas Rangers logo sat next to Japanese art prints and Victorian candlesticks. Somehow, it worked, providing an overall impression of a homely, lived-in man cave. Jade's father, Kensuke Akiyama, known simply as Ken to his friends and work colleagues, was a small genial man with the lean frame of a seasoned martial artist. Huge calluses on his knuckles gave away his lifelong passion for

Wado Ryu karate. Training kept his body active away from his desk job, and also allowed him to pound out any frustrations against imaginary opponents rather than real ones. It seemed to calm him; he had a relaxed way of doing things that made him both engaging and easy to get along with.

Ken met Jade and Turner warmly at the door and ushered them into the front living room. The room normally enjoyed great views across the city, but today the vertical blinds were closed. Motioning them to sit down on the deep leather sofa, Ken grabbed a remote and pressed a button. With a little jolt and electronic whirr, the blinds slowly folded back. There, outside on the terrace, Lee Melone stood coolly puffing on a cigar next to Sandra Vaughan, who was waving enthusiastically through the double-glazed patio windows.

Ken hopped on the spot with excitement, delighted with his dramatic unveiling of the two travelling housemates, and said, 'Surprise!'

Turner couldn't help himself – he rushed to the door and yanked it back quickly to open it, losing his grip and falling down hard on his backside. The handle had a security catch, and, in his haste, he'd forgotten to flick it up. As Ken opened the door, the sound of Lee's laughter burst in from outside, billowing clouds of cigar smoke in the air. Stubbing out the long cigar, he reached down to Turner.

'Glad to see you haven't changed. Still falling on your arse without me, eh?' Lee pulled Turner to his feet. The pair embraced warmly, patting each other on the back in typical man-hug fashion.

Turner looked into the face of his oldest friend. They'd

known each other since school, sharing adventures, seeing each other through the best and worst of times. An outsider watching them together could be forgiven for thinking they were brothers, so strong was the bond between them. Lee's pale features were an almond glow, bronzed by the Australian sun, sitting atop a yellow T-shirt with an illustration of a kangaroo wearing a sun hat bobbing with corks. Typical, thought Turner – if ever there was a shirt that said 'Look, I've been to Australia', that was the one.

'You don't phone, you don't write – anyone would think we were the ones who were married,' Turner jibed back. He'd had no response to his email – now he knew why. The crafty pal had obviously planned this with Jade's father.

'Man, it's good to see you,' Lee said, patting Turner on the back again. 'I tell you one thing – those Australians don't know how to make proper beer …' And on Lee went to decry anything and everything he'd found different on his travels. Jade and Sandra looked on at the pair, smiling; it was like they'd never been apart.

Over a noisy buffet, they all swapped stories and caught up on the latest news. From Lee and Sandra's arrival in Sydney, with its double-decker trains and the friendly bars, to their journeys through the barren outback and its never-ending roads.

Lee ravenously munched through a sandwich and took a slug of beer. 'We were on the Stuart Highway, heading to Alice Springs, in this broken-down rental truck. It was all we could afford. Anyway, we stopped at this diner place offering "the best steak in town", which was a joke as the "town" was about three buildings.' Lee looked over at Sandra, who was nodding in agreement. 'I ordered a rare steak, same as usual. Rare! I'm not kidding, a good vet could have got that bugger back on its feet.'

Turner gagged on his sausage roll, choking.

'So I says to the guy, "I think I've just heard it go 'moo'. Any chance of getting a dead one?"'

Jade slammed Turner on the back, dislodging the last of his food, allowing his croaking laughter to fill the room.

'Anyway he sulks off and brings me back the same steak, burnt to a crisp. I mean, you could have used the thing as shoe leather. Without a word – just puts this blackened lump in front of me.' Lee took another long pull from his beer.

'Turns out they were winding me up. The chef came out peeing himself at their little joke, carrying some free beers and a perfect steak. Man, you've got to love Australians.' Lee grabbed a handful of cheese sandwiches, daintily cut into neat triangles.

'There is one thing they don't put in the brochures though. The size of the sodding insects. Everywhere we went there was some mutant bug wanting to bite you, or crawl all over you,' Lee said, miming an insect slithering across the table. Jade put her spoon of rice down and imagined it wriggling and crawling off the plate.

'Lee, that's enough! We're trying to eat here,' Sandra said, glaring at him from across the table. Sandra was a mini Australian powerhouse and Lee knew better than to argue with her. Lee mumbled an apology and changed the subject.

'So, when's the wedding and who's coming? You got it planned yet?' Lee sat straight-faced, and glanced hopefully over at Sandra to see whether his change of conversation was more suitable. Almost imperceptibly she nodded 'yes'.

Turner, now clear of his sausage roll, was helping himself to a cocktail sausage with a lump of cheese on the top. 'We're thinking Whitby, maybe Easter next year. There're some people I met in Scotland I'd like to ask down. Should be better weather by then, make it easier for them to travel. You remember Hulk, right? My dad's old partner.'

Lee mimed a muscle pose across the table. 'That beast! He's not exactly hard to forget. You've seen him? How is he?'

Turner told Lee about his brief stay with the giant and a short version of his Scottish trip. Lee could sense that Turner was holding back on him – he'd known him too long – but didn't say anything. After more chat about the wedding, they all helped clean up, and before long were ready to hit the town. Ken was a gracious host, insisting on paying for everything as they trooped around the pubs in Chinatown and the West End, before staggering back on the Docklands Light Railway in the early hours of the morning.

Up first the next day, Turner decided to try and catch Hulk before he headed out on his morning fishing trip. Hulk answered the phone after one ring.

A slightly sleepy voice said, 'Hello?'

'Hulk, that you? It's Nathen, Nathen Turner. How's things?'

Turner could hear a woman's voice vaguely in the background asking who was on the phone. 'Fine ... well better than fine. Remember I was on about my neighbour, Ruth? Well, we've hooked up, all thanks to that dog of yours.'

Turner was delighted. Hopefully this one might be a

keeper. 'Great, I'm pleased for you. Listen, I'm getting married next year, probably around Easter. Can you come down to Whitby?'

'Yes, love to. Let me know the dates – can I bring Ruth?' Hulk looked back into the bedroom at his neighbour, quickly pulling on her clothes to keep out the morning chill.

Turner told him that of course it was OK, and thought that this was an incredibly positive sign from the guy who normally couldn't cope with a woman for more than a few weeks. He asked about getting hold of Callum, Maggie and Mike at the estate lodge, saying it would be great if he could repay their brief hospitality.

'Callum won't come, I'll tell you now. He doesn't do weddings. Maggie might – I'll ask her and let you know. Mike Fletcher's gone back home. Hang on, I've got his number somewhere.' Hulk fished out the telephone number and read it down the phone. 'How come you didn't ask about Julian? Do you know he's not here anymore? Vanished overnight – nobody knows where he's gone. Callum found a note nailed to the door of Julian's place, literally giving him the rights to the property. Weird, if you ask me; Callum's been in a foul mood ever since.'

Turner didn't answer immediately; he needed to cover his tracks a little. Of course, he knew Julian wouldn't be there – the man himself told him he was leaving. After glossing over it, saying he'd forgotten, they swapped a few bawdy stories of Hulk's courting exploits with Ruth, the giant keeping his voice low so she couldn't overhear, then hung up.

So, if Mike Fletcher had gone home already, his leg

must have healed pretty fast, which was great news, and Turner felt happy for him. He had taken an instant liking to Fletcher; he seemed like a nice, decent guy, dealing bravely with his own demons. Whistling happily, Turner set about preparing a large fry-up for everyone, the perfect cure for a morning hangover.

CHAPTER 25: THE BELLS RING OUT

Christmas came and went in a blur of alcohol, food and laughter, with heavy emphasis on the alcohol part of the festivities. After reuniting, the four housemates had barely been apart, either wandering around to friends' houses in Whitby, or quietly enjoying each other's company. With the upcoming wedding, Turner had ditched his goatee beard in favour of a smooth look, and had his mess of blond locks fashioned into some kind of respectable order.

They'd booked St Austin's for the service itself, a small parish church just out of town. Nestled inland in a quiet run off the main coast road, it suited Turner perfectly. After a spooky graveyard walk to access the small church, the visitor faced an imposing oak door topped with a serpent-like dragon motif carved below the lintel, and two smiling gargoyle heads sitting either side. Inside, the church itself was like walking into history, the main building over six hundred years old. Norman arches mixed with Jacobean woodwork and modern stained-glass windows, the entire interior reminiscent of a Gothic horror movie set.

Jade and Turner sat uncomfortably, and with some trepidation, as they listened to 'the talk' from Mr Stephens, the local vicar. Stephens was a slight man who took himself incredibly seriously. Dressed in a brown corduroy sports coat, underneath his immaculately pressed dog collar, he poured Earl Grey tea into polished china cups before steepling his fingers together to talk about the sanctity of marriage. It wasn't so much what he was saying, which made perfect sense; it was how he was saying it, which made the pair feel like they'd been summoned to the headmaster's office for a scolding.

'True marriage signifies love, sacrifice, obedience, devotion; two people that are one in all things,' Stephens said earnestly, crossing his legs, highlighting the light grass stains on his knees from his morning spent gardening in the ample vicarage plot. Leaning forwards, he changed his tone to talk more in the style of a polite evangelist converting heathens to his cause. 'But let us not forget what our Lord says in Romans 8:13 and 1 Corinthians 6:18.' Stephens read at length from a dog-eared open Bible on his lap, reminding the pair about the evil of sexual immorality and the curse of living in sin.

Turner flushed slightly and glanced over at Jade, who refused to meet his eye. 'Where the hell is he going with this?' Turner muttered across to his bride-to-be. Jade elbowed him to keep quiet.

Stephens's probing eyes scanned the couple like a truth-seeking radar. 'Can I take it the two of you do not live together currently? You are aware, I assume, that I cannot condone a church wedding if you are living together in sin.'

'Er … no, vicar. I have a place in Whitby, and Jade lives in London,' Turner said truthfully, though in reality Jade had barely spent a day at her flat in the past six months, staying with him whenever she was home from work.

Stephens stared across at the couple again, truth-seeking radar on full beam. 'I'll need proof of that, of course. Merely a formality, but things must be done correctly, don't you agree?'

The pair nodded in unison like naughty schoolchildren accepting a punishment.

'Good, good. To continue …'

And he did. For another thirty minutes, Stephens moved on to a series of eloquently spoken hellfire and damnation speeches, centred mainly around being faithful to each other and living a Christian life. Turner knew the vicar had a job to do, and respected his beliefs, but the experience left him in awe of the power of the church to create fear if you dared step out of line or challenge the accepted dogma. As he listened, he connected his current feelings of anxiety to those he assumed had been felt during the witch trials at North Berwick that Julian had talked about. Turner wondered whether modern culture was any less superstitious than the one Julian had lived through. Perhaps, he thought, but maybe the current Internet-savvy generation were more cautious in openly disclosing their beliefs. Turner knew people who publicly called themselves witches, but they were all nature-loving pagan types, accepted as part of the great British eccentric culture. Again, he was reminded of Julian, and the man's life in a different era and less tolerant place in history, and for the first time felt a true appreciation of the pain and suffering he must have lived through. Shaking his head to clear his morose thoughts, he unconsciously crossed himself and said his thanks and farewells to the vicar. Once outside again and out of earshot, Turner laughed nervously, muttering, 'If he delivers our wedding vows like that, I'll be too scared to say "I do", provoking a giggling fit from Jade, who nodded in agreement.

Later, Lee and Turner almost caused a riot in the traditional wedding-hire store by ordering white velvet double-breasted suits, pink shirts and black skinny ties. Jade went for a tight-fitting, above-the-knee, white velvet dress to complement the boys' attire, and a matching one in pink for her only bridesmaid, Sandra. Jade's father, Ken, couldn't face the prospect of wearing the velvet suits, so he went for a more traditional James Bond approach, with a smart black dinner jacket and bow tie.

Months turned into weeks, which in turn dwindled to days, until finally the big day arrived. Turner stood nervously in the church, asking Lee for the fourteenth time whether he had the rings. Vicar Stephens was pacing around the pulpit in his green, black and white flowing robes as if working himself up to deliver the wedding service of his life. Watching the vicar pacing around was making Turner's nerves worse.

After what felt like hours of waiting, an out-of-tune organ began to play 'Here Comes the Bride' and everybody stood in unison to watch Jade make her dramatic entrance, arm in arm with her father. Turner couldn't resist looking back to the doorway. He could see the huge frame of Hulk towering at the back of the congregation, Maggie on one side and Hulk's girlfriend, Ruth, on the other. There was no sign of Mike Fletcher, but he knew he would be here somewhere, and he was looking forward to catching up with him later. He'd managed to get hold of Mike Fletcher's sister on the phone, who'd told him she was sure Mike would be delighted to come. The rest of their collective friends were scattered in the crowd, with Turner's mother standing proudly next to him, a tear in her eye.

True to form, Stephens delivered a straight-faced and incredibly serious wedding service that left the couple in no doubt that they were taking a solemn vow before God, to be betrayed at their peril. The congregation, who knew neither the words nor the tunes to the obligatory hymns, sang half-heartedly or simply made the words up. Rings exchanged, register signed, they headed out of the huge oak door to be drowned in a sea of colourful confetti, the vicar tut-tutting loudly in the background at the amount of litter he'd need to clean up.

As the bride and groom made their way down past the row of guests, lined snake-like along the graveyard path, eager to congratulate them, a forlorn figure in an electric wheelchair took his place awkwardly in the line. One by one, the married couple shook hands or gave manly hugs, sometimes the occasional peck on the cheek, as they weaved their smiling way down the path. Hulk almost crushed Turner's hand as he pulled him into an awkward bear hug. It looked like the giant had been crying, but Turner thought it best not to mention it. Maggie greeted him warmly, her freckled features covered by makeup, red hair curled and styled elegantly. She looked every part the city girl after swapping her normal dumpy clothing for a short blue dress with a low neckline.

'You remember Mike Fletcher?' Maggie said, and turned

to her left to introduce the figure seated in the electric wheelchair. 'And this is his sister, Rose.' Rose offered a 'nice to meet you' smile and shook Turner's hand.

Mike looked up like a man who'd given up on the world, gazing unresponsively into Turner's smiling face. His right hand rested awkwardly on the wheelchair's joystick control, almost as if it didn't know it was there. The left was cradled in his lap, disappearing under a cream blanket covering both of his legs. There was a slightly musky smell of urine about the man, coming from a catheter tube discreetly tucked next to the wheelchair's seat, linked to a bag at the back. Turner couldn't tell how Mike's leg had healed because of the blanket, but it seemed the least of his problems.

Spotting the look of shock on Nathen Turner's face, Mike spoke slowly and deliberately, as if he had to concentrate on every syllable. 'Sorry about this, Nathen, but I wanted to come. Rose had to bring me. I hope it's OK.'

Turner desperately wanted to find out what on earth had happened to him, but one look from Mike's sister made him pause. Instead, he put a smile on his face and said, 'Of course. Rose, you are more than welcome. It is great to see you, Mike. Thank you so much for coming. Jade, this is Mike Fletcher, the photographer I told you about from Scotland.'

Jade was just as shocked, but followed Turner's lead. The Mike Fletcher her newlywed husband had described was a strong man with an injured leg, nothing more. Composing herself, she looked straight into Mike's forlorn face and smiled. 'Nathen's told me a lot about you, Mike. I'm glad you could come – you too, Rose.' And she meant it. As Jade leant forward to hug Rose, she whispered in her ear, 'Is he OK?

What's happened to him?'

Rose hugged her back, and said, keeping her voice low, 'Multiple sclerosis,' before returning to her standing position at Mike's side, forcing a smile back on her face.

The newlyweds finished the line and jumped into Jade's ribbon-adorned mini as they were waved off, heading to the reception at Oswin Hall Hotel in town. As soon as they'd pulled in their waving hands from the open car windows and driven out of sight, Turner blurted out, 'What the hell's happened to him?'

Jade knew immediately that he meant Mike Fletcher. 'It's MS. Well, that's what his sister whispered to me.'

'Poor bugger.' Turner simply didn't know what else to say.

They sat in relative silence for the rest of the short trip, Turner lost in his thoughts. The mood changed as soon as they arrived at Oswin Hall Hotel, warmly greeted by a beaming David Laslett, the new owner. David was an amiable man, with a body built for comfort not speed, smartly dressed for the occasion in a navy-blue suit. Ushered in swiftly through the oak-beamed lobby, within minutes the pair had a chilled glass of champagne and were toasting each other's health as the guests began to trickle in.

Four courses and multiple bottles of wine later, everyone was in high spirits, poised ready to heckle the speeches. Jade's father and Turner got away fairly lightly, but the best man, Lee, with his normal tongue-in-cheek style, was absolutely roasted. Lee decided to begin on a serious note about the importance of family, before unleashing his set of prepared jokes about his best friend. Things didn't quite get that far.

'As most of you know, I never knew who my real father was,' Lee began, raising himself to his feet at the top table. This was true; Lee had been brought up by a series of his mother's boyfriends, his existence caused by some previous relationship his mother would never talk about. Lee hoped that starting this way would pull in the sympathy vote and get the boisterous crowd on his side, perhaps feeling a little sorry for him.

Hulk spotted the opportunity from his seat two places down from Lee, shouting out, 'Yes, but your mother didn't half cry when the milkman died.' The room erupted.

Lee kept plugging on over the screams of laughter, eventually changing the subject to the evening's entertainment. 'Later we've arranged a special performance of Nathen's favourite blues tunes, featuring yours truly on guitar.' Lee mimed playing air guitar, accompanied by cheers and the odd wolf whistle from the crowd. 'And Sandra on vocals.' More cat calls and wolf whistles as Sandra stood and gave a little shimmying bow to the guests. 'Can't beat blues music – I think music has been crap since BB King passed away.'

Hulk spotted his opportunity again, calling out, 'Aren't you being a bit unfair on the Bay City Rollers?' More mass hysteria.

Lee took it all in good spirit and sat down to the biggest round of applause of the afternoon, Turner laughing and patting him on the back in congratulations.

Later, the music was a huge hit, Lee's blistering guitar style, and Sandra's sultry voice, keeping everyone on their feet, boogying the night away.

Turner and Jade slipped quietly away, leaving the revellers to party on into the early hours. Opening the door to the honeymoon suite of the hotel, Turner whisked Jade off her feet and gently placed her onto the large four-poster bed. As he stripped of his sticky white velvet jacket and carelessly threw it over a chair, Jade was already way ahead of him, pulling her short white dress quickly over her head. When they made love it was like the first time, each holding the other tenderly, stroking and kissing gently.

Afterwards, exhausted, they drifted into a deep, satisfied sleep in each other's arms.

Turner woke as usual with the dawn light flooding into the room. He never bothered to close the curtains, preferring instead to live by nature's natural pattern of dark and light. Hurriedly he scribbled a note to Jade, saying 'back in an hour or two', and headed out across the swing bridge on the short walk to his house. At least this time he'd left a note, so hopefully the new Mrs Turner wouldn't worry about his absence when she woke up.

It was a crisp fresh morning, half the fishing boats already motoring out across the bay. Within ten minutes, Turner was carefully unlocking his front door, hoping the short squeak from the rusty hinges wouldn't disturb those inside. Sneaking through the kitchen, he tiptoed past his sleeping hound and then up onto the second-floor landing, listening intently outside Lee and Sandra's room. They were both still gently snoring, so he kept going upstairs to his bedroom. Heading straight to the locked cupboard next to his bed, Turner pulled out his small Gladstone briefcase with the stealth of a master thief. Carefully, he rooted around for the carved box Julian had given him. Later that week he'd be heading off on honeymoon with Jade, but for now Turner only had one thing on his mind – find Mike Fletcher and give him the red powder inside the box.

CHAPTER 26: HOPE OF LIFE

Turner wasn't sure whether he felt pleased with his ability to burgle his own home in broad daylight. If a psychic could do it, what on earth would an experienced criminal be able to achieve? Pushing away an old memory, when two thugs had managed to break into his house, he picked up the pace and headed back to Oswin Hall Hotel. Initially, he'd thought about giving the red powder to his mother, but she was counting her days, ready in her mind to join her loving husband in whatever corner of the afterlife he'd ended up. Prolonging her wait seemed cruel to Turner, and he didn't think she'd thank him for it. Fletcher, on the other hand, looked like a man without hope, someone who'd simply given up on the world. Seeing him in the wheelchair had affected Turner deeply, and he desperately wanted to help him in some way. Julian's red powder seemed the only option he could offer, and he felt sure it was worth the risk. He also thought that Julian, with his lifelong commitment to helping others, would definitely approve.

As Turner approached the small courtyard next to the main entrance of the hotel, he stopped. Somewhere close by, he could hear the sound of a woman sobbing quietly, another female voice trying gently to console her. Not wishing to intrude on what sounded like a very personal scene, Turner half crept, half tiptoed forward. Inside, Maggie Douglas sat with her arm around Rose Fletcher on the small leather settee that filled the space under the arching stairs leading up to the guest rooms. Both women were still in nightclothes, faces devoid of makeup, and house slippers on their feet. Neither noticed Turner's quiet approach, his footsteps drowned out by the sound of vacuuming coming from the bar next door. Rose wept openly into a crumpled handkerchief, her puffed red eyes staring down at the floor. The vacuuming stopped and Maggie spotted Turner as he tried to sneak past them up the stairs. Both women instinctively pulled their clothing tighter, feeling embarrassed.

'Er … erm … we came down for more milk. We've run out, you see … can't approach the morning without a strong coffee,' Maggie lied, not wanting to put a dampener on Turner's first morning as a married man.

'And I've been out for a paper,' Turner lied back, blatantly opening his arms to show he was not holding a newspaper in his hands. 'What's wrong? I hate to see you both upset like this. Something happen last night after we went to bed? It's Lee, isn't it? What has he done?' Nathen Turner jumped to his usual, normally correct, conclusion that Lee had managed to get into some drunken trouble or other.

'No, no – it's nothing like that. Don't worry, Nathen. Rose has a few personal issues. Women's troubles, you know,' Maggie said, looking up to see whether the new half-lie would stop Turner digging any deeper. Usually, throwing in the 'women's troubles' line would send most men running for cover.

Having spent his adult life reading people for a living,

Turner wasn't buying it. 'How about I order us some coffee, eh? They've finished cleaning the bar; maybe they'll let us sit in there – nobody else is around yet.' Without waiting for an answer, Turner headed to reception to order coffee, plus a green tea for him, then ushered the two ladies next door. He was still convinced that Lee would be somewhere at the bottom of this; the sooner he found out, the sooner he could go and sort his friend out and prevent any further drama.

The trio sat in silence, waiting for the drinks to arrive, Rose wiping her face and pulling herself upright, trying hard to regain control of her emotions. With no serving staff on duty yet, the bleary-eyed hotel owner, David Laslett, brought in the drinks. Spotting the sombre mood, he quietly said his good mornings and then left, closing the door behind him to allow them some privacy.

Rose seemed to have made a decision. 'Mike's going to kill himself,' she said, the statement causing her sobbing to start again. Maggie grasped her hand under the table.

Without thinking, Turner said, 'What, here? I'd better get to him,' and stood up to leave at a half run.

Maggie pulled him back in mid-stride, pushing him back in his chair with a strength that belied her stature. 'No, next month. Listen.' Maggie's freckled features were imploring Turner to shut the hell up and sit down. He did, amazed at the shepherdess's ability to control her emotions as she explained all that had happened.

After the night of the attack at the estate lodge, things had returned to relative normality within the week – Maggie back on the hills, glad to be alive and reunited with her flock, and Callum more relaxed now that the threat had been found and, as he saw it, 'exterminated'. Mike Fletcher had busied himself helping as much as he could around the house, the leg recovering well as he'd pushed harder to walk on it unaided.

Then, within a matter of days, things went from calm to crisis. Fletcher complained of feeling a little unwell and began to slur his words, forgetting how to do the simplest of things. Fletcher's left arm seemed to struggle to move, as if he was pushing hard against a heavy weight, his fingers unable to grip anything. Things came to a head when they found him on the floor in his bedroom, unable to get up, the left side of his face drooping slightly. Fearing blood poisoning from his leg wound and a possible stroke, Callum had literally run to Julian's house for help. Julian had always been their rock in times of crisis and seemed to have an eclectic but effective knowledge of medicine. Callum returned furious – Julian had simply left without a word of goodbye, leaving a note nailed to the door, giving Callum the rights to the property.

With no other options available, Maggie and Callum had loaded Fletcher into a Land Rover and driven him three hours to the nearest major hospital, in Inverness. After a nervy wait, the pair were asked to come back in the morning, the medical crew no further forward in explaining Fletcher's symptoms. During the night, Fletcher had woken and was lucid enough to explain his prior multiple sclerosis diagnosis to the medical team. So fixated were Maggie and Callum on the possibility of blood poisoning or stroke that neither had thought to mention MS when they'd arrived. From there on, things progressed quickly. MRI scan, lumbar puncture, visual acuity test – all were completed in short order, before finally the doctors seemed satisfied as they pumped Fletcher full of steroids.

'Turns out he'd had a massive multiple sclerosis relapse at the lodge. We'd never seen anything like that before. I mean, how were we to know what was going on?' Maggie said, talking quickly to Turner as if looking for his acceptance of their ignorance of the disease. Turner said nothing and kept listening.

'His MS had deteriorated to a progressive form while he stayed with us. They said it was nothing we'd done, and it would have happened anyway, but I still feel responsible somehow.' Maggie had stopped looking at Turner and was gazing at Rose as if asking forgiveness. 'Apparently, it's rare for this to happen so quickly, but all the tests showed that it's running riot. A very aggressive form.'

Rose spoke for the first time since they'd entered the bar. 'They've given him three to six months to live if it keeps going the way it is. He's been back with me since before Christmas, getting steadily worse. I've had to quit my job to look after him. I mean, how are we supposed to afford twenty-four-hour medical care?' Rose was bitter about the lack of support and financial help she'd been offered through official channels. Weeks filling in forms and doing interviews had resulted in no real support for the pair, who'd spent their entire lives doing nothing more than working hard and paying into the system – a system meant to help them in times of crisis. All it had done so far was make them fill in endless bits of paper with a load of stupid questions.

Turner could see Rose's resentment growing and realised that none of it was going to help Mike Fletcher. Trying to get her back onto why and how he was going to kill himself, Turner simply asked her outright.

'Next month. He's made an appointment at DIGNITAS in Switzerland,' Rose said, crying again. 'He won't let me come, says I could be prosecuted for helping him.'

Turner knew DIGNITAS were an organisation that allowed people with critical conditions to die with dignity at a time of their choosing. UK law prohibited anyone attempting to assist a suicide attempt, so he could understand Fletcher wanting to protect his sister.

Turner had a plan. He'd already made it as soon as he'd seen Mike Fletcher yesterday, but he couldn't tell anybody about it. Nobody, that is, except Mike Fletcher. 'Would you let me talk to him? Alone, I mean,' Turner asked hopefully.

Rose happily agreed, even though she'd never met Turner until yesterday. There was something about him that seemed different. She knew Turner was some kind of psychic, but in truth she had no time for such things. Any faith Rose may have had in anything supernatural disappeared long ago in a series of broken relationships, failed careers, and now the devastation of her only brother. Leaving Maggie and Turner alone, Rose headed up to raise Mike Fletcher and get him presentable for a visitor.

Turner looked across at Maggie. 'You know, from what little I saw, I thought you and Mike Fletcher might become an item. I hope you don't mind me saying so.' He was sipping at his lukewarm tea, watching Maggie's response. She went bright red, her freckles positively jumping out from her pink skin. 'Sorry, I didn't mean to embarrass you.'

Maggie was trying to cover her unease by pouring more

coffee from the cafetière. 'It's OK – I'm not good with personal stuff. But, yes, I thought so too, for what it's worth. We have such different lives though, even if he was well. I know it could never happen now.'

Turner could see the conversation was making her uncomfortable, so he offered his apologies again and headed up to Mike Fletcher's room, hoping he'd left enough time for Rose to get him ready and out of bed. Knocking gently on the door, he was ushered in to a waiting chair, opposite the despondent figure of Fletcher propped in his wheelchair. Rose excused herself, saying she was heading back down to see Maggie and finish her coffee.

Turner could detect the faint smell of urine again, clinging to the depressed figure opposite him. What it must be like to be stripped of your dignity, totally dependent on the care of others, Turner had no idea. Now was not the time for such thoughts; now was the time to put his sketchy plan into action.

'Mike, remember back at the estate lodge you asked me whether I have any special powers, or could see into the future?' Turner got no response from Mike Fletcher; it looked like he wasn't listening. Turner reached out and grabbed Fletcher's hand, hard. 'Mike, are you listening to me?'

Fletcher looked up despondently at the lanky figure of the psychic sitting opposite, as if noticing him for the first time. 'Yes, I remember.'

Turner was still holding onto Fletcher's hand. It was the one that controlled the joystick on the wheelchair, so the photographer couldn't move away from him, even if he wanted to. 'Well, I do have one thing, a thing I think you've lost and I'm here to give back to you.'

Fletcher snorted in disbelief. He'd gone from living the high life in the city, photographing celebrities, dining out two or three times a week, to this. A prisoner in his own body. His time in Scotland had refreshed him, making him feel positive again about rebuilding his life. He'd thought about moving up there, maybe making a go of things with Maggie – if she'd have him. Changing the pace of his life to the slower ebb and flow of countryside living. Even the chance of that had been taken away. Now he had nothing. Just increasing disability and, no doubt, a painful and humiliating death. Rather than let that happen, he wanted to end his days with some dignity, some respect, and he'd already made his mind up how to do it.

Lifting his head up in defiance, he said, 'What can you give me? I've lost everything and nobody can give me it back, not even God himself.' If he could have, Fletcher would have moved away, but Turner's grip prevented him.

'Faith, Mike, faith,' Turner said softly to counter Fletcher's frustration. 'If you don't have faith, then you truly have nothing.' Turner stood up, towering over the wheelchair to make his point. 'Ever heard of the Placebo effect? It's where people believe they've taken something that can cure them, and then they get better. But in reality they've had a sugar pill or something, nothing that would do them any harm or any good. Thing is, they believed they'd taken a cure. They had faith and they got better. Their mind cured them. We can make every chemical known to man in our brains, if only we can tap into it – faith and belief let us do that. Do you understand me?'

'So what are you going to do – give me a sugar lump and cure me?' Fletcher sneered back.

Turner shook his head in a 'no' gesture, smiling down at the seated figure looking scornfully up at him. 'I'm going to do better than that – I'm going to prove you have faith and you're going to be well again.' Turner fished in his pocket for the deck of tarot cards he'd taken out from his Gladstone briefcase, and the vial of red powder from the carved box Julian had given him. Holding the cards and the vial under Fletcher's nose, he said, 'We're going to play a game. If you win, you get to live again as you want. If not, then things stay exactly as they are. You have nothing to lose, and everything to gain.'

Fletcher watched as Turner spread the tarot cards face up across the dressing table in front of them. Each one held a different colourful design, some with ancient figures, others with bizarre motifs. 'Some believe that the tarot hold the hidden secrets of the ancients coded in their images. It is this one card that you need to find if you want your life back.'

Turner held up a card showing a hooded lady travelling in a boat shaped as a crescent moon. Her right arm cradled a closed book with a green cover, her left hand raised with a single finger to her lips in a gesture of silence. On her head sat a decorated crown, again in the shape of a crescent moon, and in the sky above shone a full moon looking down across the scene.

'This card is the High Priestess of the tarot. She is the symbol of our unconscious mind, a gateway to the deepest parts of our soul. With her help, we can find the power hidden within us, and use it to heal.' Turner was relieved to find that he had Fletcher's full attention and so far his plan was working. Turner knew that if he'd just showed up with the red powder and given it to Fletcher, questions would be asked later if it did work and he got well again. Somehow he needed to convince Fletcher it was the power of his mind helping him, and the red powder was inconsequential. Calling on his years of experience, when he'd been a sham psychic act, Turner had come up with this idea and prayed it would work. So far, so good. Looking at the cards was taking Fletcher's mind off his feelings of resentment, and he watched silently as Turner continued.

'There are seventy-eight cards here.' Turner flipped them all face down and mixed them haphazardly on the smooth surface of the table. Slowly and deliberately he placed the High Priestess card amongst the pack and then kept mixing. After about a minute, Turner carelessly stacked them into a tall face-down pile directly in front of Fletcher.

'I want you to give me a number between one and seventy-eight. Don't make a conscious choice – let your instinct guide you. You must feel somehow that this number is right for you; you must have faith in making the right choice.' Turner was an expert at this kind of performance and Fletcher was completely hooked. 'Whatever number you pick, that will be the card that will govern your fate. If you can find the High Priestess, then you will be well again if you have faith in yourself and believe you can get better. If not, then things will be exactly the same as they are. Remember, your chances are only seventy-eight to one to find the card.'

Fletcher closed his eyes briefly as if trying to visualise a number. In truth, he thought the odds of finding the card

Turner had so eloquently described were between nil and nothing. Gradually he felt, rather than saw, two numbers appearing in his head. Surprised and slightly baffled he said, 'Thirty-six.'

Carefully, as if handling the most precious material on earth, Turner picked up the cards and began dealing one at a time face up, counting out loud as he went. Turn after turn the exotic images flashed by, Fletcher clumsily trying to lean forward as they reached thirty-three.

'Thirty-four … thirty-five … and this is the card at the number you felt was right for you.' Turner placed it face down on the table away from the others. 'Tell me, Mike, do you have faith? Do you truly believe the card you've chosen is the High Priestess and that you can heal yourself?'

For a reason Mike Fletcher would never truly understand, he felt compelled to say yes. Watching Turner work like this was mesmerising, and he was completely drawn in by the man's sheer presence. There was something different about him that drew the attention, made him forget his pain and suffering, and gave him a feeling he hadn't had in living memory – hope.

'Then prove it to me.' Turner walked to the bedside table and poured a glass of water from a large jug. Deliberately, he tipped in the vial of red powder Julian had given him, and swirled it slowly in the glass until it dissolved. 'Drink this – if you truly believe, then this will heal you. It may taste a little bitter, but you must drink all of it.' Turner offered the pale red liquid to Fletcher's good hand.

'But we haven't seen the card.'

'I asked whether you had faith, Mike. If you do, then you

don't need to see the card – you already know what it is. You must have faith in yourself. Trust that you made the right choice.' Turner steadied Fletcher's hand and motioned him to drink.

Fletcher looked straight into Turner's eyes. There was a certainty there, knowledge beyond anything he'd felt before. Without any further hesitation, Fletcher downed the ruddy liquid. It tasted mildly of salt with a slightly bitter aftertaste.

Turner cleared the tarot deck and put it back in his pocket, leaving only Fletcher's chosen card face down on the table. 'I'll ask your sister to come back up if that's OK. I think you need to rest. I believe you'll feel a lot better tomorrow. Will you do one thing for me?'

Fletcher nodded that he would, feeling a little sleepy after taking the drink.

Turner helped Fletcher reposition himself more comfortably in his wheelchair after he'd leant forward to watch the tarot cards. 'I want you to cancel your appointment at DIGNITAS. Promise me you will do that today.'

'I will, Nathen, I promise. Thank you for everything – thanks for trying to give me some hope again.' The pair hugged warmly but slightly awkwardly with Fletcher in the chair.

Turner fetched Rose from downstairs and then headed back to his room to find Jade still asleep. Tossing the note he'd left in the bin, he shrugged off his clothes and snuggled back into bed next to his snoozing bride. By the time Mike Fletcher was feeling better, Turner would be away on honeymoon in Japan, staying with Jade's grandparents. If Turner's plan worked, then Fletcher would believe he was 'thinking' himself better and any memory of their brief time together that morning would be long forgotten. Hopefully, Fletcher would believe he'd drunk something like red sherbet dissolved in water that was of no real value to his recovery. Feeling satisfied with his morning's clandestine mission, Turner nuzzled into his beautiful bride and drifted back to sleep.

Three doors away, Rose was settling Fletcher back into bed. He seemed different somehow, more at peace with himself, less angry and resentful. Tidying around, she grabbed the empty glass and noticed the strange face-down card, with its half-chequerboard, half red back design, on the table. Pointing to it, she called over to her brother, 'Mike, what's this? Do you want it?'

Fletcher sleepily opened one eye to see Rose pointing at the tarot card and said, 'Can you show it to me?'

Rose lifted the card up so he could see it. Fletcher looked over to see the High Priestess card gazing unemotionally back at him. Smiling contentedly, he drifted off to sleep, new hope filling his mind, draining away the darkness drowning his thoughts.

Not sure what else to do with it, Rose threw the strange card in the bin and continued her cleaning.

CHAPTER 27: RETURN TO THE WILD

Callum Benvie crawled silently through the dense heather with panther-like skill as he edged slowly forward. Six feet behind him, another figure was trying to emulate his approach, but the end result sounded like a herd of raging buffaloes stamping in a particularly bad mood. Scowling back, the trailing figure froze in Callum's glare, mouthing a feeble 'sorry'.

Raising his brass spotting scope and wedging it in a cleft in the heather, Callum scoured the hillside ahead, looking for the huge red deer stag they'd been tracking all morning. Callum signalled behind, and the two stalkers changed course to keep downwind of their prey. After a prickly thirty minutes more, as they rode the tide of springy foliage, they were finally in range. Raising a camera with a large lens to his eye, the trailing figure sighted the animal, and carefully tucked his elbows into the heather to form a stable base. Taking a deep breath in, so as not to cause any movement, the man gently squeezed down.

Click followed by a muffled cry of 'Got it' and the pair retreated, their steps taking them back over the ridgeline. Out of sight of the deer herd, Callum exploded.

'You're like a bull in a china shop out there.' Callum's face was flushed with rage. 'If you want to do this stuff, you'd better learn fast, son. We've done mountain hare, pine marten, red grouse and red deer, and you're still bloody hopeless.'

The slim figure at the centre of Callum's wrath just laughed. 'Keep talking like that and people will think you're starting to like me.'

Callum frowned and stared at the figure nonplussed, then burst out laughing. Nobody ever dared to speak to him like this except one man. And that man was Mike Fletcher. Putting his huge camera lens back in his backpack, Fletcher purposefully strode up to Callum and hugged him warmly.

'That was brilliant, thanks. I think I'm starting to get the hang of this wildlife photography lark – what do you think?' Fletcher smiled happily at the grumpy keeper.

'I'd rather shoot them than photograph them, but each to their own, I suppose.' Callum couldn't deny that the photographs Fletcher had taken over the past few months were pretty good. Better than good, in fact, but he didn't want to admit that. As Callum taught Fletcher how to track and spot field signs, the photographer was repaying him in whisky. So far, the arrangement was working well, the pair growing used to each other's company, but not at the firm-friends level yet.

In the week following the wedding, Fletcher had started to feel a lot better, much to the amazement of his sister and Maggie Douglas. Fighting for independence, he'd removed the catheter, determined to get back some of his lost dignity. When he stood from his chair on the fourth day to dash to the bathroom, Maggie nicknamed him 'Whizzing Lazarus' as she listened to him peeing contentedly in the bathroom. The desire to stand and walk had been totally unconscious, simply driven by a full bladder and a sense of urgency. From that point on, Whizzing Lazarus never went back in the wheelchair.

Maggie decided to stay with him for a while, part in curiosity, and part in hope that the man she'd met in Scotland would return to her. The kind man, the man who'd nursed her through the nightmare in the wild.

Back at his sister's house, Fletcher played incessantly with his camera equipment, like a child who'd been given his toys back after a spell on the naughty step. He was in high spirits when his weekly home visit by the MS nurse caught him by surprise. Opening the door to the slightly dumpy uniformed visitor, carrying her medical reports under her arms, he smiled happily, jumped out, and hugged her warmly. Not used to this kind of physical welcome, the nurse ran screaming down the path, papers flying in the wind. Whizzing Lazarus had struck again.

'You realise, Mr Fletcher, that we can't condone this degree of physical contact between a patient and a member of the medical profession,' the bespectacled neurologist chided a few days later, peering over the top of his thick horn rims. Fletcher had been instantly summoned for a full review, including psychological evaluation, following his inappropriate embrace. 'Can you explain to me how you come to be walking again? Have you been dabbling in … erm … how can I say … illegal substances?'

'No, I just decided to get better,' Fletcher replied innocently. As Turner had predicted, the photographer had made no link between the drink he'd taken and his recovery.

'Simple as that, doctor. Anyway, aren't you supposed to be the one telling me why I feel better?'

A quiet cough to clear invisible phlegm cracked the silence of the room. 'Well … erm … yes, of course … but …' The neurologist flicked the MRI scans deftly into the lightbox on the wall. 'You see here – your lesions are exactly the same. If anything, you've got more than you had a month ago.' He pointed to the small blobs of white on the black and white plates.

After a further twenty-minute examination, where Fletcher was stuck with tiny pins, banged with a reflex hammer and asked to grab and push various parts of the neurologist, all that his bespectacled expert could say was 'remarkable' and scratch his head in irritation.

So it went on – day by day, hour by hour, Fletcher was improving, causing much confusion in the medical profession. In their world of science and the strict rules of cause and effect, there was no space for miracles, no room for hope unless it came out of a bottle, or a fancy bit of space-age kit. A powerless neurologist is not a happy neurologist, and Fletcher simply loved it. In conversation, he was upbeat and incredibly positive. So upbeat, in fact, that he asked Maggie whether he could come and visit the estate lodge again and try his hand at wildlife photography. Seeing the change in him, Maggie positively jumped at the chance of them spending more time together. The problem would be Callum.

Armed with four bottles of the best Scotch Mike Fletcher could afford, Maggie returned to the Highlands and tentatively asked the sullen stalker whether he'd mind having

Fletcher around for a while again. After half of the first bottle of whisky, Callum reluctantly agreed, on the basis that the photographer earn his keep by helping on the estate, which inevitably meant manual labour. Callum doubted that Fletcher would be up to it, so the visit would be called off.

Six weeks later, Fletcher arrived, camera in hand and with a huge grin on his face. Callum was lost for words. The last time he'd seen the dark-haired guest, he was comatose on a hospital bed, barely able to speak.

Fletcher had been at the estate lodge for two months now, with no sign of him leaving anytime soon. If Callum was being truthful, he was growing fond of having the pleasant character around, and it certainly was a big benefit as he couldn't call on Julian for help anymore. Besides, Fletcher didn't want any money, just his bed and board. As a true old-school Scotsman, that suited Callum perfectly.

Fletcher's sister, Rose, had gone back to work, regaining her own financial stability and security. Seeing the change in her brother had inspired her. She happily spent each day putting the house back together, removing all the disability hoists and handles they'd put in when Fletcher was there. As each one came down, her mood lifted. With no mobile signal at the estate lodge, the siblings kept in touch the old fashioned way with long loving letters at least twice a week. Bizarrely, Fletcher's health crisis had served to bring them closer together, and he seemed a better man because of it.

Callum and Fletcher trudged back across the moor, enjoying the afternoon sunshine. The only thing Fletcher was struggling to get used to in his new mountain home were the midges, the small biting flies that plague the Highlands in the summer months. Swarms surrounded him as he crossed the peaty ground, the tiny bites turning his face red in what the locals jokingly called 'midge glow'. Callum was immune, the tiny insects preferring the taste of the soft southerner to the leathery-skinned highlander.

Callum led Fletcher into the outbuilding and threw a small plastic bottle labelled Avon Skin So Soft at the photographer.

'Here – cover yourself in that. The little buggers don't like it,' Callum said, referring to the cloud of midges still circling Fletcher's head.

Fletcher tentatively sniffed at the lemony bottle in his hand. 'This is a joke, right? You've given me a woman's skin product. What I need is a vat of insect repellent and a tiny shotgun to kill them all.'

Callum shrugged and headed into the house. Not sure exactly what the shrug meant, Fletcher decided to give the bottle a go and slapped half of it all over his face, neck and exposed forearms, practically drowning himself in the stuff. The midges didn't go away, but they stopped biting. Little sod – this has been his secret all along and he's watched me be midge bait, thought Fletcher. Still muttering under his breath, he made his way into the house and dumped his camera gear in the living room.

Sneaking up on Maggie in the kitchen, Fletcher hugged her warmly and the pair kissed passionately out of the sight of Callum. In the past month, their relationship had grown stronger, to the extent that they now shared Maggie's bedroom. Callum had been surprisingly relaxed about the arrangement, as long as they didn't start drooling over each other in front of him.

After a beautiful roast lamb dinner, the three sat chatting in front of the open fire in the living room, each cradling a tot of whisky in their warming hands. Maggie reached over to grab an envelope off the bookcase and passed it to Fletcher.

'Sorry, forgot to tell you. Picked this up in Benlogan today when I got the supplies. I think it's from Nathen Turner.' Maggie took an appreciative sip of her drink, slowly letting the amber liquid seep down her throat, warming her as she stretched and relaxed.

Eagerly, Mike Fletcher tore open the blue envelope written in Turner's distinctive hand, and read it silently to himself:

Mike,
I hope this letter finds you well and at peace with yourself. We had a great time on honeymoon, visiting Jade's grandparents in Japan and reliving old memories. My wish is that you find the same love for life that we share, and can reinvent yourself in a way that truly fulfils you. I know how hard that can be – trust me, I've been there. But if you have faith, anything can happen. You've proved that to yourself already. If my guess is correct, you and Maggie will be an item by now, and I send you both my best wishes for the future.
Keep well, keep safe and above all, keep in touch.
Live in hope,
Nathen Turner
PS The dog says 'woof.'

PPS Jade, Lee and Sandra say 'Hi' and don't do anything they wouldn't do. So basically do anything you want …

Inside the letter, Nathen Turner had put a single tarot card. A card that meant more to Mike Fletcher than any fancy present. It was the High Priestess card that symbolised Fletcher's faith in himself and his belief in the future. Carefully, he stood and placed it centrally on the fireplace above the roaring blaze. At the sight of the hooded figure in the crescent-shaped boat, Callum harrumphed quietly and headed to bed. He'd seen enough hooded ladies for one lifetime and didn't want to spend the evening gazing at another.

'What's that?' Maggie asked, looking up at the card illuminated by the flickering flames.

Fletcher smiled at the card. 'That's hope, Maggie. Well, at least, it is to me.' Hope that Mike Fletcher had found, and Julian had so tragically lost.

Fletcher looked around the cosy living room, taking in the basic decor, the antler-lined walls and the muddy boots tucked away in the corner. He thought of his past life in the city, surrounded by the latest gadgets like his high-definition TV, and the way he'd spend more time sending texts on his phone than talking to people face-to-face. Memories of his old friends drifted through his mind, like projected photographs sliding by, one after the other. The same friends that had disappeared when he'd become ill, offering him their deepest sympathy and lifelong support, never to be seen again. He thought of the dirt and the constant noise in the city, the hustle and bustle as everybody rushed by in a hurry to do something. Something unknown but vitally important that made them push and shove and jump queues in their haste to get on with it. The darkest days of his illness came flooding back to him, his complete and utter loss of hope. Feelings of worthlessness that gnawed at him like a cancer. He understood what depression was, and how it felt, how difficult it was to escape once it had you in its grasp. But then he'd met Nathen Turner, a strange enigma of a man who seemed to understand things he couldn't possibly know, a man who seemed to know the right things to say at just the right time. Turner had given him back a belief in himself that he'd lost completely. Here he was, surrounded by wild nature, cocooned it its welcoming embrace, completely at home with the colourful characters it attracted.

Maggie moved over to sit next to him and snuggled warmly into his side, her freckled face resting on his shoulder. Softly stroking her red hair, he had never felt so content and at peace in his life. In a strange way, his illness had turned out to be a blessing rather than a curse, giving him the push to reinvent his life in a way he could never have foreseen. Above all else, he had faith in the future, knowing that deep down, whatever life threw at him, he'd get past it.

He thought back to how he'd felt so alone, walking along the path to the croft for the first time. How he'd embraced the loneliness and isolation as he'd tried to clear his mind. He looked down at Maggie, then across at the tarot card on the mantelpiece, breathing in his new life. Mike Fletcher was no longer alone … and he liked it.

CHAPTER 28: MAGIC BY CANDLELIGHT

Kenny Florian gazed up at the tall figure in the Hawaiian shirt like he'd just won the lottery. Shuffling enthusiastically through the myriad handwritten notes in his hand, he tossed them with a flourish onto the glass shop counter below.

'I've got to hand it to you – this psychic coaching thing is a gold mine,' he beamed, picking up a few of the tatty sheets on the counter. 'I mean, look at this – I've had four enquiries this morning.'

Nathen Turner accepted the bundle of notes and stuffed them in the chest pocket of his shirt. 'Thanks, Kenny. It was a gamble, but people seem to like what I'm doing. So far, anyway. I couldn't have done it without you. That advert you made makes me sound like I'm an angel sent from God.'

Kenny laughed, looking across at the large poster in the shop window of The Alchemist, advertising Turner's psychic coaching services. 'Well, maybe I did get a little carried away. How can I help today?'

With the wedding planning and the honeymoon, Turner had spent little time reflecting on his time in the wilderness. Now back in his regular routine, he was dwelling more and more on his trip and wondering why his psychic radar had been so off beam. He'd travelled to Scotland based on the belief that his father's old fishing partner was under threat from something supernatural. But he'd found nothing to back that up. Turner had given Kenny the edited version of his Highland adventure, not mentioning the crypt or the hooded figure, determined to keep the promise he'd made to Julian. He couldn't shake the feeling that he'd missed something around the croft, and thought talking it through with his old friend might help him unravel the mystery.

Turner knew that Isobel was not the cause of his unease – she was human, of this mortal world, albeit extremely old; so was Julian. The bodies of the monks were just that, skeletal remains, more of interest to archaeologists than psychics. The only person from Julian's original group of friends who Turner hadn't come across was the lady who'd owned the crystal ball they'd used in the crypt to view visions from Julian's long life – the lady Julian had called Caitlin Smith, who he'd said had the power to make nature do her bidding. Proof of that was in the enchantment she'd put on the crystal, giving it the ability to manifest visions – if, that is, the diviner had the power to use it. Something kept gnawing at Turner; he felt a connection with this lady that he couldn't explain. When he'd first held the quartz ball in his hand, he'd felt it was alive somehow. Perhaps something of her presence remained in the quartz, and he felt connected to her in a strange way – almost like they'd met before, perhaps crossed paths somewhere on his travels. Julian had told him she'd never been caught, but was vague about what had happened to her. Turner needed to know; he must know. Thinking about it was giving him sleepless nights. Still in pursuit of an answer, he'd thought up an unconventional way of getting to the bottom of it.

Leaning in, so he wouldn't be overheard by other customers in the shop, Turner said, 'Well, you know we talked about that bleeding pentagram thing …' leaving the end of the sentence hanging.

'Yes,' Kenny said quietly, picking up on Turner's implied need for secrecy from his body language, 'and then got a chemistry lesson from The Terminator about the effects of high-voltage static electricity on paints containing iron oxide.'

Kenny was referring to Turner's old science teacher, who also worked as the school's intimidating rugby coach. It was for the latter that he'd earned his not too affectionate nickname of The Terminator. They'd bumped into him in the local pub and decided to put his knowledge to the test. After describing the 'bleeding' paint on the ancient pentagram symbol to his old teacher, Turner believed he finally had the answer. According to The Terminator, lightning, plus red ochre, plus whatever else had been mixed in, equalled red goo. Apparently, the iron contained in the ochre paint had set off the reaction when it was charged with the electricity from the lightning. Solving this still didn't explain why he'd sensed something strange and mysterious about the place.

'Yes, I know. It's not that,' Turner said, keeping his voice low. 'When I headed up to Scotland, I genuinely believed there was something supernatural going on, not just some bizarre chemical reaction that caused a symbol to apparently "bleed". I felt it, you know?' Kenny did know, and trusted Turner's feelings; they'd always proved right in the past. 'I can't get past the feeling that I've missed something. I know I have. Something felt weird to me. Like not of this world.'

'You can't get it right all the time, Nate,' Kenny said sympathetically, still refusing to call him Nathen as it wasn't cool in hippy speak. 'When you say weird, do you mean weird as in "ghostly", or weird as in "a bunch of nutcases"?'

Turner chuckled back, 'Not so much ghostly, something else. Like an ancient magic surrounding the place somehow. Can't put my finger on it. Have you got any texts on old magic? Maybe around the Elizabethan period.'

Turner felt a little embarrassed asking. He'd never put much store in books of this type, believing them littered with made-up rituals from a more superstitious time. Now he was rethinking and changing his attitude. He'd found the supernatural real enough, and the knowledge in his own bizarre book collection had saved his skin more than once. Trouble was, he didn't own any magical texts, hence Kenny was his go-to guy.

Kenny led the psychic to a large glass-fronted cabinet tucked away at the rear of the shop. Pulling off the large bunch of keys attached to his belt, he picked out an antique-looking one and opened the doors. Waving his hand across the books, in a mock gesture of a magician taking a bow, he said, 'All the old magic stuff is in here. Go ahead, knock yourself out.' With another flourish of his arms, Kenny headed back to the counter.

Thanking him, Turner began to carefully scan the titles of each of the leather-bound volumes. Kenny had got them all rebound in matching burgundy leather with gold foil titling. It totally destroyed their value to book collectors, but Kenny didn't care about that. On the third shelf down, Turner spotted what he was looking for.

'Can I borrow this for a day or two?' he asked, waving the small book over at Kenny, who was back behind the counter, serving another customer.

Kenny nodded in reply so as not to interrupt his new customer, who was in full flow, talking excitedly about Wiccan herbs and potions. With a quick wave and a nod of thanks, Turner clip-clopped his way back into the street.

Later that evening, after the other housemates had gone to bed, Turner quietly sneaked out his Gladstone briefcase, tiptoed past a snoring Jade, and headed downstairs to the lounge. Sleep wouldn't come to him; something was clawing at the back of his mind like an old memory just out of reach. Carefully, he laid out a black cloth on the table, then two tall purple candles in old bronze holders. Finally, from the briefcase, he lifted the heavy crystal ball Julian had given him, easing it gently from the dusty bag before placing it on its stand in the centre of the table.

Flicking off the light, he breathed deeply, staring at the flaming illumination from the candles, allowing his eyes to adjust to the gloom. As he reached forward to cradle the shimmering quartz, tiny rainbows jumped and danced inside it, like some sort of enchanted light show for the fairy realm. Slowly, he allowed the energy from the crystal to pour into him, breathing in its power, and breathing out all the thoughts clouding his mind. After placing it back reverently on the stand, he opened the book, borrowed from Kenny, at the place he'd marked earlier.

The text was an ancient grimoire containing hundreds of handwritten spells in small, neat handwriting. Turner had never tried to do any form of magic before, and thought it best that his first attempt was done alone in case anything went badly wrong. Also, if nothing happened, then at least he would save himself the embarrassment. Scanning through the words, tracing his finger gently under the brown ink as he read, he checked for the tenth time that this was the spell he wanted.

Quietly at first, he began to chant the words written in the book, pulling smoke from the candles over the crystal. After long reflection, he'd chosen a variation on a summoning spell to show things that were lost. The theory, if it worked, was that the current whereabouts of the crystal's owner would appear in its clouded depths and Turner would finally figure out the mystery and put his mind at ease. Cautiously, he leant forward, peering deep into the heart of the quartz, looking for any recognisable shapes and patterns. The hairs on the back of his neck prickled and he felt a surge of energy in the room. Orange flames bent and twisted above the candles, flaring brightly, making the crystal shimmer and bloom. Turner felt, rather than saw, two green eyes peering out curiously at him from the heart of the glistening stone. It was the cat, the huge wildcat that had shared his Highland dwelling and feasted on his food.

Confused, he leant back a little, taking in a wider view of the vision unfolding in front of him. The image changed to show a woman. Young and beautiful, with flowing black hair, much taller than Isobel. This must be her – Caitlin Smith – he thought, satisfied that his summoning spell to find the crystal's owner was working. She walked through the forest next to the croft, her mouth moving like she was singing.

Behind, a huge man on a horse appeared, thundering down the path, making a direct line towards her. He looked intent on trampling the woman underfoot, the horse's hooves scattering clouds of pine needles as it galloped forward. Twisting around slowly, the lady smiled. Turner wanted to shout at her to get out of the way, beads of sweat breaking out on his forehead. But she stood her ground, as if waiting for something. Then, within seconds, the brown linen dress draped around the pretty figure dropped, fluttering to the ground, empty, leaving no trace of the lady it had been so neatly wrapped around. Bucking and kicking, the horse pulled up short, the man looking around desperately for his quarry. Out from the pile of linen on the forest floor padded a huge wildcat, hissing and snarling at its hoofed aggressor. The horse fled desperately back down the path, the man clinging on for dear life. Calmly, the cat slinked off out of sight into the forest, a linen heap left piled in amidst the pine needles the only remnant of what had once been the beautiful woman.

Things were beginning to clear in Turner's mind. The woman in the glass was a shape-shifter, able to transform into animal form. Intrigued, he watched on as the vision changed in the sphere. He saw himself, asleep in a foetal position, dozing deeply on the fish crates and straw mattress in the croft. Through the open bedroom door, the wildcat padded in and sprang effortlessly onto the bed, flopping against his chest. Snuggling against his rumpled clothing, the furry companion closed its eyes, stretched out a long paw and joined him in his slumber.

'Hello again,' Turner said to no one in particular,

scanning around the empty living room as if expecting the cat to leap out from behind the couch. Tearing his gaze from the crystal, he scanned the grimoire to check whether the theory forming in his head was correct. After fumbling around and losing his place a couple of times, he found what he was looking for. Slowly, he read to himself the section on animal enchantments and shape-shifting. Many times he'd come across tales of the like in his research, but, as with most things of this type, he took them with a pinch of salt. It appeared there was more to this than he'd thought possible. Julian had said that the crystal could only show the truth to those that could use its power, and Turner believed him. Reading through the text he was more certain. The spells detailed methods for transforming into different animals and suggested a cat was the safest one to use as a host. Cats were fiercely independent and chances of survival, if anything went wrong, were much higher. The actual spell for the feline transformation lay in a sub-section titled *'Cait Sidhe'*. The words tumbled through his mind – *Cait Sidhe* – Caitlin Smith. They sounded similar. Too similar to be a mere coincidence. Had the choice of name been her little joke? Turner thought it likely.

At the end of the shape-shifting spell there was a warning spelt out in red ink. It highlighted that the feline transformation could only be carried out nine times. On the ninth time the change would remain permanent. Turner remembered some old folk tale like this, and believed that this was where the legend of a cat having nine lives originally came from. So, he assumed, by some tragic miscalculation, Caitlin had transformed herself too many times and roamed her way through life permanently fixed in her feline form. If she were still able to change back, Turner felt sure she would have done so and spent her days living and working with Julian. To what extent the ancient moggy retained Caitlin's thoughts and emotions, Turner could only guess. After so long in the new shape, he felt certain that the hairy beast was pretty much one hundred per cent cat, with no memory of what, or rather who, it had been.

Sinking into his chair, Turner exhaled deeply, bringing his thoughts back into the present and shifting his attention back into the room. So he was right. There *was* something supernatural around the croft. A thing he'd sensed but couldn't put his finger on. A feeling he'd interpreted as danger, when it was nothing of the sort. Nathen Turner, the famed psychic medium, in tune with all things supernatural, had been happily snoozing with a wildcat that had once been a woman, Caitlin Smith, and he'd had no idea – so in touch with his psychic 'sixth sense' was he that he openly talked about his special abilities to those who would listen. Realising he'd unwittingly slept with a shape-shifter who was stuck in animal form, and was hundreds of years old, he laughed – a roaring laugh – into the silence of the room. Once he'd started, he couldn't stop, hysteria overcoming him.

Jade's head popped round the doorway, woken by the noise. 'You OK? What's so funny? And why are you sitting here in the dark?'

Trying to control himself, the best he could manage in reply was, 'You wouldn't believe me if I told you. Let's just say that my psychic radar is not as good as I thought, and I'm now a firm believer in magic. Maybe the Elizabethan tales of witchcraft weren't as far off the mark as we think these days.'

Looking around the room for a cauldron and evidence of some weird sacrifice, Jade stepped in, thinking her new husband had finally lost the plot. Switching on the light, she blew out the candles and pulled Turner over to the couch.

'You are one strange man, Nathen Turner. I think maybe you've been reading too much of your *Mall Metaphor*.'

'*Malleus Maleficarum*.'

'Whatever,' Jade said sleepily, hitching down the edge of the Hawaiian shirt she was using as a nightie and then snuggling in next to him. 'Why can't you read something that normal people read for a change? Come back to bed – I think you're overtired.'

Pulling him up by the arm, she kissed him on the cheek and pushed him gently towards the door. As they walked, she remembered something.

'Oh, I forgot to tell you. Dad rang last night. He's thinking of getting a cat to keep him company.'

Turner's laughter followed them up the stairs.

DISCOVER MORE ABOUT THE NATHEN TURNER THRILLERS:

Want to read more about the background to the Nathen Turner stories and explore the haunting settings? Sign up for the ***Haunting Tales*** newsletter at **www.andrewlangley.co.uk** and join the growing group of Nathen Turner fans.

Andrew also posts regular updates and special offers on Twitter. Connect with him **@mirroronthesoul** to keep right up-to-date with the latest news.

If you liked this book, please tell others about it! We really appreciate all the positive reviews from readers on Amazon, Barnes & Noble, Goodreads etc. Thank you for your support; it is very much appreciated.

Nathen Turner returns in ***Silence of the Soul***.

Praise for Andrew Langley and his Nathen Turner thrillers:
'Gripping and original, with unforgettable characters … a frighteningly good read.' – *Jack Magnus for US review site, Readers' Favorite.*

'Atmospheric and entertaining thriller, told with style and humour.' – *Karol Griffiths, Hollywood script editor.*

'A fun romp for any reader.' – *Amanda Monell for US review site, Readers' Favorite.*